CRUISE LINES

"Postcards from the orgy Deck"
David Wolf
June 30, 2008

CRUISE LINES

Erotic Tales
from
Ship to Shore

Edited by Sean Fisher

alyson books
NEW YORK

© 2008 BY ALYSON BOOKS

AUTHORS RETAIN RIGHTS TO THEIR INDIVIDUAL PIECES OF WORK.

ALL RIGHTS RESERVE

MANUFACTURED IN THE UNITED STATES OF AMERICA

PUBLISHED BY ALYSON BOOKS
245 WEST 17TH STREET, NEW YORK, NY 10011
DISTRIBUTION IN THE UNITED KINGDOM
BY TURNAROUND PUBLISHER SERVICES LTD.
UNIT 3, OLYMPIA TRADING ESTATE, COBURG ROAD, WOOD GREEN
LONDON N22 6TZ ENGLAND

FIRST EDITION: MAY 2008

08 09 10 11 12 a 10 9 8 7 6 5 4 3 2 1

ISBN: 1-59350-056-4
ISBN-13: 978-1-59350-056-6

LIBRARY OF CONGRESS CATALOGING-IN-PUBLICATION DATA ARE ON FILE.

COVER DESIGN BY VICTOR MINGOVITS

Contents

Introduction

Did you ever see those ads for cruises—you know, the ones that show hot guys in barely-there swimsuits, smiling their bright white teeth at each other while simultaneously checking each other out? Did you ever say to yourself: "I want to be a part of that?" Well, now you can go cruising anytime you want, with Alyson's hot, all-new collection.

I had a great time putting this anthology together. Previously I've edited both of the *Dorm Porn* titles for Alyson and I've got to say, it sure is nice to get out of the classroom and off campus! Because with these eighteen stories I got to travel, in my mind at least, to all sorts of locations. The Caribbean, Mexico, Alaska, the Mediterranean, even deep under the sea. Hot times aboard huge cruises, with the hottest guys imaginable.

Some of erotica's top writers are represented here—Simon Sheppard, who is "Learning to Do the Cha-cha-cha," and Lew Bull, who takes us on an "Italian Rendezvous." We've got some newer voices, too, like Jeff Funk and his "Two If By Sea," and Keith Williams, who knows a thing or two about "Cold Night Visitor Hot." And then there's a bunch of our regulars, all of whom know how to please an editor . . . and a man.

But you can't close out your reading experience without delving into T. Hitman's "The Strange Case of Brody Thomas Boyce." It's an epic short story (if there is such a thing) about a horny detective on the trail of a runaway porn star. Finally, as a coda to the rest of the collection, comes Christopher Pierce's ethereal, erotic "Ocean in His Eyes."

Enjoy your journey to seas as deep and blue and wild as the men you'll meet. Who knows, maybe that next cruise ad I come across will feature you—your smile grinning back at me, checking me out. Hey, I'll be doing the same. Then I'll see you on board!

—Sean Fisher

Italian Rendezvous
Lew Bull

The long, low, sonorous sound of a ship's horn reverberated across the harbor as the stark white cruise liner slowly began to edge away from the quay at precisely 5:00 p.m. Streamers floated through the air as passengers pelted their friends left on dry land with streams of color. On board a band played some of the latest pieces of music. Competing with the ship's hooter were shouts and screams from the departing passengers, as they waved frantically, hugged each other, and generally started what was to become a non-stop party.

I stood on the jogging track, which formed part of Deck 10, alone, but bounded by happy, singing, and cheering young men, some also alone, and others with their partners and friends. Although a part of me was somewhat depressed, I couldn't help but be swept up by the camaraderie that surrounded me. The stark whiteness of the ship stood out against the turquoise of the sea as it sailed slowly from the port, and objects that seemed large on the quay gradually became smaller as we drifted farther away from land on our way to our two-night, three-day cruise.

My depression had come about by the break-up of my eight-month relationship with Barry Jones, a young man aged twenty-two, eight years my junior. Some of my friends had said that our relationship was doomed to failure because of our age differences, but I was determined to overlook an aspect like that. I was naïve to think that Barry wouldn't be attracted to anyone else. Barry was extremely good-looking and was a catch for anyone. The result was that it didn't take long for Barry to get hooked up with a muscle-bound guy his own age, pack his bags, and flit off to some foreign place, possibly until he found some even bigger muscle-bound guy and flit off with him. I had already booked a cabin on the *S.S. Majestic* for Barry and me, but now as the great white ship sailed majestically out to sea, living up to its name, I was very much alone in my luxurious cabin with its quaint balcony.

Once the ship was a fair way from shore, I decided to make my way around the ship to seek out where everything was. At first, I followed the sound of the band, which was playing alongside the swimming pool, and found myself confronted by what seemed like hundreds of dancing, happy, partying men. The cruise, on which I had booked, was ostensibly a gay cruise for men, but I did see a couple of women on board, all staff, but very much in the minority.

I made my way indoors and found the "Schooner Bar" where I decided to have a drink. I strolled up to the bar counter where a young barman asked me what I would like to drink. I ordered a beer. With my hand clasped around the cool glass of the bottle, I sipped my beer, watching the various people who were passing through the bar and the lounge, keeping an eye on my Italian barman.

"Hi, I'm James," I said, stretching a hand across the bar counter.

The barman took my hand and I felt the firm grip as he shook it.

"Hi, my name is Marco," he said in broken English, smiling at me.

I suddenly felt weak at the knees when I heard the seductive Italian accent. His pearly white teeth glistened with his smile while his eyes twinkled with delight. His handshake wasn't brief. He held onto my hand, not releasing his grip, his green eyes burying into mine with his smile becoming broader and broader. Marco was of average height and build, at least with his clothes on, with olive-tanned skin and looked about late twenties or early thirties—just what I needed, someone my age!

As I sat staring lovingly into Marco's eyes, an announcement came over the loudspeaker informing everyone that a lifeboat drill was about to take place and that we must report to our various stations. I looked a little bewildered, but Marco was quick to inform me what I had to do and where to go. He said that he would keep my beer for me and once we were finished with the drill, I could return to the bar. I hurried off in the direction that Marco had told me and met up with hundreds of others, equally lost like myself.

Instructions were given, explaining what we were to do in the unlikely event of us having to abandon ship. It goes without saying that when you have a ship full of gay men, taking things like rescuing and abandoning ship take on a hilarious aspect. Putting on life jackets became more of a fashion show than a life rescue and when we were informed that there were whistles attached to our life jackets it was like an invitation to set off a cacophony of whistling all around the ship. I stood among this noise of whistles and laughter and wondered just what the captain thought about all this behavior—a ship full of gay men. Once the exercise was over, we were free to return to whatever we were doing prior to the drill. I made my way back to the bar and found Marco nursing my beer bottle.

"I've kept it cold for you, James."

"Thanks Marco, that was kind of you," I said, sitting at one of the bar stools. "Have you ever had a group of passengers like this before?" I asked.

A smile as big as a crescent moon emerged across Marco's face.

"Once before, but I like it because it livens up the trip . . . And they are good tippers here at the bar," he added as an afterthought.

I wasn't sure whether this was a hint, but I wasn't about to take it that way, after all, Marco seemed a genuine sort of guy.

"Are you with someone on the ship?" he enquired.

I think he realized my answer before I said anything, as my face took on a depressed look.

"I'm afraid, I'm alone, Marco," I replied.

"Do not be afraid to be alone," he joked, laughing. "It means you can have much more fun," he said, giving me a wink.

"I suppose you're right. It's just that sometimes it's nice to be able to talk to someone that you know and not spend every evening on your own."

"I can't see you being on your own for long," continued Marco. "You are good-looking and there are many men on this ship who would be happy to be with you. You'll see."

I smiled at Marco, realizing that he was trying his best to make me feel at home, but without having a physical body to cuddle at night and to talk to in the early mornings, it still made me feel empty inside.

"Who is your cabin steward?" he enquired, placing another beer in front of me.

"I didn't order this, Marco."

"No. It is on me," he said grinning at me. "But you haven't answered my question."

"Oh, sorry. There was a card in my cabin and it had the name Giovanni on it."

"Ooooh!" cooed Marco. "You'll like him; he's *very* good."

I looked a little surprised by Marco's reaction and I'm sure that he could see my reaction, but chose not to elaborate.

"He's my best friend on the ship," he continued. "I'll tell him to look after you."

"Thanks Marco," I said, not knowing what to expect.

I must have spent at least another half an hour chatting to Marco and watching the passing trade, then said that I was going to my cabin on Deck 7 to unpack, which I did.

I slid open the balcony door and allowed the brisk sea air to infiltrate the stuffiness of the cabin, which was really a suite. Apart from a double bed, there was a sofa, easy chair, telephone, and a TV in the sitting area. On the balcony was a deck chair, for those moments when I could stretch out, perhaps in the nude, and watch the passing sea.

I kicked off my shoes and socks, stripped down to my

briefs, and whipped off my shirt. I was busy unpacking when there was a rap on the cabin door. Since I knew this ship was made up of men, I didn't bother to pull on some shorts, and went to open the cabin door. A tall, dark-haired man in a neatly pressed white shirt, a black bow tie, and a pair of tight-fitting black pants stood in the doorway. My eyes moved from the tip of his head to the shoes on his feet, but I must admit I did hover rather long when my eyes reached the crotch area, which was protruding heftily. When our eyes met again, we were both smiling at each other.

"Mr. Elliot?" he asked extending a hand.

"Yes," I replied grasping his warm hand and feeling a gentle crunch as his fingers wrapped around my hand.

"I am Giovanni, your cabin steward. Marco telephoned me. I am here to be of any assistance to you throughout this voyage. Anything and I mean *anything* . . ." he hesitated, smiling at me. ". . . Anything you want, you call me and I will be here for you."

"Thank you Giovanni; that's very kind of you."

"Do you need help with your unpacking, sir?"

I was a little flabbergasted, as it was not what I expected of a cabin steward, but I was also becoming perturbed because I could feel a rise developing in my briefs as I stood staring at this hunk of a man with his broad shoulders tapering to a trim waist. I stammered a little, not really knowing what to say to Giovanni, but then he broke the ice.

"May I come in, sir?"

"Oh, yes, yes, of course," I stammered, closing the door behind him.

We were now facing each other, barely a foot apart. I could feel my boner growing in my briefs but I couldn't take my eyes off this man.

His eyes twinkled and he smiled one of those all-knowing smiles as if to say, "Have I embarrassed you?"

"Do you need a hand?" he whispered.

Suddenly I felt his gentle touch on my engorged cock.

"Aaah," I gasped and retreated a little way from him. His smile never vanished nor did he advance towards me. "I think I'll manage, thanks Giovanni." I didn't know what else to say. Here was this young man coming onto me and I was rejecting his advances; what was wrong with me?

"Well if you change your mind and do need help, please call me," he whispered seductively as only an Italian can do, and ran a hand over his tightly encased crotch.

I knew that I was blushing, but being the gentleman that he was, Giovanni excused himself and departed my cabin. I stood breathless for a moment, taking in what had just happened and how I had thrown away a perfectly good chance to have sex with a perfectly beautiful man. What was wrong with me? I looked at myself in the full-length mirror in the cabin and saw myself—good-looking, neat, trim body and a roaring erection—so what was wrong with that? I reprimanded myself for being such a fool, but I consoled myself by saying, "I have got his number and I can call him any time."

The first evening on board was very festive with a stunning dinner followed by a floorshow. After the show, I made my way to Marco's bar to find him busily pouring drinks for what appeared to be hundreds of men of varying sizes and ages. He caught my eye and shouted across some heads to find out if I wanted a beer, to which I nodded. As I pushed through the crowd to get to the bar counter, I could feel bodies and crotches pushed up against me. At length, I reached Marco.

"Hi. Seems like you're busy tonight."

"This is fun," he shouted above the din of the people.

"I met Giovanni earlier," I shouted back, but then thought that perhaps that wasn't quite the thing to do, but it was now too late.

Marco smiled. "And what do you think?"

I blushed. I didn't know whether Giovanni had said anything to Marco about what happened in the cabin.

"He seems very nice," I replied, but I think my face gave my true feelings away.

"You like more than nice?" shouted Marco.

Again I merely blushed and took a swig of beer to avoid answering the question.

After having consumed a couple of beers and having spoken mainly to Marco all evening, I decided to turn in early. I excused myself and made my way back to my cabin. On entering, I noticed that the bed had been turned down and a chocolate lay on my pillow accompanied by a note, which read *Sleep well. Giovanni.* I stripped off, opened the sliding door to my balcony, switched off the cabin light, and then lay on my bed allowing the gentle sea breeze and the rock and roll of the ship to lull me to sleep.

At 7:00 a.m. there was a gentle tap on my cabin door. I opened my eyes, stretched, and threw back the bed covers. I stood up with a morning pride and padded to the cabin door. I opened it and peered out. Giovanni stood outside with a tray of tea and some small biscuits.

"Good morning Mr. Elliot. I hope that you slept well," he said, entering my cabin and placing the tray on a small table. He turned to face me and saw my morning erection, which I hadn't taken the trouble to hide.

"You look incredibly well, this morning, sir."

"Thank you, Giovanni," I replied trying now to hide my hard-on.

Giovanni smiled and neared me. I felt his hand grab my balls and give them a gentle squeeze. His eyes never left my face, as if to watch for my reaction.

"You like that?" he whispered.

I didn't know what to say. Yes, of course I liked it. No, I lie. I loved it! I extended my hand and felt for his crotch. My fingers found a semi-erect firmness hidden in his tight black pants. I slowly slid my fingers along the slowly growing length covered by soft material. Giovanni suddenly sank to his knees as if worshipping me. I felt his warm breath on my cock and then I felt his tender lips caress the tip of my cock. His tongue licked slowly around my cock head circling where I had been cut, then the warmth of his mouth engulfed the head. He held it in his mouth allowing it to become salivated, and then he steadily sank down my length, slowly swallowing each inch until his chin jabbed against my balls. He held his position and sucked. A tight vacuum effect was created and I groaned as I felt his tongue attempting to lick up my stem while his mouth remained glued to the base of my cock. After a while, his mouth began a slow and sensual journey up to the tip. He released his grip on my cock and smiled up at me, his eyes twinkling with pleasure. His tongue then rasped under the length of my throbbing cock and balls, and I thought I would shoot because the feeling was so intense. Giovanni sank once more down my length, licking and sucking as he did so, creating a feeling of tightness around my stem. I held his dark hair in both hands and began a slow, gentle face-fuck. I thrust deeply into his throat, moaning as I did so, and his mouth slurped my every inch.

"Giovanni, you're getting me close," I groaned, as I increased my pace.

As if not to hear me, he continued pleasuring me until I gasped out aloud and fired a shot of warm cum down his Italian throat. He immediately released his grip on my cock, allowing it to fire across his tanned face. His hand took over bringing me again and again to climax, as his tanned face received strands of white cum. Once I had exhausted my supply and my groaning had become minimal, I placed my hands under his armpits and hoisted him to his feet. I kissed him tenderly taking in my own cum from his face as I did so. I could taste my salty-sweet love-juice and as we pressed close together, I could feel his hard-on throbbing in his pants.

"Thank you, Giovanni," I whispered in his ear. "That was wonderful."

He released his grip on me, and smiling into my face said,

"Treat that as only the antipasto. The main course will come later!"

I brought a towel from the bathroom and gently cleaned Giovanni's face of my evidence, then kissed him on his full Italian lips, feeling his tongue immerse itself in my mouth, causing my subsiding cock to jerk with excitement again.

"Oh, and one other thing," I said, releasing my mouth from his. "Please call me 'James.'"

He smiled once more, kissed my forehead, and exited my cabin without a word. I fell onto the bed, grinning from ear to ear, pleased with myself and now felt ready to face the rest of the day.

I pulled on my Speedo under a pair of shorts, slipped on a vest, and made my way to the main deck for breakfast al fresco. After a hearty meal, I made my way to the swimming pool. When I arrived I surveyed the scene, which resembled a body-building conference. Extremely well-built men, all in brightly colored Speedos, were either seductively massaging tanning oil into their pecs or six-pack abs, or parading in front of others, like peacocks. I knew that Barry would have lusted for a sight like this. I truly admired their beauty, but I was a more subtle man. I liked my men to have good bodies but not overdone, but I cannot deny the thought that went through my head wondering what it would be like to be sexually domineered by one of these muscle-bound men. Oooh, I quivered. I found myself a deck chair, threw down my towel onto it, whipped off my shorts and vest, and settled down to some serious tanning. If I say so myself, I was proud of my physique; lean with slightly enlarged pecs, a flat, trim stomach, long, firm legs, and a healthy package packed into my Speedo.

As the morning progressed, the number of men who approached me to have a casual chat surprised me. I was beginning to feel less depressed. I realized that things could happen on this cruise, provided I was willing to let it happen, but at the moment I was not ready.

During the evening there were the usual on-board entertainment such as variety shows and quizzes, discos, and gambling. I mingled with others and had a few drinks with Marco and then at about midnight, decided to retire to my cabin. When I entered, I found two chocolates and a red rose placed on the pillows of the double bed along with a note in Giovanni's handwriting: *Call me if you need anything. Giovanni.*

I had spent a horny day in the sun admiring all those men and had enjoyed an equally horny evening watching Marco so now I was ready to explode with passion. I picked up the telephone in my cabin and dialed the magic number. I heard the strong Italian accent.

"Hi, Giovanni, it's James here. Are you free later tonight?"

"Hello James," came the reply. "Is there anything I can get for you?"

"I just wondered whether you'd like to come round to my cabin when you're free."

"I'll be there at about 1:00 a.m., if that's fine with you."

"I can't wait," I replied, putting down the phone, smiling to myself, and stripping off my clothes.

At precisely 1:00 a.m., there was a gentle rap on my cabin door. I rose from my bed and opened the door but received a shock on doing so: Giovanni and Marco were both standing there. I wondered why they were both there.

"I decided to bring Marco with me, I hope you don't mind," whispered Giovanni.

"Come in, come in," I said, quickly ushering them in and closing the door behind them and then standing naked in front of both of them.

"James we could be in big trouble if we are caught in the passengers' cabins," said Marco, seeming a little agitated.

"I'm certainly not going to tell anyone," I replied. "Would either of you like a drink?"

Both rejected the offer but Giovanni said that he needed to go to the bathroom, which he duly did.

When he returned he was naked and I looked at his taut, muscular body admiringly. His long, pendulous uncut cock hung tantalizingly between his legs as he moved from the bathroom and slipped onto the bed. Just seeing him naked got me aroused and I was semi-hard. Marco immediately stripped and lay on the bed next to Giovanni. I looked at the two beautiful Italian studs as they began caressing each other's body. Marco scuttled down Giovanni's muscular chest, taking Giovanni's hardened cock into his mouth. Just watching them was a turn on for me, but I had no intention of being the voyeur; I wanted in.

I moved onto the bed and lay next to Giovanni; his hand took hold of my stiff cock and started sliding it along my length, while our mouths found each other. Marco then moved onto my cock and I felt his warmness encircle my stem, while Giovanni took Marco's slim, yet long cock down his throat. Of the two I would say that Giovanni had the thicker and longer cock, but each was a beauty to admire.

I nibbled at Giovanni's foreskin with my teeth, inserting my tongue tip into this opening and lathering his cock-head. To watch their foreskins peel back to reveal their swollen cock heads was enchanting to me. Pre-cum began to ooze from their piss slits and I couldn't resist licking it off for them.

"What do you like?" breathed Giovanni in my ear as his tongue explored my neck and face.

"I want you to fuck me," I gasped. "I want you both," I continued, breathing heavily. "But take it slow," I said to Giovanni, hoping that he wouldn't. I needed his cock and I was determined to have it deep inside of me.

Giovanni shifted us around and lay on his back on the bed. "Sit on me, James."

Before I sat on his bobbing cock, I reached for a condom, placed it on his tip and unrolled it down his length with my mouth, then I got some lube and spread it on my ass, then I slowly sank onto his waiting bargepole. There was no restraint on my part and I sank straight down to its base, causing Giovanni to groan in ecstasy as I did so. Marco came around and started sucking my cock as I rose and fell on Giovanni's length.

"Marco, get ready," commanded Giovanni.

Marco knew exactly what to do. He wrapped his erection in a condom, rubbed some lube over his length and aimed for my ass. We froze as Marco slowly began pushing his cock into me alongside Giovanni's. I felt an intense pain as I was stretched, but Giovanni's face was a picture of pleasure as he felt the tightness of Marco's cock rub up against his and my ass muscles tighten around his length. When both young Italian studs were embedded in me, they began a slow, rhythmic movement, which emulated that of the gently rolling ship.

Their tightness was bringing me close to a climax that I knew would explode at any minute. I warned them both, but they continued plowing into my ass with more Italian gusto. My breathing became fast and intensified until finally I gasped out loud and fired my first shots of warm cum across Giovanni's smooth chest. On feeling my ass muscles clamping tighter around their cocks, both men thrust deeper, then Marco suddenly pulled out, ripped off his condom and fired onto my back. I could feel the warm trickles as his shots ran down my ass crack and onto Giovanni's cock as he continued to thrust in and out, pushing me high into the air. Giovanni's muscular arms gripped my waist and lifted me to the tip of his cock. As he shot, he pulled me back down onto his throbbing cock, plowing it deep into me as I felt the constant throbs as his condom filled with warm liquid.

That evening we slept, fucked, and slept; but that night remained embedded in my mind and every time I've gone on a cruise, I've always hoped that I would find my two Italian men, but so far without any luck.

Oh, What a Friend I Have in Jesus

Todd Gregory

I watched as the storm rolled in from the ocean into Acapulco Bay. The lightning flashes at the mouth of the horseshoe shaped inlet lit up the night sky. In the distance, the black water below the jagged white strings turned green. I sat on the balcony of a beachfront high-rise, smoking a cigarette, unable to sleep. It was about four o'clock in the morning, and I knew I was going to have to let myself out relatively soon to catch a cab back to the *S. S. Adonis,* which was setting sail for Mazatlan at promptly eight in the morning. Part of me was tempted to just go on to the airport and catch the next flight back to Los Angeles. I wasn't enjoying the cruise, as I'd known I wouldn't. It seemed now, as it had in the days before departure, like an incredible waste of time.

Inside the apartment, beyond the open sliding glass doors, Jesus muttered something in his sleep and rolled over onto his back. I looked inside, noting the long thick brown cock resting off to the side of the large balls. His flat, perfectly smooth stomach rose and fell with every breath. I felt my own cock stir again inside my underwear, but ignored it and turned back to look out to sea. There wasn't time for another round, and besides, he was asleep. When he woke, I would most likely be out to sea, on the cruise I regretted taking. *It's only five more days,* I reminded myself. *After Mazatlan, we turn back north and head straight back to LA. You can get through it, surely.*

The cruise hadn't been my idea. Whenever I thought about going on a cruise, my mind automatically returned to movies like *The Poseidon Adventure* and *Titanic*. It had been Mark's idea, one of his harebrained schemes born out of his own boredom and need for change. Maybe that wasn't quite fair—Mark was just more adventurous than I was, always had been, and I was usually more than happy to go along for the ride. It was Mark who'd dragged me to Gay Days at Disney, Southern Decadence in New Orleans, and IML in Chicago. I'd never regretted letting Mark serve as my vacation planner, having a great time every time I went anywhere with him. It was hard not to have fun with Mark; Mark drew people to him everywhere he went with his infectious big smile, sexy blue eyes, and his ripped muscular body. Everyone always looked at Mark, everyone always wanted to meet him, everyone always wanted to fuck him. Maybe I was a little jealous of him, but he'd worked long and hard on his body, and the work showed. He was always prone to take his shirt off whenever he got the chance, displaying the huge mouth watering pecs and gigantic biceps that everyone wanted to touch, to see flexed. But I'd known Mark before he'd dedicated himself to turning himself, as he said, "Into the hottest man over forty in Southern California." When he suggested going on the *Adonis* cruise, I'd been more than happy to fork over the several thousand dollars, despite my aversion to being on the high seas.

Mark made everything more fun.

I flicked my cigarette over the edge of the balcony and watched the little glowing red ember tumble end over end down eleven stories before exploding into sparks on the marble walkway below. The wind was picking up as the storm crossed the bay toward land, and I shivered a little. I debated lighting another one; debated getting dressed and slipping out the elevator and heading back to the ship.

Instead, I went inside and got back into the bed, feeling Jesus' warmth as he breathed shallowly in his sleep. There was a bedside lamp on, and as I drew on his body heat to warm my chilled skin, I looked back at the semi-hard cock with a little drop of liquid in the slit. It was a beautiful cock, purplish-brown and gigantic when flaccid. When erect, it was the stuff of pornographic dreams. I stared at it wonderingly. *That thing was inside of me about an hour ago,* I thought, resisting the urge to shake my head. *It made me feel like no other cock ever had before. I came three times while he pounded into my ass—no one's ever done that before. I came the first time without even touching my own cock.*

Mark had been forced to cancel his cruise at the last minute—a medical emergency. He'd overdone it at the gym and created a rupture inside his own ball sack, and his doctor had insisted on operating on it right away. The surgery itself was minor and routine—an outpatient procedure I'd driven him to and home from—but the doctor forbade him to leave the country. And when I said I'd cancel, too—Mark wouldn't hear of it. "*No,* you go on without me," my best friend had insisted. "I'd never forgive myself if you didn't go because of me. You go on. You'll have a blast, you'll see."

It was impossible to argue with him. If I didn't go, he would feel bad, which then would make me feel bad. So it was easier just to go ahead and pack, head down to the port, and get settled in. Mark drove me to the pier, all the way insisting I would have a good time.

But I'm not you, I wanted to say. *I won't know anyone, and I'm too shy to just start talking to strangers. I'll be a wallflower and bored the whole time. I'm not beautiful the way you are, with the body of a god and a smile that is so bright it could draw bugs in the dark to its radiance. Without you, I'll just be bored to death and have a miserable time.*

But I didn't say any of that, instead I talked about how I was looking forward to seeing Cabo and Acapulco and Mazatlán, gambling in the on-board casino, and going to the disco to dance the night away with my shirt off and my jeans riding low on my hips. I pretended an excitement I didn't feel. I smiled and laughed and joked, knowing that if I let him know how much I didn't want to go, he'd feel bad—and even though his surgery wasn't a serious one, I wanted him to focus on getting better. So, I got out of the car, checked in, checked my bags, and waved good-bye from the deck of the ship as the horns blew and the big ship pulled away from the dock.

And then I became invisible.

I had my meals. I tanned on the deck while reading books, watching the other men laughing and having fun with their friends. I went into the disco in the evenings and sipped at margaritas while watching guys make new friends, hit on each other, walk past me like I wasn't there. I walked around aimlessly, watching the moon in the night sky and wishing there was someone with me, all the time thinking how much more fun it would be if Mark were only there. Within minutes of walking into a bar together, Mark's smile and body and charisma would have a crowd of people around us.

Without him I was nothing.

When we docked in Acapulco yesterday afternoon, I went ashore along with everyone else—although everyone else seemed to be a part of a crowd talking and laughing and making plans for their day. Me, I just grabbed a cab with no real idea of where to go, so I just instructed the driver to take me somewhere *los Americanos* rarely went. He just nodded, and after about twenty minutes he let me out in a business area, full of restaurants and bars and shops. As I walked around, I slowly began to realize that this was the part of Acapulco that the Mexican tourists came to—white faces were few and far between. I did some shopping, ate dinner at an Italian restaurant, and walked a little further up the street. It was getting late, and I was just thinking about hailing a cab and heading back to the boat when I glanced up a side street and saw a place called *Club Caliente*.

"You speak English?" a young man beside me said.

I turned and looked at him. He was young, maybe seventeen or so, short and stocky with a face burned reddish brown by the sun. He was smiling. I smiled back. "Yes." I replied.

He nodded at *Club Caliente*. "Is club with dancers. For men. Upstairs, the women dance. Downstairs, the boys." His smile grew bigger. "You like the boys?"

I nodded.

"The boys dance. You will like."

"Thank you." I replied, and started watching the traffic for a cab. But as I saw one approaching and started to raise my hand to wave it down, I stopped. I looked back over my shoulder.

Mark would go to the club. You owe it to Mark to go in there and check it out. If it's scary and dirty or whatever, you can always leave and walk back up here to get a cab. But you'll have a story to tell Mark, for sure—and wouldn't it be nice if one of the stories of this trip was actually true rather than made up?

So, without really expecting too much, I walked down the side street, paid a five hundred peso cover charge, and walked into the bar.

It was dark, as all gay bars are; a few lights here and there breaking through the gloom. I could see that there were less than ten people inside. I walked up to the bar and ordered a bottle of Bud Lite, and made my way to a table in the corner. The music was playing rather loudly, and I was kind of amused to note that a gay bar is a gay bar, regardless of the country. I sat down on a stool and nursed my beer as someone leapt up onto the bar and started dancing. My jaw dropped.

He was stark naked except for his boots.

So, a gay bar is not the same everywhere, I smiled to myself. He was short, and looked like he was in his late teens, with cinnamon skin and that smooth, lean youthful type of body that some boys are just blessed with. He danced his way around the top of the bar, his big dick flopping, kneeling down and letting some of the guys seated play with it. He was rewarded with folded bills being stuffed into his socks. He made his way around the bar a few times, before jumping down and heading for patrons seated at the tables. When he reached me, he stood in between my legs, reached down and rubbed his dick against the bare skin of my legs. He tilted his head down, then raised his eyes to mine shyly. "You like?" he said, slapping it against my leg again.

"Very nice," I replied, thinking, *He's thinking, American with money, isn't he?*

He moved away after another moment, and I watched as he plied his wares at another table. I shook my head, wondering how Mark would react to the boy. I picked up my beer and out of the corner of my eye, I saw another dancer climbing up onto the bar. I had the bottle up to my mouth as I turned my head and just stopped short.

The dancer on the bar was without question one of the most beautiful men I'd ever seen—which is saying a lot.

He was much taller than the previous one; maybe about six two with thick shoulder-length blue-black hair, big, round, brown eyes, and his skin was tanned a dark copper. His shoulders were broad and his torso layered with corded muscle. His waist was small and his hips narrow, with long muscular legs that looked solid as stone. His entire body was hairless except for the patch of hair at his crotch, and his cock—

His cock was fully erect, long and thick, one of the biggest I'd ever seen outside of a porn film.

He danced around on top of the bar, turning around now and then to show a round, muscular pair of buttocks.

I gaped at him, unable to take my eyes off him.

He was magnificent.

He hopped down from the bar and made his way around the tables. I watched him—he didn't linger for long at any of them, and I could hear my heart pounding in my ears as he approached my table.

He flashed a dazzling smile of even white teeth at me. "Hola! I am Jesus."

"Hi." I somehow managed to mumble.

He stepped in close between my legs, his big, thick, hard cock brushing against the bare skin of my upper legs. "This place is a dump, no?" His English was perfect, only lightly accented. I stared into his eyes. How old could he be, I wondered, resisting the urge to reach out and touch his lean torso, to reach down and put my hand on that gigantic cock. He tossed his hair back, and placed his hands on my chest. They felt hot through the T-shirt fabric, as though they would burn right through it. "If I had better offer, I would get my clothes and leave right now." He flashed that smile at me again.

My heart sank. Stupidly, I had allowed myself to hope he might actually be interested in me. No, he was for hire, and he targeted me as what he hoped would turn out to be a rich American. "Oh." I said, looking away from his eyes. "I see."

He watched my face for a moment, then he opened his mouth and shouted with laughter. "You think I am a *puta?* What you call a whore?"

My cheeks flamed with embarrassment. "I—uh—"

He leaned into me and whispered into my ear. "I think you sexy. Very sexy. I watch you come in, and I decide, I want that one." He brushed his lips against my cheek. "I have apartment two blocks from here—is beautiful place. You come?"

"Um . . ."

"I get clothes."

He reached down and squeezed my cock through my shorts, smiled at me again, and turned and walked away. I watched him until he disappeared through a door off to one side of the bar— the same door another short dancer, who could have been a clone of the first one other than his hair was too short—and stared.

This couldn't be happening. This kind of thing happened to Mark, but not to me.

I had just finished my beer when Jesus came back out through the door wearing a pair of faded torn jeans and no shirt. He walked right over to me, and smiled. "Come on—" he stopped and laughed again, a joyous sound. "I don't know name."

"Stacy." I replied.

"Come on, Stacy." He grabbed me by the hand and dragged me out the hallway and out the front door.

As we walked the two blocks or so, he talked—an incessant stream that I couldn't have interrupted had I wanted to. He wasn't wearing a belt, and the worn jeans kept sliding down his hips until he would notice and yank them back up. I kept glancing out of the side of my eyes as the jeans worked their way down his hips with each step he took, revealing the tantalizing crack, the beautiful curve of his cheeks. My cock was rock hard, and then he led me across the street to a stunningly beautiful high-rise that looked like it was made of solid marble. "You live here?" I asked.

He laughed again. "I am what you would call 'kept,' is that the right word? My lover lives in the capital and only comes here every other week or so. I dance at *Caliente* when I get bored." He pushed open the huge glass doors, and the older man working at the front desk called out "Hola, Jesus!" He waved and led me to the elevator, pushing me inside one and hitting the 8 button. Once the elevator doors shut, he shoved me back against the glass wall and put his lips on mine, his hands wandering down into the front of my shorts. He wrapped a hand around my cock and started teasing the head with his fingertips, just as he slid his tongue deep inside my mouth and pressed his entire body against mine.

I would have let him fuck me right there in the elevator if he'd wanted to.

But then the elevator stopped and the doors opened. He laughed again and grabbed my hand, pulling me down a hallway to a cast-iron gate. He paused and unlocked it, then stepped inside and unlocked the inside wooden door, then pulled me in as he turned on the lights.

The apartment was stunning. The furniture was all white, matching the white marble floors and walls. A ceiling fan turned over the couch, and on the walls were paintings, splashes of magnificent color that looked expensive.

He shut the door behind us and undid his pants. They dropped to his ankles and he stepped out of them. His cock was hard, a drop of wetness at the tip. He knelt down and untied his boots and tossed them aside as I pulled my shirt over my head. On his knees, he scooted across the floor and untied my shoes, and I lifted one foot than the other as he removed them. He reached up and undid my belt, next my fly, and then he gently slid my pants down and off.

He smiled up at me. "Is very nice." He said, and then took my hardness into his mouth.

His tongue felt like silk against my cock, and I closed my eyes and moaned as he began to work his mouth over it, going gently and slow as he worked his mouth back and forth on my cock. After a few moments, though, he stopped, kissing the head, and got to his feet. "Come," he said, taking me by the hand and leading me through a door into the bedroom. He switched on the overhead light and ceiling fan, and I was stunned. The curtains in the living room had been closed, but in the bedroom they were pulled back, and all of Acapulco Bay spread out before me.

"What a view." I gasped out as he went around me, and then moaned as he spread my cheeks and slipped his tongue into my asshole.

Oh . . . my . . . God.

My entire body went rigid as he went to work on my asshole. His tongue was ravenous, licking and probing, darting in and out, his lips working on the skin around. I couldn't help myself, I bent over and leaned on the bed as my entire body shuddered with pleasure. I could barely keep my eyes open as the pleasure swept through my body in waves, and my balls began to ache with desire.

And then he stopped.

"You taste so good," he whispered into my ear from behind as a probing finger went into my asshole. "And your ass is so beautiful . . ."

He pushed me onto the bed, and I rolled over onto my back as he slipped a condom over that huge cock.

My eyes widened.

There was just no way that could fit inside me.

He squirted lube onto the condom, and then onto his hand. He smiled down at me. "You will like," he insisted, and then he got on the bed, raised my legs and pressed the huge head against my entry.

Relax, relax, relax, don't fight it.

Come began leaking from my own cock as he slowly and gently began to work himself into me.

I'd never felt anything like it before, he was filling me and stretching me . . . I took a deep breath and focused again on relaxing.

"Oh my god." I breathed the words out as he went deeper inside me. I bit my lip to keep from crying out, trying to stay relaxed, trying not to resist this massive invasion, bigger than anyone I'd ever had inside me before.

"Oh you feel so good," he cooed, smiling at me as he began gently tugging on my nipples, as he kept moving deeper into me, slowly, ever so slowly.

And then, with a final thrust, he buried himself.

All of my breath rushed out of me in a moan, and I came.

Oh . . . my . . . God.

And then he started slowly pulling back, pulling himself out of me.

It was indescribable. I'd never felt so amazing, so good, so much pleasure . . . and when all that was left inside me was the head, he slammed back into me and I cried out as I came yet a second time . . . but I didn't want him to stop, I never wanted him to stop, I just wanted him to pound me, to keep pounding me with that god-like cock, to pound on me until every drop of come inside of me was drained, till my balls were empty, and I heard myself growl, "Fuck me . . . fuck me . . . fuck me . . ."

And as he slammed back into me, I rammed myself against him. I wanted him inside of me as far as he could go. I wanted that cock to fill me, to fuck me.

He smiled and we developed a rhythm, pulling away from each other before slamming together again.

I started stroking my own cock, already sticky from the two times I'd already come, and kept murmuring, "Yeah, fuck me man, keep fucking me . . ."

I'd never been this way before.

I'd never felt like this.

I didn't want him to ever stop. I wanted him to fuck me until I died, because there was no way I would ever feel like this again, I wanted to die and go to heaven with his huge monstrous cock inside of me, pounding, pounding, pounding . . .

And just as I came a third time, he let out a cry and his entire body convulsed . . . and when he was finished, he pulled himself out of me, stripped the dripping condom off his cock, and smiled down at me.

"Oh, papi, what a wonderful ass." He breathed as he took a towel and wiped my come off me.

And then, he lay down next to me and within a matter of moments, was asleep.

And I had gone out to the balcony to smoke and watch the storm roll in.

I dressed quietly, retrieving my clothes from the floor in the living room where they'd been scattered. I walked back into the bedroom, knelt down, and brushed my lips against his cheek. "Thank you, Jesus." I whispered. He shifted in his sleep, but didn't wake up.

I walked back to the elevator, and out to the street to flag down a cab. All the way back to the dock, I couldn't stop thinking about him.

He wanted *me.*

Maybe . . . maybe I wasn't such a loser after all.

And as I climbed the walkway back onto the boat, the storm broke around the boat, drenching me in warm rain. But I didn't care. It felt good.

I glanced at my watch as I got back to my room. Five in the

morning. I had just put the keycard into the slot when a door directly across the hall from mine opened, and a guy wearing a pair of jogging shorts, socks, and shoes stepped out.

He had a magnificent body.

"Morning." I said, nodding my head. "Going out for a jog?"

One of his eyebrows went up, and he smiled at me. "I want some exercise, at any rate."

I pushed my door open, and stood aside. "Well, come on then."

His hand brushed against my crotch as he went into my room.

I closed my eyes. *Thank you, Jesus.* I thought quickly as I shut the door behind me.

Maybe this cruise wasn't going to be so bad after all.

Postcards from the Orgy Deck
David Holly

March 23
Frank Worthing & Paul Shields
868 Spring St.
San Juan Capistrano, CA 92675

Dear Frank and Paul,

I finally convinced Bill to come on an All Gay Cruise. Oh, the eye-candy! You've never seen so many fabulous guys (with constant hard-ons) wearing slinky swimsuits. My new red Speedo looks modest in comparison. Ole' stick-in-the-mud Bill is sporting 22-inch-long sunburst boardshorts, but his thick cock makes an appealing profile.

Wish you were here,
Dave

March 23
Mrs. Prudence Danforth
347 Colonial Drive
Montpelier, VT 05602

Dear Aunt Prudence,

Greetings from the Port of Miami. My chum Bill and I are on a cruise ship preparing to depart for the French Caribbean. After boarding, selecting our dinner hour, and booking our excursions, we are relaxing poolside with platters of coconut shrimp and scrumptious frozen banana daiquiris.

Wish you were here,
Your Nephew Dave

March 23
Elizabeth McKee
2105 SE Ash St., Apt. 4
Portland, OR 97214

Dear Mackie,

Bill and I no sooner hit the pool deck (I'm wearing the red Speedo—too early to spring the thongs you helped me select) then a steward arrived with "Spank the Monkey Banana Daiquiris": white rum, dark rum, banana liqueur, and crème de cacao. Surrounding me are thousands of guys in skimpy swimsuits, thongs, and sarongs. Oh, Mackie, you'd be in fag hag heaven.

Wish you were here,
Dave

March 23
Frank Worthing & Paul Shields
868 Spring St.
San Juan Capistrano, CA 92675

Dear Frank and Paul,

This afternoon has been loaded with outrageously campy activities—a bon voyage party, gay bingo (huh?), drag queen comedians, karaoke, gay themed movies, piano bar, pop vocalists, a gay cabaret, porn star parties, underwear fashion shows, tea dances, and themed dance parties. Nice, but where's the sex? My travel agent hinted that the crowd would be sexually stimulating, but not that many guys got laid. Screw that—I'm here for whoopee!

Dave

March 23
Elizabeth McKee
2105 SE Ash St., Apt. 4
Portland, OR 97214

Hey, Mackie,

I'm busy reading tourist guidebooks so I can write bogus cards to my old Aunt Prudence. She controls the purse strings, as you well know, and I want to inherit the family fortune when she kicks the bucket. If Aunt Prudence knew a fraction of my activities, she'd stop my allowance and disinherit me. I might have to WORK for a living. THE HORROR!

Dave

March 24
Frank Worthing & Paul Shields
868 Spring St.
San Juan Capistrano, CA 92675

Dear Frank and Paul,

We're under way (or is it weigh?), and the sexual tension is so thick you couldn't cut it with a machete. While we were watching a cabaret, standing room only, some old fart kept feeling up my ass—a compliment to my stunning derrière, but sheesh! Funny thing—I thought Bill would gripe, but he encouraged the senior butt pincher.

Dave

March 24
Mrs. Prudence Danforth
347 Colonial Drive
Montpelier, VT 05602

Dear Aunt,

We embarked at sunset, and it was quite the festive event. The boat was gaily bedecked with streamers and colored flags, while many of the lads had decorated the doors and windows of their cabins. The breeze quickened from the Atlantic as we slid from the dock with a happy blast of the ship's horn. White seagulls rose around us with their glad cries and brown pelicans swooped. My heart leaped up with excitement at the beautiful scene. I hope that you can join me on a future cruise.

Your loving nephew,
Dave

March 25
Elizabeth McKee
2105 SE Ash St., Apt. 4
Portland, OR 97214

Dear Mackie,

Bill and I and a bunch of other guys flogged our dolphins while we watched a Texas college student putting out. The guys have been sticking sexual advertising on their doors, but this kid one-upped the lot by propping his door open and putting on his own sex show titled "Banged from Both Ends." The guy fucking the kid had an ass that could've powered a jackhammer. Bill and I could see his thick cock sliding in and out of the college kid's butt hole. Meanwhile the kid's mouth was slurping a young black cock. Didn't take long before the passage outside the room was slick with semen, Bill's and mine included.

Love and kisses,
Dave

March 26
Frank Worthing & Paul Shields
868 Spring St.
San Juan Capistrano, CA 92675

Dear Frank and Paul,

Didn't get a chance to finish a card yesterday. The ship steamed along like stink and we docked in Haiti. Bill vowed he wouldn't set foot on the "Magic Island," so we stayed aboard, though I quizzed the guys who went so I could pretend. We were tanning by the pool when Mike from Dover called for a game of "Bare-Assed Leap Frog." You get the idea? Whee!

Dave

March 26
Mrs. Prudence Danforth
347 Colonial Drive
Montpelier, VT 05602

Dear Aunt Prudence,

Late yesterday afternoon, the ship docked at Cap Haitien. The city looked pretty, rather pastel and delicate. The Haitians rely upon the tourist trade, selling paintings, wood carvings, and baskets, and retain the French panache for producing delicious cuisine. Outside of the town stand the ruins of King Christophe's Sans Souci palace, and on the top of the mountain, Citadelle Laferrière.La Citadelle is clearly visible from the ship, hewn of stone, and shaped so that it looks like a ship itself floating upon the clouds.

With warmest regard,
Dave

March 26
Elizabeth McKee
2105 SE Ash St., Apt. 4
Portland, OR 97214

Hey, Mackie,

I ended up wearing so much splooge, you wouldn't believe. First there was a game of "Bare-Assed Leap Frog," and a "Jack and Jill Party" followed it. No Jills turned up, to my relief. Imagine twenty guys stroking their hard cocks and popping anal beads and butt plugs up their asses while watching other guys play. Bill couldn't hold out thirty strokes before he decorated my chest, while Mike blasted his jizz onto my butt. Everybody was squirting spunk and getting showered. The magic of a circle jerk is in watching fellows spasm and feeling them come on you. Group sex is hot, hot, hot.

Dave

March 27
Elizabeth McKee
2105 SE Ash St., Apt. 4
Portland, OR 97214

Hey, Mackie,

This afternoon the guys took over one pool for a grab ass game of "Gay Marco Polo." You ever played "Marco Polo?" Imagine a hundred horny gayboys in a pool, and when you're caught your swimsuit comes off! Caught naked, and your cock gets sucked. I wanted to catch this deliciously slim guy named Fidel. Fidel is a mixed race Cuban with golden skin and jet-black hair and he was wearing a green swim slip with a tight seam up his ass crack. (I cheated a little by peeking through my eyelashes). No luck, though I glommed onto some hunky butts and torsos and some fresh gayboys got their hands on my red bikini. Then, can you believe it??—Fidel caught Bill!!! Fidel seized Bill's buns with both hands and off came Bill's board-shorts from the tent factory. Good thing that Bill had already been loosened up by four watermelon margaritas, 'cause for a few minutes, his dick was the most available hard-on in the pool.

Dave

March 28
Mrs. Prudence Danforth
347 Colonial Drive
Montpelier, VT 05602

Dear Aunt Prudence,

We spent yesterday steaming toward our southernmost des-tination, Martinique. For the most part we were traveling over the open Caribbean Sea, though we passed a few small islands, most only sandbars. For much of the afternoon, the sky and the sea maintained the same hue so I could see no horizon. However, life is never dull aboard the ship. There is a constant stream of new chaps to meet, each with his own interests, and we get together for games to pass the time.

Your adoring nephew,
Dave

March 28
Frank Worthing & Paul Shields
868 Spring St.
San Juan Capistrano, CA 92675

Dear Frank and Paul,

Following a hot game of "Gay Marco Polo" yesterday, Bill and I had the best sex we've had all year. Our sex life had been getting a little stale, so this cruise is part of the cure. Anyway, getting sucked off in the pool got Bill in the mood, and he gave me the blow job of a lifetime—better even than the first time he sucked me. When our cabin door clicked behind us, he dropped to his knees and kissed my cock through my wet Speedo. Then he pulled it down, groped my ass cheeks with his smooth hands, and touched his lips to my cock head. The way he popped his lips over my cock head and took it down his throat was sheer bliss. I begged him to hold off so I could suck him some too, but he showed me no mercy. I blasted my load down his throat.

Dave

March 28
Elizabeth McKee
2105 SE Ash St., Apt. 4
Portland, OR 97214

Hey, Mackie,

Bill has been loosening up ever since we embarked. They say that everybody goes to pieces in the tropics. Whatever!—his button-down inhibitions have been dropping like beachgoers assailed by the no-see-ums. This morning he tossed aside his board shorts and claimed my red Speedo.

Dave

March 28
Elizabeth McKee
2105 SE Ash St., Apt. 4
Portland, OR 97214

Hey, Mackie,

I had the most awesome orgasm. When Bill sucked me off after the "Marco Polo" game, my whole body went off like a fire truck. He started sucking me, and his mouth was a relentless tug massage on my cock. My cock head was tingling right off, loving the way Bill's lips, tongue, mouth, and throat were loving the penetration of my cock. The tingles turned into waves of pleasure, and I gripped his head to fuck his mouth while his hands played with my wanton gay ass. Then the hot explosion of orgasm, like my heart stopped and my brain exploded. My body was frozen in the instant of ultimate rush and at the same time it was a molten pulsing magma, and I was coming like a bitch into the mouth of the man I love.

Dave

March 30
Frank Worthing & Paul Shields
868 Spring St.
San Juan Capistrano, CA 92675

Dear Frank and Paul,

Rats! Martinique didn't have a single nude beach. The dykes went topless but where's the thrill in that? I was hoping for bare male asses and swinging dicks. Still, the place was easy on the eyes because the people are gorgeous. I don't think I've ever seen so many beautiful men speaking French or Creole. Bill and I sampled rum from all eleven of the island's distilleries; then we went back to the ship and danced half the night at our little onboard fairy carnival. Bill and I wore green tights, green vests, and green Robin Hood hats.

Hungover from the tips of my artfully frosted hair down to my green polished toenails.

Dave

March 30
Elizabeth McKee
2105 SE Ash St., Apt. 4
Portland, OR 97214

Mackie,

Went to a Green Party last night. No, I never heard of it either, but it had a Green Man or a Jack o' the Wood theme. Bill and I were already feeling no pain after the rum on Martinique. Bill's inhibitions being loosened, we went commando under our green tights, which showed off our assets. I must've freak danced with thirty guys, grabbing my ankles and wiggling my ass to the music while those hunky boys humped my butt.

Some of them got off too, because the seam of my tights was sticky and stained.

Dave

March 30
Mrs. Prudence Danforth
347 Colonial Drive
Montpelier, VT 05602

Dear Aunt Prudence,

My high school French may be rusty. On Martinique, we thought we booked a catamaran to a black sand beach, but the vessel delivered us to a bat cave. *Incroyable!* The bats were neither congenial nor photogenic. Still, Martinique has fabulous museums with an inspiring collection of Paul Gauguin's paintings (he lived and painted on this island before going to the South Seas). Knowing your love for your flower garden, I can report that Martinique's flowers are *magnifiques,* as are its perfumes, pastries, cheeses, and wines.

Wish you were here,
Dave

March 31
Frank Worthing & Paul Shields
868 Spring St.
San Juan Capistrano, CA 92675

Dear Frank and Paul,

Heading north by northeast toward Marie Galante. On the ship, we're eating rice and crabs (no, not those kind), and listening to *Zouk,* French Caribbean music with a West African rhythm. I'm sunbathing in a hibiscus thong. All afternoon we've been sucking down *ti'punch,* a potent rum concoction with sugarcane syrup and fresh lime, and listening to some senior citizen from Wichita endeavor to get into Bill's red Speedo. The bikini does hug Bill's firm buns deliciously—the old queen called it Tansie's Formal.

Sure as shit doesn't look like Kansas, Toto,
Dave

April 1
Elizabeth McKee
2105 SE Ash St., Apt. 4
Portland, OR 97214

Holy fuck, Mackie,

Bill and I ended up playing "Choo-Choo" last night. That's a bunch of guys in a line, each plugged into the ass of the guy in front. Seth from Cleveland had some wicked, homegrown weed that got us totally wasted, and we threw caution to the trade winds. Having a stupendous orgasm while stoned and while having a big cock sliding in and out of your ass is an experience you can't imagine. The orgasm is deeper and richer, somehow, and does it last! After the "Choo-Choo got off, we watched the engine fuck the caboose. What a show! Could those horny gayboys fuck! Then we showered as a group, each guy soaping every cock and butt crack he could reach.

Dave

April 1
Mrs. Prudence Danforth
347 Colonial Drive
Montpelier, VT 05602

Dear Aunt Prudence,
    We stopped briefly at Marie Galante. Locals call it *La Grande Galette* because the island is round and fairly flat. The highest hill *Morne Constant* is 670 feet. We saw hundred-year-old windmills, and ox-drawn carts are common. Ashore we dined on *bebele* and *court bouillon de poisson frais.*

Miss you,
Dave

April 2
Elizabeth McKee
2105 SE Ash St., Apt. 4
Portland, OR 97214

Hey, Mackie,
    After playing Marco Polo all day and Choo-Choo two nights in a row, Bill and I were complaining of sore crotches. So we flossed our butt cracks on Guadeloupe's Caravelle Beach, an uncluttered stretch of powdery sand when it's not cluttered with a thousand hungover homosexuals.

Love,
Dave

April 2
Mrs. Prudence Danforth
347 Colonial Drive
Montpelier, VT 05602

Dear Aunt Prudence,
   We docked at Pointe-a-Pitre, Guadeloupe, last night. You
and I should move here! Wide tree-lined boulevards, first-rate
schools, universal health care, a social safety net, and leisure
time for self-actualization add up to a higher standard of living
than we enjoy at home. The inhabitants are a jolly crowd, celebrating Bastille Day, Arts Fest, All Saints' Day, Fête des
Cuisinieres, and Carnival. The island-grown coffee is black as
midnight and sweet with Guadeloupean sugar. The trade winds
blow over sugar cane and banana plantations, the 4,977 foot La
Soufrière volcano, pristine rainforest, rainbow-crowned water-
falls, precipitous canyons, rock formations like fairy castles,
sapphire waters, and silvery beaches.

Your nephew,
Dave

April 3
Frank Worthing & Paul Shields
868 Spring St.
San Juan Capistrano, CA 92675

Dear Frank and Paul,
   Here we are on St. Barts, playground of celebrities. Bill
caught a glimpse of Paris Hilton and David Letterman, and I
spotted three gay porn stars. The world-famous Saline Beach is
clothing-optional and it has a gay area. Of lesser importance,
it's a great beach for sunning and seeing crystal clear water. One

POSTCARDS FROM THE ORGY DECK

local gayboy told me that the beach is usually occupied only by the locals and far from crowded. Not today.

Dave

April 3
Mrs. Prudence Danforth
347 Colonial Drive
Montpelier, VT 05602

Dear Aunt,
   Semi-arid and extremely hilly, St. Barthélemy did not support large plantations, so while there were domestic slaves, the island never developed the taint of a slave economy. Its beaches are so dazzling that they are nearly perfect and très européenne.

Votre neveu aimé,
Dave

April 4
Frank Worthing & Paul Shields
868 Spring St.
San Juan Capistrano, CA 92675

My travel agent is clueless. Debauchery such as you would not believe occurred on the night we left St. Barts. The upper pool deck turned into the orgy deck. Everything started out normally (normal for our group) with a '60's Mod Party—picture guys wearing love beads and flowered bell-bottoms—or miniskirts. I went in drag in a psychedelic minidress. We had a whole bale of pot and as it vanished, the pants came off. Those of us in miniskirts tossed our hems over our backs, bent over, and grabbed the ship rails.

Fucked on the Orgy Deck,
Dave

April 4
Elizabeth McKee
2105 SE Ash St., Apt. 4
Portland, OR 97214

So far the Mod Party has been the biggest orgy of the trip. I got wasted in so many ways that I won first prize as the cruise's most promiscuous slut (that's hard to believe considering how available these guys are). Bill got gang-banged too, and he sucked too many cocks to nitpick about my behavior. Funny thing was, when we fell into bed, we cuddled, made love, and declared undying devotion. The guys we fucked on the side just didn't count.

Dave

April 4
Elizabeth McKee
2105 SE Ash St., Apt. 4
Portland, OR 97214

You would have found St. Barthélemy so charmingly French: the police even wore kepis. The town of St. Jean was jam-packed with European bistros, French brasseries, lavish villas, and stylish boutiques. In the hills east of town we discovered the old St. Barthélemy where the red-roofed houses have walls of stone. Nearby rose the highest peak, from which I caught a glimpse of the British Virgin Islands.

Pensées,
Dave

April 4
Mrs. Prudence Danforth
347 Colonial Drive
Montpelier, VT 05602

The hard-core butt fucking and daisy-chain cocksucking went on and on. There were big bowls of extra-strength condoms, flavored condoms, and assorted lubricants. The bars were pumping out tropical drinks and Caribbean beers at top speed, and the bale of pot had appeared again. Seth from Cleveland better ditch that shit before we meet U.S. Customs in Miami.

Like I said, I was in drag in a '60s minidress, made of paper, I think, and it was pulled over my hips so I could take on a gang of horny studs. Some of the crew also must've fucked me, because they were smirky at the breakfast buffet this morning. I had to send them back to the kitchen for more Bananas Foster, which took way too long to arrive and were not *flambées* at the table.

High-maintenance Dave

April 5
Frank Worthing & Paul Shields
868 Spring St.
San Juan Capistrano, CA 92675

Dear Frank and Paul,
   I'm still drunk and stoned after last night's orgy. Bill and I are chilling out with triple sec-flavored margaritas and enjoying nude sunbathing at Orient Beach on St. Martin. I'm so wrecked that I haven't seen anything of the island, though I cribbed some crap from the guidebook and sent it on to my aunt. Oh, shit! I fucked up—I gotta get to the post office.

Dave

April 5
Elizabeth McKee
2105 SE Ash St., Apt. 4
Portland, OR 97214

Hey, Mackie,
   By any chance did a card come to you that went on and on with a load of tourist crap? If so, I am so screwed. It means I sent a card describing a gay sex orgy to my Aunt Prudence. I can't believe that I fucked up so royally. If the old prune gets that card, I can kiss my allowance and my inheritance good-bye. Unless I get lucky and she drops dead the second she reads it.

Alcohol and postcards do not mix,
Dave

April 5
Mrs. Prudence Danforth
347 Colonial Drive
Montpelier, VT 05602

Dear Aunt Prudence,

I suspect some degenerate person stole a postcard I had addressed to you. I attempted to intercept it, but the French postal authorities refused to permit me a look. If you receive a card with a foul message, even if it appears to be in my handwriting (FAKED), please destroy it unread.

À bientôt,
Dave

April 5
Mrs. Prudence Danforth
347 Colonial Drive
Montpelier, VT 05602

Chère Tante,

I remember when you took me to France for my twelfth birthday and I was so amazed that dogs were welcome guests all over. Well, Marigot is *très chique* and *très française*, so we were not surprised to find the island's dogs accompanying their masters everywhere, even into restaurants. St. Martin is rich with mango, almond, and guava groves, and there are farms, including a butterfly farm with 40 species. On the Dutch side I saw a windmill.

Again, *ignore* any card that could not have come from me. *Anansi le trickster est parmi nous.*

À bientôt,
Dave

April 6
Elizabeth McKee
2105 SE Ash St., Apt. 4
Portland, OR 97214

Our last night at sea included a fabled White Party. Bill and I wore the traditional white short-shorts and tee shirts of a clingy fabric. Imagine three thousand guys in white, dancing to a throbbing rhythm under the pulsating lights. The sexual tension grew until guys were dropping in groups. Bill and I finally hit our bed around three. Mackie, I gave him a two-hour blowjob, bringing him almost over the edge time and again until he had the most explosive orgasm ever. Afterward, he wanted me to fuck him, which was incredible. We were still fucking and sucking when the sun came up. In my postcards I may have stretched the truth about some of my sexual exploits, but I'm not exaggerating now. I feel like I've been reborn, and Bill agrees.

Dave

April 6
Frank Worthing & Paul Shields
868 Spring St.
San Juan Capistrano, CA 92675

Just heard that a group of Russian Charismatic Christians have booked the ship after us. Do you think they'll exorcize the decks of our evil influence?

Dave

April 6
Mrs. Prudence Danforth
347 Colonial Drive
Montpelier, VT 05602

Chère Tante,
   In a few hours we will disembark in Miami, Florida. It has been a wonderful voyage, though I thought of you virtually every minute. I miss you desperately and hope that we will be together again very soon. Perhaps you and I can together make the next journey to the French West Indies.
   Once again, should you receive some despicable card with a message that you know I could never have written, *please destroy it unread.* It wounds me deeply that a fiend could have played such a foul prank upon us.

Votre neveu affectueux,
Dave

Sunset on the Nebula Deck
Joel A. Nichols

Kip Daniels stood in the crowded causeway, resting his arm atop his roll-along suitcase. Men crowded the gleaming, curved hallway, looking each other up and down. At the front of the line, the broad, metal hatchway lurched open and two stewards with deep tans and bright white teeth began collecting tickets and motioning with their heads. Kip nudged ahead his suitcase. The stewards glanced at each passport and then ran a hand scanner over the barcode on the ticket. When the scanner chirped, the two over beautiful men smiled bleached teeth and sent a passenger through the hatch. Kip was wearing tight Y-fronts that clenched his balls and pushed up his cock so it would show big in his trousers. His friends Cash and Ben had given him two pairs for the cruise.

"Thanks," Kip said as they motioned him past. The line moved faster on the other side of the doorway, and he tugged his suitcase behind him. It thudded over the seams on the causeway floor. Long oblong windows showed the dull charcoal skin of the ship floating in front of a dense black curtain with few stars.

More stewards stood just inside the ship, pointing passengers right and left. Kip flashed his ticket at one of them—a tall man with dark brown skin and a neat black goatee, and the steward leaned in and put his hand on Kip's shoulder. "Right over there—follow the blue lines on the deck to the 'Mercury Mezzanine,' cabin number 443. Enjoy your cruise with us!"

Before Kip could mumble thanks, the man had shoved him in the direction of the blue tracks snaking off around a corner. Inside the ship thrummed. Kip followed the blue line up a short ramp that fed into a lighted hallway. Info-screens up and down the hallway showed the twinkling star field alternating with a list of scheduled events. As he stood reading one, someone rolled a suitcase wheel over his foot. Kip stepped out of the way.

"I'm so sorry!" The man who had run into him had a short red beard and a deep voice. "I didn't see you . . . too busy looking at this schedule."

"Don't worry about it," Kip said. He pointed. "Yeah, it's like the army."

The redhead smiled. "Sorry, I'm clumsy. See you around, OK?" He twisted his suitcase handle in his hands and strode away. Kip stared after him, watching the muscles work in the back of his thick legs. As the man disappeared around the corner, Kip remembered that he should have introduced himself. He sighed and looked at the info-screen.

2100	Captain and Crew's Welcome
2145	Captain's Cocktails
2300	Dinner in the Star Deck Dining Room—(vegan buffet)
	Dinner in the Comet Lounge—(vegetarian buffet)
	Dinner in the Orbit Deck Dining Room—(buffet)
	"Who Needs Dinner" Cocktail Party (Nebula Deck)
0100	Pool Party at the Moonlight Lagoon (Star Deck)
	Dancing at the Gas Giant (Orbit Deck)
	Anything Goes Party at the Black Hole (Nebula Deck)
0900	Speed Dating Breakfast, locations TBA

Kip stopped reading, and concentrated on the blue line. Why did everything have to have such cartoonish names! The brochures had been overwhelming enough, when his pushy friends Cash and Ben had given him the cruise as a thirtieth birthday present. Kip wasn't getting any younger, though, and was getting sick of going out to the same bars. So Cash and Ben had sent him on a Starliner Voyage, a kitschy singles' cruise around the Russjo Nebula.

***

Kip molded his sandy brown hair into a front flip, imitating that actor. It took him almost an hour, fretting and fussing in front of the mirror inside the miniature bathroom in his cabin, the counter of which had vanished under his gels, waxes, hairdryer, and curling iron. It reminded him of his younger days. Cash and Ben had made him promise he'd try on this cruise. And fixing his hair into this elaborate twink shape was step one.

He'd missed the Captain's Welcome and figured he'd be better just heading straight to the cocktail party. He traced his steps back toward the main fork, following the blue line as it curved along the ship's interior. As he made his way toward the banquet hall, the crowd grew thicker. Men tall and fat, skinny and short, black and brown, all wearing smart, gay outfits thronged the hallway. They wore sleeveless shirts that revealed arms with ropy muscles and big slabs of bicep, tight and shiny tunics, and patterned, designer oxfords that Kip knew cost as much as a week's wages. He came up to a group of guys standing around an observation window. Stars streaked past as the ship slipped faster and faster toward the Russjo Nebula Corridor. The men were laughing, and one was clapping another on the back. They all had tattoos: Two wore ink on their temples that traced around the backs of their necks in intricate lines, and the others with pictures on their arms and hands. One brilliant Virgin, all blue and pink and yellow, rose from a crease of elbow and bloomed over an upper arm. Kip tried not to stare—tried to glance at the men while watching the star field, but one of the handsomer ones looked over and locked eyes with him.

Kip smiled. The man looked away blankly, scratched his wrist where a filigree of thorns snaked around the bone and ignored Kip. Kip blushed, and pushed on. Up ahead stood a tall, lithe man with oval eyes. The man was alone and watching the crowd around the doorway to the Captain's Lounge. His T-shirt was a rhinestone-studded screen-print of Princess Rosanna as she had looked six or seven years ago, when she spent her nights dancing in queer bars and snorting club drugs off the shoulders and backs of her hunkier subjects. Since then, she'd been the style icon for the whole planet even though her father had threatened to disinherit her and Parliament had censured her—their future queen—for her embarrassing and lewd behavior. Underneath her rhinestone smile was her famous response to the censure: "Let them eat my ass." That had endeared her to Kip, who was a staunch anti-royalist despite the princess's homo-friendly partying.

Kip walked in the man's direction, thinking up something to say about the T-shirt. But as he stepped around a guy yelling into a phone and plugging up his other ear, he saw that someone else was already talking to the tall man. He swore on his way to the bar.

The captain leaned against the bar railing. His smooth and unlined face suggested plastics rejuvenation, since his thick salt-and-pepper hair curled over his forehead with a jaunty maturity. His teeth were just as white as the stewards. Too white. He wore a white uniform with the silver captain's stripes around both forearms. His round, brimmed cap sat on the bar next to a sweating martini with a long, curling twist of lime peel reaching toward the bottom of the shallow glass like seaweed. His shoulders were wide and his chest firm and broad. Big hands with shiny nails gestured to the giant triangle-shaped porthole behind the shirtless bartenders. A crowd of younger men—boys almost, certainly university or academy students spending a term break on this party cruise—ringed him, rapt. Kip saw what they were watching: the captain leaked sex in his throaty voice and white uniform pants that bulged at his crotch and hugged juicy thighs and ass. Even the shirtless bartenders couldn't help but watch the powerful man seduce this group of young men as other passengers lusted after them, adding exorbitant tips to their checks for a few more seconds of attention from their sweating, sculpted chests.

"What you'll see between here and there is really nothing. The systems between the planet at the Nebula Corridor are empty, full of dusty rocks and asteroids that have been mined dead. But," he flicked his powerful wrist to check the silver-plated dials strapped underneath the hem of his shirtsleeves, "When we decelerate in just over seven hours from now, you will begin to see the first clouds of the Russjo."

Kip listened to his meager description of the gasses and colored dust as he keyed in his cabin number on the pad the shirtless bartender held out to him. When the code cleared, he handed Kip his margarita. Hazy wisps of vapor drifted from the iced glass. It was all in the book Cash and Ben had given him along with the cruise. It was much more interesting than the captain seemed to care about, especially because more than half of it had been seeded by tourist companies when the original eddies of the incubating stars hadn't been big enough or bright enough to keep drawing cruise money. Most of the brilliant colors they'd be seeing in fifteen hours had been planned by a marketing department and nobody but the driest astronomers—and a handful of reference librarians—knew what the Nebula had looked like when it was first discovered more than a hundred years before.

It had been beautiful, with bright green explosions curving gently through the rim of a dying galaxy that was slowly feeding the emerald and jade fire. Kip drank his margarita quickly and ordered another one, and moved away from where the captain was holding court. Kip drank another cocktail and followed a herd of men toward one of the buffets, not stopping to see which one it was. He ate a salty meal from the buffet, mak-

ing polite but disinterested conversation with a beefy account-
ant who talked of nothing but balance sheets and free weights.
At first Kip thought he might want to try and sleep with him,
but—Cash and Ben be damned—he wanted a real conversation
first.

"Attention. All passengers and crew. This is the captain. We
regret to interrupt your dinner, but very disturbing news has
just come over the wireless. Just after our launch, there was an
incident in the City—a bomb." The captain paused. Kip
thought he heard the man take a sip, or choke on a sob, it was
hard to tell over the intercom. "A terrorist bomb exploded on
Broome Street." The crowd gasped. Broome Street was the
core of the gay City, the high street for a queer neighborhood
that reached all the way from the center to the western sub-
urbs. "We know you may be worried about loved ones and
friends, and will make our long-ranges available as quickly as we
can on the control deck. But information may be slow—the
initial report had confirmed only a handful of dead." Again the
captain stopped. This time his sob was clear over the speakers.
"Among the victims were P-Prin-Princess Rosanna and her driv-
ers. We will continue our cruise as planned."

Men all over the dining room screwed up their faces. Many
began weeping, others wailing. Kip felt his stomach lurch. He
scanned the crowd for the willowy man wearing the Princess
Ro T-shirt, but didn't see him. The room had become chaotic
with people frantically dialing their phones. Most were out of
range of the planet by now, and people scowled and clutched at
the keypads with white knuckles. They hugged each other,
holding onto to their friends who were sobbing and squeezing
the arms and hands of mourning strangers. Kip stood up and
tasted a slug of tequila repeat in the back of his throat. He staggered across the room and out into the hallway. As he searched
the colorful lines crisscrossing in the hallway, wondering where
to go, he tripped on a pair of heavy brown boots.

It was the husky redhead who had bumped into him on the

way to his cabin. The man had sunk against the red-carpeted deck, and was holding his hairy face in both hands.

Kip picked himself up on his elbows. The man looked at him through his fingers. Kip started to stand up. "Are you alright? I know a lot of people loved her."

The man scoffed. "What?"

"Princess Rosanna. Didn't you hear the announcement?"

"No." The man pushed himself to his feet. He reached out and grabbed Kip's hand. "I was just sitting there—it was getting so loud in that dining room. And I think I had too much to drink earlier."

"It's the artificial gravity—it can make you pretty sick. Is this your first cruise?" The redhead nodded.

"I'm Jasper. Hey, didn't I run you over when we got here? It was you, wasn't it?" Kip shook his head up and down.

"Kip." He was a few inches taller, and looked down at the man's coarse red hair that trailed into silky sideburns. Kip noticed then that the man had two thin silver hoops in each pink earlobe. The info-screens along the hallways to the control room had been displaying the network coverage of the disaster, and the men in the hallway watched as rescue crews buzzed around the giant hole in the middle of downtown, near the Broome Street subway station.

Kip pointed to one of them. "There was a bomb. The Princess is dead."

"No shit," said Jasper. "A lot of other people dead?"

"Didn't say. But the guys inside are really upset. Even the captain sounded like he was crying."

The redhead twisted his head around toward the door to the banquet hall. "I never really got into Rosanna that much. Now her brother—he's something to look at."

Kip laughed. "You're not serious? He wears tie-dye—and he's a prince!!"

"He's just finding himself. I wore tie-dye like that once."

"Me too, I guess," said Kip. He sighed.

Jasper winked at him. "Do you want go to one of the other buffets?"

As the ship slid closer and closer to the Nebula, Jasper and Kip shared a plate of hot seitan and sour noodles piled with bright pink soy shrimp. Jasper kept pouring cups of steaming tea. Kip told him how they'd made the Nebula.

"I'm not sure I would have come here if I'd known," he said. He offered Kip the last soy shrimp. "How'd you find that out?"

Kip looked down in his teacup. The leaves undulated like milfoil. "I'm a librarian—and these friends of mine from work, this couple, they sent me on this cruise and gave me a tour book."

"No way!" Jasper's voice rose in excitement. A solemn man at the next turned to look and he dropped his voice to a whisper. "I'm a book-maker."

Kip's eyes lit up. Nobody had paper books anymore—even his library branch had gotten rid of most of them. He had a few at home he'd gotten as presents from his parents. "You can make a living?"

"I have a few excellent private clients. They pay the bills—and enough left over to buy a cruise."

Kip told him about the handful of books on his shelf, and asked him about his work. "I've seen that one! In a shop window." Kip had been pressing his toes against Jasper's under the table, and suddenly Jasper reached over and laid his hand on Kip's chin.

He leaned over the table and kissed Kip. His lips were firm and his tongue wet and warm. Kip's face chafed against his short beard. The redhead's hairy upper lip tickled his nose. They pulled apart.

"Let's get out of here," Jasper said, tugging Kip by the arm. On the way out, they walked past the tall man wearing a Princess Rosanna T-shirt. He was slumped over a table.

***

They made their way to the Nebula Deck, which had a large, dark bar and lounge with low couches bolted under huge portholes. "Sunset Lounge" burned bright in a neon sign over the door. Men stood in twos and threes, drinking and talking about Princess Rosanna in hushed tones.

Jasper pulled Kip across the lounge, into a dark room. A group of men stood in a circle, pulling at their dicks, a couple of them reaching to stroke another, two kissing, one reaching across the group to squeeze at a nipple. Kip stared at them as Jasper dragged him by the wrist. Kip's cheeks flushed. At the end of the room were doors to private booths.

"We'll see the first traces of the Nebula soon," Jasper said as he chose one of the booths and they slipped inside. "Human made and all."

Kip took a sharp breath—one entire wall of the booth was a clear window open to the black soup of space. In the distance, stars were floating by.

"Hope you're not afraid of heights."

"No," Kip said. "Just surprised. This is a great view."

There was padded cushion on the floor, and the two of them sank against each other on top of it, still holding hands.

Jasper grabbed hold of Kip's shoulders and pushed him back on the cushion. He crawled between his legs and traced his fingers down Kip's chest, playing at his nipples through his shirt and then drawing a straight line to his belt. Kip was holding his breath and could hear his own pulse.

He tried to sit up, but Jasper pushed him down. "Just relax," he said, and Kip threw back his head and thought, if Ben and Cash could see me now.

Jasper laid his cheek against Kip's crotch, grinding his jaw against the flap of zipper. Kip sprang hard. "It's been a while," he mumbled.

He ran his fingers through Jasper's close cropped hair, burying his nails in the red whorls as the other man nudged open Kip's fly and pulled it open. In the tight underwear, Kip's cock lay fat in his lap. Jasper cupped his package and peeled back the briefs. He sucked at Kip, drawing it all the way in and letting it slide slowly back out, so that the ring of his lips caught it around the head. Kip moaned.

Jasper let Kip fall out of his mouth. He kissed his hipbone, licking his salty skin. His beard tickled Kip's thigh, and he squirmed back and forth. Jasper grabbed Kip's dick around the bottom and shook its weight back and forth. As he licked down around his balls, he smacked the cock against his furry cheek.

He drew each of his balls between his lips, still squeezing and stroking Kip. With his other hand he traced down the curve of Kip's ass, letting his wet finger tease up and down Kip's crack. He pressed against his hole.

Kip groaned and ground himself down on Jasper's finger. He guided himself back into Jasper's mouth. As he sank into Jasper's throat and onto his finger, Kip moaned and a spider-quick shock ran up his spine. He clenched his muscles and pushed on the back of Jasper's head. Kip opened his eyes and saw Jasper looking up at him. He started leaking, then coming with shaking legs and a quivering ass. Over Jasper's bent head, Kip watched the first silky strands of the Nebula drift past the window. They two of them lay there, watching the clouds.

Time Sharing
Rob Rosen

I was sitting in the hotel lobby, a drink in one hand, my speech in the other. I've always hated conferences, especially when I'm the one doing all the talking in front of a group of strangers. Hence the drink, and a rather stiff one at that.

So when she smiled, sat down, and introduced herself, I thought she was just another attendee, equally as bored as I was. But man was I wrong. Because the only thing worse than working on a weekend, even at an oceanfront resort in Fort Lauderdale, is someone trying to sell you time-sharing at an oceanfront resort in Fort Lauderdale.

She began her spiel, all smiles, of course. "All I ask is for two hours of your time, and then dinner and drinks are on the house for the rest of your stay."

I quickly downed the remainder of my cocktail. "Sorry, ma'am, my work is already paying for everything. But thanks and . . ."

"And a show at the Copa," she interrupted.

"Gloria Estefan is performing at the conference. Who's at the Copa?"

The smile briefly wavered. "And a cruise."

"A cruise?" I felt the familiar tug as she began to reel me in. I regained my senses quickly enough, though. "No thanks, but . . ."

"But the cruise is two nights and a day in the Bahamas. All expenses paid." She looked me up and down, appraising her prey, deciding which was the best bait to lure me in with. "Your choice: An all-straight or an all-*gay* cruise."

She had me hook, line, and sinker. "When do you want me there?"

Truth be told, she almost had me at "cruise." She definitely had me at "gay." She also had me the next day. I bought the time-share unit. In my defense, it was a really nice resort. Plus, there was an open bar at the presentation. In other words, I should've just handed her my checkbook when I walked through the door.

The cruise was legit, though. Sort of. It was all gay. It was all expenses paid, too. It was even a nice ship, large and sleek and chock full of amenities. But I had to pay my way back to Fort Lauderdale, and I had to take the trip on a Tuesday through a Thursday, any week from June to November. If it sounded fishy, remember who they were dealing with.

June to November: hurricane season.

The boat was half empty. A boat half full of idiots, like myself, who didn't bother to check the weather at sea during the month of August. It was the only week I could take off, though. I hoped, nay prayed, I'd make it back in one piece.

Everything started out nicely enough. The weather in Florida was okay: hot, humid, blue skies for miles—out to the horizon, at any rate. And the guys were attractive, the single ones that is, which there seemed to be scant few of. Well, at least they were all wearing skimpy bathing suits, and not much else. Eye candy is better than no candy at all, I like to think.

The ship pulled out of port at five at night. It was due in Nassau at eight the next morning, which left me a whole evening to eat, drink, and cavort. Eating started promptly at six, drinking soon after, and thundering gray clouds rolled in just after that. Cavorting was scratched right off the list, barely making an indentation in the paper. As was frolicking, romping, and, yes, even dancing. It was, by all intents and purposes, a lost cause. The ship heaved and hoed me right back down towards my itty, bitty below-deck cabin at just after nine.

My body swayed from side to side as I made my way down the corridor. Dinner was great, but it was quickly returning for an encore. I made it to the cabin just in time. Just in time to catch the guy next-door reaching for his handle the same split second I did.

I looked up. He looked up. "Fun, huh?" I quipped.

"Like a barrel of seasick monkeys," he said, with a grimace. "Is my face as green as yours?"

Actually, his face, though slightly sweaty, was downright cute. "Maybe just a little bit," I confessed. But the green went so well with his sparkling blue eyes. Still, I had little time to add that little tidbit. A certain porcelain potty was screaming my name. I hurried inside, and not a minute too soon. The floor of the miniscule bathroom felt like the coolest place on the ship, not that my wobbly legs were taking me anyplace else to test this theory.

Ten minutes later, having still not moved except to take a giant swish of Listerine, I heard a knock coming from the divider that separated our two cabins. I grasped the edge of the sink and pulled myself up. The ocean lurched and tossed me the few feet I needed to reach the door.

I unlocked and opened it. He was standing there in a towel, his hair wet from a shower, droplets of water still clinging to his compact, lean, tight, sparsely haired frame. The eyes beamed and twinkled. "You all right?" he asked, holding each of his hands up, adding, "Pepto-Bismol or Tums?"

I leaned down to the mini-fridge and returned with my own hands now full. "Gin or Vodka?"

"An odd combination, yours and mine." He grinned, revealing a neat row of pearly whites.

"Then let's skip the former and go for the latter. You get the tonic and the ice, I'll scrounge up some rope to batten us down with." I blushed at the joke. He seemed not to notice, or at least to care. "Never mind, just come in."

"We don't have a hurricane season in Phoenix," he said, walking in and taking the only seat in the house, namely the bed. Thank God for cheap accommodations.

"Not in San Francisco either, only earthquakes. And even then, the rocking generally stops after a few seconds." I fixed us our drinks and sat on the floor looking up at him. "Name's Josh," I said, leaning over to shake his hand.

"Steve," he said, with a firm grasp that lingered a few seconds too long. But who was counting. "Great weather we're having. Let me know when Noah arrives and I'll break out the animals." I laughed, as did he. "Serves us right. Time-sharing?" he asked, knowingly.

I nodded. "Time-sharing." He downed his drink. The waves rocked my tiny room. His defined legs parted with the sudden jolt, offering me a view up his towel. His massive balls bounced to the ship's rhythm. I quickly looked away, and then just as quickly looked back. "Did the shower help?" I asked.

"Briefly. But I kept dropping the soap. No pun intended. The cold water did shake off some of the queezies, though."

I knew what he meant. The motion of the ocean was doing quite a number on my sensitive tummy. And him sitting there practically naked like that was simply adding fuel to the fire. I stood back up. "Mind if I . . ." I didn't get a chance to finish my thought. The boat rocked, yet again, and I went tumbling forward, my hand landing in his lap.

"I don't mind at all," he whispered, his face now a few inches away, those eyes locking in on mine. I could feel his cock twitch beneath the thin towel.

"I was gonna say, *take a shower,*" I said, in between ragged breathes.

"I know what you were gonna say," he replied, moving in closer and then closer still, until his lips just barely brushed my own, sending a burst of electricity down my spine that bolted right out through my crotch.

"Bon voyage," he said, pressing his lips harder against my own. His were soft and wet. I parted his mouth so that our tongues could do a casual swirl.

When we separated, I informed, "That's what they say when you take off. We've already left."

He chuckled, ran his tongue done my chin, across my neck and around my earlobe, which he took between his teeth, before saying, "So *take off* your clothes then."

"And fuck the shower?"

"Or just fuck me." He reached down and removed the towel. His cock jutted up and out, a thick, veined, rigid seven inches that glistened at the tip of his fat mushroom head. I couldn't wait to get my mouth wrapped around it, not to mention all the rest of him. Big things, apparently, do come in small packages.

I jumped into bed. Sitting next to him, I pulled my shirt up and off. He massaged my chest. "Hard, hairy pecs," he said, appraising me. "Yum."

I reached over and returned the favor. "Tight, hairless ones. Yum."

His hand moved farther down, gliding across my tummy hair, sending tingles through my belly. "And killer abs, dude."

"Sweet talker," I said, with a chuckle, and then a kiss on his neck. His own stomach looked and felt flat as a washboard, with just a slight treasure trail that disappeared into his trimmed bush. I rubbed the firm muscles. He leaned back to allow the attention. Then I slipped out of my slacks and boxers, until we were both naked and hard, sitting next to each other, hip to hip. The boat still swayed ever so slightly, not that I noticed anymore.

I leaned in again, our faces an inch apart, "Hey," I whispered.

"Hey," he whispered back, his stunning blues boring into my muddy browns.

I leaned back on the bed. He lay down on top of me, his body fitting snuggly into mine. He kissed me, sending the familiar waves of pleasure coursing through my stomach and pulsing dick, sending my nerve endings into overdrive. I reached around and caressed the small of his back. Soft, taught skin. Hairless, so unlike my own. My hands traveled further south, cupping his round, hard ass, also hairless, save for the groove, which I parted and stroked. My index fingers found the crinkled center, circled with fine, soft hairs. He moaned, gently, as I prodded his hole, working the rim.

"What you gonna do with that?" he rasped into my ear before biting down on my lobe.

I laughed and rolled him over so I could stare down at his beautiful face. "Well," I replied. "I was thinking about licking it first, getting it good and wet, then maybe sliding one or two fingers inside, you know, to get you ready for the real deal."

He looked down at my cock. "Better make it three fingers then."

Again I laughed. "Good idea. And then, well, that'll be a surprise."

He craned his neck up to kiss me. "I like surprises."

"Then you're gonna love this one."

My mouth worked its way to his neck, which I sucked on, instantly creating goose pimples down his sinewy arms. His nipples were next. They were small but hard, and I could tell that they liked to be sucked and licked and tweaked because each time I pulled and slapped and bit them, he'd arch his back and kick at the bunched up sheets down by his feet. I grabbed his hands and pinned him down. He grasped my fingers and writhed beneath me.

"Yeah," he moaned, as I bit hard, harder, first on one then the other nipple. They pulsed after every suck and slurp. Each time he rasped the word, a shiver went down my back. My mouth continued on its merry way, stopping at each granite-hard, little ab-pack, and then down and around his belly button, surrounded with the hair that led to the treasure in the center.

The tip of his rigid cock now rested on my lips. I licked the salty syrup off the top and then downed the head, filling my mouth with the pulsing helmet. I cupped his heavy balls in my hand, tickling the fine hairs before giving a gentle pull on the sack. Again his back arched and again the *yeah* escaped his mouth, rumbling through me like a locomotive.

Inch by thick inch I maneuvered the length of his formidable member inside my mouth, slicking it with spit, making my way down his shaft. In and out it went, each time farther down, until he was piston fucking my face as I tugged harder on his balls. His back and butt were now almost completely off the bed while I used my mouth on his prick and worked his nipples with my free hand.

"I'll take this over an open bar and a drag show any day," he groaned.

"And your cock is way better than that buffet upstairs."

He raised his legs and ass into the air. "Try the dessert."

His asshole now winked up at me, pretty and pink and puckered with a whirl of light brown hair circling it like a halo. I smacked each cheek in turn, then licked the hole and blew a cool breath of air across it before diving back in, sucking at it, making out with it like it was his mouth, tonguing it with a deep, long French kiss. His moaning continued. The bed and his balls rocked and swayed, whether from the ocean or him, I hadn't a clue.

I spit on the ring and then wet a finger, which I glided, slowly, evenly, up and in and back. Again my mouth found his heavenly prick, which throbbed each time I slid my index finger to the farthest reaches of his asshole. Soon I found my rhythm, mouth on cock, finger up ass, both going up and down, in and out, in perfect unison. Then one finger became two. But there was room for a third, or at least that's what he pled for. The guy liked having his ass worked over even more than his nipples. I sensed he could've taken four, but I had better things to fuck him silly with.

I jumped out of bed and returned with some lube and a rubber already wrapped around my bouncing, fat cock. His ass was still up in the air upon my return. It was a beautiful sight, hard and white like alabaster. I got back on top of him, swinging his calves over my shoulders and staring at those pools of blue again. "Who needs the ocean when I have those to swim in," I said, my breath mixing with his, and then my lips pushing hard on his lips.

My prick instinctively found his hole, pressing on the edge before making its way within, slowly, gently, slower still, until just half my thick head was inside. He sucked in his breath and his ass clenched before he finally relaxed and gave way. He gazed into my eyes the whole time, and then pushed his ass against my cock, sending it farther, farther, farther to the back, until my balls were nuzzled up against his cheeks.

The familiar *yeah,* half sigh half groan, again escaped from his soft lips. I echoed it with one of my own and then kissed him just as gently as I fucked him. He was tight, but his asshole accommodated my cock like a glove, wrapping around it with nary a millimeter to spare. With each thrust of my prick he'd rock his ass into me, until we were like one well-oiled, or at least well-lubed, machine. A machine whose gears gradually began to speed up. Faster and faster my cock went in and then, with a *pop,* out, ultimately slamming into his rapidly hardening prostate like a battering ram.

I circled my fist around his rock-solid prick and pumped it as I fucked his ass with abandon. Drops of sweat trickled off my brow and landed on his belly, which tensed and relaxed with each and every thrust.

"Gonna. Come. Gonna. Come." He moaned the words in between exhales. And then he shot, rope after rope of hot, white come, which spewed from his cock and onto his stomach, his chest, his chin, cascading over his sides like a sticky, salty waterfall. I popped my cock out of his ass and slid the rubber off so he could watch me shoot as well. And then I did, in a torrent of steamy jizz that mixed and mingled with his own, until his torso was as white as the sheets beneath us.

Collapsing on top of him, I sighed and covered his mouth with darting kisses. Then we lay there, motionless, save for the heaving of our chests as our hearts and lungs struggled to return to their normal tempos. Spent, we fell asleep like that, rocked into dreamland by the churning waters just outside the cabin walls.

When we awoke, it was hours later. The come had dried, gluing us nicely together. Slowly, we got our bodies out of bed and managed to squeeze ourselves in the shower together—no mean feat, mind you. He went back through the divider to his cabin and got dressed. I did the same. Then, hand in hand, we walked back down the corridor and up to the deck. The air was damp, thick with the aroma of salt and fish. The sky was an azure blue and the Nassau port was directly in front of us.

The storm had subsided, at least for the time being. We had nine hours to shop, to eat, to sightsee. I looked over at him, his eyes like emeralds sparkling beneath the intense overhead sun, and then I turned around and stared at the door we had just come through. He laughed, and said, "You've seen one paradise, you've seen them all." Then he grabbed my hand and led me back to the cabin. "Screw it," he added, as we got out of our clothes and back into bed.

"And then screw me," I told him.

He laughed, a chuckle that filled my heart with a deep, profound sense of joy. "Man," he finally said. "If that lady had offered me this, I might've actually bought one of those time-sharing units."

I didn't tell him about my purchase. But I figured I got off lucky. If she had offered what lay before me, I would've found a way to buy two units.

"Bon voyage," I moaned as he began a slow nibble down my neck. "Bon fucking voyage."

We Traded Fucks
BEARMUFFIN

I once had this crazy blonde secretary. Now, I don't know what she was doing that day. Maybe she was sniffing too much white out. Well, she accidentally booked me on a gay cruise. Yeah, really. Now, I'm straight—or at least I thought I was. You see, I'm in sales and I had gone on this cruise for some much-needed relaxation. But once I was on board I couldn't help but notice that there were gays having sex all over the place.

As I sat in a deck chair and listened to my iPod, I just couldn't keep my eyes off all these hot men, their hard muscled bodies writhing under the hot sun. I even saw three hot, sweaty studs meet and jerk off together. I couldn't believe my eyes when I saw them hitting each other's cocks, laughing joyously, so completely and totally at ease with their sexuality and so obviously caught up in the joy of being with each other.

The more I watched them the more it reminded me of an episode in my old college days. I once had an affair with a guy named John, a college roommate who was on the wrestling team. He later got married and I never saw him again. That was the one and only time I had experimented with homosexuality.

Well, I like to keep in shape when I go on a cruise so I spend a lot of time in the gym or on the jogger's track. So I was standing on one of the upper decks with the rest of the knob-gobblers watching the joggers do their thing on the deck below. As I watched the joggers with their trim well-muscled bodies, I kept on thinking of John who himself was a hard-muscled humpy stud with a super-developed body, thick thighs, and a nice, firm bubble-butt. I found myself getting a hard-on in spite of myself.

That's when I spotted Lars Nilsson, a Swedish hottie, jogging on the track. I couldn't help but think of my old college roommate, he looked so much like him. Lars must have sensed me staring at him because when he saw me ogling him he broke out in a winning smile that would have melted a heart of stone.

Lars was in his mid-twenties, devilishly handsome with green eyes, smooth fair skin, and curly blonde hair. He had your classic chiseled features and a lantern jaw. His broad back tapered into a narrow waist. His well-honed tree-trunk thighs and sturdy calves were awesomely impressive even to so jaded a muscle-lover as myself. The upward curve of his powerful buttocks took my breath away.

Lars's chest was powerfully sculpted. His abs were super defined. My heart pounded and my pulse raced when my eyes roamed over his superb, six pack down to the crotch of his silky red jogging shorts, which were high cut and showed off his muscular legs. They clung tenaciously to his heavy balls, thick cock, and sumptuously curved buttocks like a passionate lover. My heart raced when I saw his huge dangling cock flip-flop inside his shorts. Fuck! I couldn't wait to run my tongue over the family jewels! Yeah, it looked like the better part of me was coming out again. And I decided to act on it.

So I went down to the jogging track and joined Lars. He saw me and grinned. I jogged behind him keeping up a steady pace. I was drawn to the power and beauty of his splendid ass as he sprinted down the track. As the sweat continued to pour down his muscles, his trunks became so transparent that I could see his ass-crack. Holy fuck! I wanted his beautiful ass so bad.

I followed Lars for several laps around the track until he stopped to cool off. Then he walked towards the elevator and I followed him. Our eyes were devouring each other as we waited for the elevator. The doors opened and we stepped inside. Luckily, we were alone. Lars quickly pulled me to him. For a moment I gazed into his mesmerizing eyes. I was hypnotized with lust. Then he began kissing me.

Lars was a great kisser! His tongue slid in and out of my mouth as he caressed my arms and upper back. Our groins were mashed together so my cock was throbbing against his spasming cock. Our tongues were battling for supremacy. And I could feel his masculine power surge through me and radiate through every fiber of my being. My hands flew down to his crotch and I gave his boner a good squeeze that made him sigh with delight.

He grunted hard and said, "I know where we can go." Lars pressed the Deck A button and the elevator started to move. My horny Swede managed to grab a few more hot kisses until the elevator stopped and we hopped out. A trio of studs waiting for the elevator eyed us with lustful envy. Of course I beamed with pride, glad to have found such a handsome stud to trick with.

I followed Lars to one of the theaters on the ship. It was two in the afternoon so the theater was dark. We went inside and made our way to the stage, slipping through the curtains.

Now we were alone. It was one hell of a stage debut but what the fuck. Lars pulled me to him and began licking my neck slowly until he reached the sensitive area behind my ears and began nibbling on my earlobe. The stud was driving me into an erotic frenzy. My cock was so hard now that pre-cum was oozing from my piss-slit.

Suddenly, he started moving down toward my pecs and he began sucking on one nipple as he tweaked and pulled the other. I was gasping with pleasure as he sucked on my tits. My hands were gliding down the small of his back and into his butt. I squeezed his tight melons and was thrilled to find them hard and muscular.

I pulled down his trunks and gasped with awe and admiration when his glorious cock surged into view. The head of his mighty cock was shrouded with thick foreskin. Fat, throbbing veins were snaking and twisting all over the pulsing shaft.

Lars was palming his cock through his shorts and I bent down and began mouthing it. "Yeah, oh yeah," he moaned as I kissed the shaft, soaking it with my spit. He held it by the root as I sucked hard on it.

I looked up at him and he smiled at me as he pulled down his shorts and out sprang his turgid cock. I gasped when it hit my face. He grabbed his splendid crank and struck my face with it, then rubbed the swollen and throbbing shaft along my cheeks, over my nose and against my lips. That's when I opened my mouth wide and swallowed it down.

Now my mouth was full of cock, my lips flattened against his balls and the root of his cock. I held his cock inside my mouth for a few seconds and then pulled up and released it only to watch it quiver up and down before my eyes.

Lars moaned when I reached down and wrapped a hand around his cock. He placed both hands on my nipples and tweaked them. Fuck, that man sure knew his foreplay. Yeah, his expert nipple work sent lusty tingles all over my body until I was dizzy with lust.

I played with Lars's cock some more until it was rock hard. Lars grabbed my head and guided me to it. "Suck," he said. So I opened my mouth as he pushed forward filling me with hot Swedish cock. I held his balls inside my hand as I lovingly sucked on his cock, stroking the shaft, while I mouthed his knob. I felt his hand stroking the back of my head as I worked on him.

I palmed Lars's impressively huge balls, which were hanging low in his scrotum. My nose was buried in the thick forest of pubes surrounding his cock. I sniffed his balls, allowing his male scent to linger in my nostrils for a moment, before taking both of his sweaty testicles into my mouth. Ah, his ripe, masculine odor was so wonderfully rich and powerful. The potent man-stink rushed up my nose until I was reeling with lust.

I slurped around the root of Lars's cock, then slowly pulled back to work upwards on the shaft until I reached the glans. As I fluttered my tongue-tip over the sensitive flesh, my hands started to roam over Lars's taut abs and upper torso. Soon my nimble fingers landed right on his thick protruding nipples sprouting from his sculpted pecs.

I made little circular licking motions with my tongue-tip and then traced it over his fat pulsating cock-veins. Lars groaned encouragingly so I stuck one of my fingers up his sweaty asshole and twirled it around. That really drove him crazy.

I looked up to his catch his reaction. He pursed his mouth as little sighs escaped his lips. "Oh fuck," Lars cried out with ecstatic pleasure. At the same time, his powerful ass-muscles sucked around my invading finger. Yeah, I could tell that he was ready for a rim job. Ever since I had laid eyes on him I'd wanted to eat his hot butt.

I moved underneath his balls, stopping a moment to inhale their rich, musky fragrance. Then I licked along the passage from his balls to his asshole. Lars moaned again and a long, lusty shudder coursed through his magnificently muscled body. I pried open his ass cheeks and he bent over and grabbed his ankles so that I could eat out his ass. I took this opportunity to check out his rosy puckers. They were spasming and twitching with anticipation as if waiting for my tongue.

I love the manly taste of sweaty butt hole, so I had hoped that his asshole was going to taste great since he had been jogging for a while. I hovered my nose over his hole and I took a deep whiff. Fuckin' fantastic! Just as I had hoped. He stank so fuckin' good. The aroma of his pungent sweat was particularly exciting. I kissed his hole a couple of times, feeling his puckers throb against my lips. I eagerly ran the full length of my tongue up and down his ass-crack. I jacked off as I munched on his butt until my cock was hard as steel.

Suddenly, Lars reached behind him, grabbed my head and forced my face into his butt. My face was jammed between his sweat-drenched ass-cheeks so I gave him the rim job of his life.

I hadn't eaten butt since college but judging from Lars' reaction it was good to see that I hadn't lost my touch. Lars zigzagged his butt across my face until my tongue was firmly lodged up his sweaty hole. My tongue was drilling, probing, and stabbing into his hole until it was totally lubricated and dilated.

I munched on his butt for a good while until the Swede cried out, "Fuck me! Oh fuck me!" It seemed that he was always prepared for a quick fuck because he fished into his shorts pocket and brought out a little tube of lube. I quickly applied some on my hefty cock and his spasming asshole. I lay on the floor and he straddled me, and slowly hunkered down as my cock flew up into his ass chute. Lars smiled gleefully as he rode my big hard cock for a good while as he masturbated.

My cock continued to plow deeper and deeper until I felt my balls hit his sweaty low-danglers. I kept my cock inside him as he worked his ass muscles over it. The hot clutching and grabbing action of his ass-muscles on my swelling cock was driving me crazy so I automatically reached over and began tweaking his nipples.

Lars moaned again as he pulled up a bit, which allowed my lust-bloated cock to slip out to just beneath the head. I held him there feeling his asshole clutch hotly around the head of my cock. Then he eased down back again so that my cock slid all the way up his steamy asshole.

His meaty butt was bouncing off my thighs and my hot turgid meat was flying up his ass chute. He just loved having my big, fat cock inside him. And so we fucked for a good hot and sweaty half hour until I felt ready to explode. I was sure he wanted my load just as much as I wanted to shoot it. So I tweaked his nipples harder. Lars howled as he shuddered. "Fuck! Ah! Fuck!" His asshole sucked around the root of my cock, milking it with his ass muscles. I cried out and felt my cock explode inside him. I reached down to touch his cock and it suddenly swelled up and erupted between my fingers covering them with his thick, potent jizz.

Lars continued to milk my cock until the last drop of cum had been drained from my balls. Then he pulled forward letting my cock slip out from his asshole. He turned around to face me. I wasn't surprised to see his rock-hard dock twitching lustily before my eyes. "Now, I fuck you!" he said.

Lars slapped my butt and pushed me down to the floor. Now I was on my knees, hands on the floor, my butt sticking out. I gasped when he yanked down my trunks. When Lars saw my bare ass he totally lost control. I mean the lube was flying all over the place. I felt his nimble fingers deftly circling my asshole, smearing my puckers with lube. It made me sigh with delight and anticipation. I clenched my eyes, waiting for his anal assault with feverish excitement. My lips trembled as a cold sweat broke out over my forehead. My heart was pounding wildly. Fuck! I was now completely at Lars's mercy.

Lars kneeled behind me, put his hands on my waist, and positioned himself for the kill. Without any warning he sank his cock up my hole. I could hear his harsh grunts as he worked his cock inside me. The pain made me scream but he continued inexorably, forcing me to take his cock deep inside me. Instinctively, I clenched my buttocks together but Lars slapped them a few times. Sharp needles of pain tore through my butt at first. But then I began to feel the first stirrings of pleasure that made my cock twitch and bolt. Now I was ready for a good, long, hot fuck. "Okay. Fuck me, Lars," I panted. "Fuck my ass!"

I pressed my sweaty palms against the floor and pushed my ass back to meet Lars's relentless pumping thrusts. He tore into me. My head was bobbing back and forth. My harsh cries of pleasure-pain were grating my throat. The loud squelching sounds of his cock pumping my asshole were punctuated with his loud, obscene grunts.

Lars's steaming groin pounded against my butt. His thick pubes scratched my butt raw. "I'll fill you with cum!" Lars said. He alternated a series of slow-fucking thrusts with sharp stiletto-like jabs that made me cry with pain.

"Fuck! Fuck! Fuck!" Lars chanted with each stroke. My ass was on fire. The pain intensified and then subsided. Then it began to feel like sheer fucking heaven. I was jerking my prick up and down, fisting my cock as he ass-fucked me. "I'll fill you with cum," he hissed again.

Lars howled as he sunk all of his mighty ten-incher inside me to the very hilt. When I felt his dick throb and swell within me and brush against my prostate, my cock stiffened. I knew I was about to shoot.

"Ah fuck! I come! I come!" Lars cried, grabbing me by the waist and slamming into me. His mighty cock swelled and I felt his first squirt shoot inside me. Lars grunted lustily as he continued to pump hot cum into my hole. His climax was relentless, like hot, molten lava. My own body became liquid fire as I joined him in a mind-shattering climax that almost blinded me with its savage intensity.

Lars popped his cock from my hole. Then he slapped his still hard cock against my butt a few times. I was kneeling on the floor, gasping for breath, my muscles swollen because of the incredible fucking I had just received at the hands of this Swedish stud.

Even so, I begged him once again to let me suck on his magnificent cock, which had just began to rise and stiffen once more in front of my anxious eyes and trembling lips.

"Yes. Do it. Suck me," Lars said.

My knees hit the ground as I wrapped my lips around his knob and cork-screwed it a few times.

"Fuck!" Lars yelled when yet another hot load spurted between my lips and rushed down my gagging throat. I fairly choked on the river of cum blasting from his beautiful cock. His cock spasmed and swelled inside my mouth, filling it with sizzling semen that overflowed and dripped down the corners of my mouth. Afterwards I got up, licking his hot cum from my lips. Lars hugged me, kissing me hard. Fuck! I wanted to spend the rest of my life with this hot Swedish stud!

So Lars and I spent the rest of the cruise together and we're still great fuck buddies. When I got back from the cruise I didn't tell my secretary about her mistake. In fact, I gave her a dozen roses and a box of candy. After all, she'd done me a big favor.

Learning to Do the Cha-cha-cha
Simon Sheppard

For W.W.A.

"Let's not," Bruce had said, "go on an all-gay cruise, OK? We're at least ten years too old, not buff enough, and we are decidedly not what you'd call 'party animals' anymore."

"But," Brucer had replied, "our friends tell us that those glossy gay-cruise ads awash with gym-bunny hunks in Speedos don't really reflect the diversity of the passenger list."

"But," Bruce had countered, "we live in San fucking Francisco. It's not like we have to board a boat to be amongst our queer brothers."

"But," Brucer said, "at least that way we'll know that our anniversary cruise won't be full of born-agains."

"Nevertheless," Bruce had concluded. And that was that. Decided.

***

As the *Dawn Princess* pulled away from Pier 35, ship's horn blaring, Bruce and Brucer went out on deck. The Golden Gate Bridge loomed up in the fog, and then, in one thrilling, tourist-postcard moment, the liner sailed beneath the span, and they were out on the open Pacific.

Brucer stood at the rail, spread his arms, and made a retro-joke. "The king of the world!" he yelled out, drawing a limited number of bemused glances from his fellow passengers.

Bruce shot him a wry look. "Let's go get a glass of over-priced champagne," he said, "then go below and fuck."

***

The ship hadn't even reached Mazatlán when Brucer, who was something of a workout addict, first encountered the stranger, the handsome stranger with the handsomer hard-on, at the gym. Brucer was something of a blowjob addict, too, and he'd been getting sucked in the steam room by Jacques, a cute little middle-aged Canadian he'd first met at the Friends of Dorothy meeting.

When he ran into Jacques at the workout room, the two of them had engaged in enough insinuating conversation to lead to a tryst in the ship's small steam room. It was, perhaps, not the safest place to get sucked off. But though Brucer had once been deprived of his 24 Hour Fitness membership upon the discovery of some unapproved hanky-panky, Princess Cruise panky seemed rather less risky. *What,* Brucer thought, *are they going to do to me? Throw me overboard?*

As the two of them entered the steam room, the stranger was already sitting there, his midsection decorously covered with a fluffy Turkish towel. For a long minute, the three of them sat around uneasily in the mist, giving one another those in-the-steam-room glances composed of equal parts wariness, desire, and exposure to high temperatures. At last, the stranger pulled aside his camouflage. His dick wasn't particularly hard at first, but it soon became so, an impressively erect shaft, its nicely swollen head still half-covered by foreskin.

Brucer had been restraining himself, out of some now-obviously misplaced sense of decorum. But being watched like that had made his cock hard, too, so he tossed his own towel aside. Jacques was on him like a shot, his damp hand stroking Brucer's hard-on. They both glanced over to the glass door, and then Jacques bent over and took Brucer's dick in his mouth. The little Canadian's technique was perfect—socialized medicine was apparently a boon to fellation—and the riskiness of the enterprise, the incessant stare of the voyeuristic stranger, and the oppressive heat all lent a sense of urgency to the churning of

Brucer's balls. This had all the benefits of being on a gay cruise, he mused, but without the necessity to exfoliate.

"Let me see your dick," he said, and the Canadian, never taking his expert mouth off Brucer's sensitive shaft, complied, undoing the towel at his waist. The stranger's equipment was large, but Jacques' cock was ginormous . . . though the contrast with his otherwise petite physique might have added to the impression of bulk. Brucer reached over for it, and the Montreal meat throbbed in his grip. It had a pronounced curve to the left, something that Brucer found a turn-on, though his dick could scarcely have gotten any harder. Without warning, the cocksucker's cock started spasming, oozing, rather than shooting, a sizable load of jizz. Brucer glanced over at the stranger, who was masturbating vigorously. It was all too much, and there was the possibility that they would be discovered at any moment, so Brucer relaxed his guard and fed a pulsing stream of protein to the attentive little Canuck. And nearly at the same exact moment, the good looking stranger leaned back and coaxed out a high-flying load, spraying ropes of cum all over his steam-slicked torso. It was then, as the man's left hand squeezed out the last few drops, that Brucer noticed it: a wedding ring.

***

They were at dinner that evening, the first formal night. It being their first cruise, Bruce and Brucer had been a bit nervous about their dinner arrangements. They'd chosen traditional dining, late seating, with some trepidation, but their assigned tablemates were working out better than expected. Edna and Ira, a retired couple in their 80s, had been to damn near every country on the globe, including a fair number that were no longer in existence, while Fran and Celeste were hearty and fun—Bruce and Brucer had hoped they were lesbians, but they turned out to be Just Friends traveling sans their hubbies. None of them seemed to have the slightest problem being seated with a gay couple, and they were all soon bonding in that temporary way that travelers do, making pledges to keep in contact after the cruise, though it was unlikely they actually would.

"That's him," Brucer said to Bruce, swallowing down one last bite of seafood terrine.

"Who?"

"The man I told you about," Brucer replied, feeling it would probably be indiscreet to add, "the one who jacked off while I was getting blown." But he had told Bruce of his steam room frolics in great detail, and felt confident he'd already figured out.

Bruce and Brucer were looking rather elegant, if they did say so themselves, in their matching black suits and red silk shirts—if people were going to mistake them for twin brothers, they might as well make the most of it. But the arriving stranger looked positively dashing in a perfectly fitting tux that reeked of Armani, and on his arm was a gorgeous, clingy blond—presumably, though not certainly, his wife—in a gorgeous, clingy sea-green gown.

"Who are you talking about?" asked Edna.

"Oh, just some guy," weaseled Brucer, but the evasion went unchallenged, for at that moment, the carpaccio arrived.

***

As the ship pulled away from Puerto Vallarta, Bruce and Brucer attended another meeting of the Friends of Dorothy, a code term for "fags" that Brucer found rather charmingly archaic, though he knew that some guys thought it stank of the closet. The cruise director had generously oiled the gathering with complimentary mimosas, but Brucer still thought his fellow FODers rather staid. While he and Bruce had gone ziplining over the jungle, most of the other guys had evidently gone shopping, or drinking around the circuit of gay bars, or both. Bruce, though, was enmeshed in conversation with a cute-enough bear who was a hairdresser back in Reno, so he excused himself and headed to the gym for a pre-dinner round of Pilates.

After a pleasant-if-strenuous hour of doing the hundreds and rolling like a ball, the only male in the overpriced Pilates class, Brucer headed to the locker room.

Once again, and not to his surprise, the stranger with the wedding ring was there. There was also a grossly obese guy there, as well as one of the few hot young passengers on the ship—there were more oxygen tanks onboard than men under thirty. But the fat guy was pulling on his clothes, and the young guy, with his perfectly trim, marvelously muscular body and low-hanging balls, went into a shower stall. So Brucer, with a Signficant Glance in the stranger's direction, walked into the steam room. And, as expected, the uncut stranger soon followed.

"I want you to suck me," the stranger said, his accent German or maybe Dutch. "I want you to suck my penis."

Brucer was happy to comply. The dick was quite a mouthful, and the ship's sudden swaying didn't help matters. But, rough seas or no, cock was cock. Brucer ran the tip of his tongue around the man's foreskin, half fearing and half hoping that the hot young jock would barge in on the proceedings before the money shot. But apparently the ministrations of his hot blonde wife hadn't done enough to cure Herr Whoever's horniness. Brucer had reached for the stranger's left hand and begun, maliciously—or perhaps kinkily—twisting around the fellow's wedding ring, when the cock in his mouth thrust spasmodically once or twice and Brucer's mouth was filled with fluid as salty as the sea on which they were being tossed.

As soon as he'd wiped his mouth, Brucer began to feel guilty about leaving his partner behind at the Friends of Dorothy do, and so was happy to later find out that Bruce had gone to the hair-burning bear's stateroom for a vigorous session of mutual masturbation.

***

The final leg of the *Dawn Princess*'s journey back to San Francisco was, as expected, rougher than the voyage south had been. The night before, Fran and Celeste had been absent from dinner, victims of mal de mer. But Bruce and Brucer had decided to celebrate their anniversary on the sailing's final sea day, and so, shortly after lunch, they puckishly split a marijuana brownie they'd smuggled aboard. The snack was pleasantly potent, and Bruce, left alone for a bit while Brucer went to book a Future Cruise Credit, was already beginning to get a warm, floaty feeling when he spotted the uncut stranger on the "Lido Deck." The day was warmer than expected and quite a few passengers were at the pool. The stranger, his blonde beside him, was lying on a chaise lounge. Bruce chose a seat catty-corner to them and, through his Ray-Bans, surveyed the man's graceful feet, hairy, slightly heavy calves and thighs, and meaty chest. The bulge in the stranger's Speedos told Bruce that Brucer had not, in fact, been exaggerating.

Bruce whisked off his shades and stared at the stranger till the stranger stared back. Out of a semi-malicious desire to freak out a closeted foreigner, Bruce shot a glance that conveyed, he hoped, *I know who you are and I know that my boyfriend ate your sperm.* But the man, rather than seeming nonplussed, glared back angrily, then turned and said something to his probably-wife.

Bruce, feeling the increasing effects of the brownie, was suddenly suffused with an oceanic, no pun intended, feeling of love for all his fellow creatures and contritely looked away. Fortuitously, the young jock that Brucer had told him he'd seen naked was standing by the pool, showing off his prodigious lats. Bruce mused upon the man's reputedly huge nuts.

***

Bruce and Brucer were avid trivia players. But they had already, with the collaboration of a pair of newlyweds from Walnut Creek, won a Princess-branded water bottle, alarm clock, tote bag, and luggage tag, which pretty much exhausted the possibilities of swag. And besides, in their current amplified state, they were in perhaps not the best shape to recall which actor first played James Bond after Sean Connery. (Answer: George Lazenby.) So they decided to pass up the final trivia game and learn to dance the cha-cha instead.

They were the only male couple in the "Vista Lounge," but no one seemed to give them a second glance as they learned the steps to the once-popular dance. *One two cha-cha-cha,* they counted to themselves, trying their best not to step on each other's toes. It might have been a long way from the testosterone-fueled frenzy of techno-disco night on an all-gay cruise, but Bruce and Brucer—both now flying very nicely—enjoyed it immensely nonetheless.

"I remember my parents doing this," said Bruce.

"Me, too," Brucer replied.

"And after this is over," Bruce said, "let's go to our room and fuck, cha-cha-cha."

"Cha-cha-cha, indeed."

***

The cabin steward—an obvious friend of Dorothy himself—had, as usual, made up their little room to perfection. "It's going to be hard to go home and make our own bed again," said Bruce.

"And speaking of hard . . ." Brucer said, grabbing for his lover's crotch.

It was mere moments till Bruce and Brucer, thoroughly buzzed on brownie, were naked in the now-disheveled bed,

Bruce on his back, Brucer nestled between Bruce's hairy thighs, sucking on his nice, thick dick. This was how sex between them usually went nowadays, but though it usually was sweet and somewhat predictable, this time it took on an urgency, a newfound sense of passion. Brucer took the cock down his throat like a starving man, and Bruce's groans were not in the slightest bit contrived.

Brucer was, in fact, one of the very greatest cocksuckers Bruce had ever known, and now, cosmically under the influence, Bruce was finding it difficult to deal with the waves of pleasure emanating from down below.

"I love you," Bruce said.

"Mmmf," Brucer replied.

"I want to fuck you," Bruce continued.

Brucer was off his dick in a shot, riffling through the luggage in search of lube and a condom—one man was positive, the other not. Once the rubber was in place, Brucer straddled Bruce, still lying on his back, and climbed aboard. The meaty cock slid up his ass with well-practiced grace, and he started to seriously tingle. Bruce raised his knees and began to thrust upward, and Brucer leaned over and kissed him hard and gratefully. After a small eternity, the two of them, as if with a single mind, rolled over, less clumsily than such things are usually accomplished, so Brucer was on his back, legs in the air, and Bruce was pounding down deeply into his lover's yielding hole.

"We haven't done it this way in forever," Brucer gasped.

"I know," Bruce gasped back. "Isn't it great?"

They knew each other's bodies by heart and, taking advantage of that fact, fucked away cosmically while the *Dawn Princess*, sailing northward against the current, pitched hard enough to rattle the wine glasses on the bedside table.

Somewhere along the line, Bruce realized he was about, irrevocably, to come, and when he informed Brucer of the fact, Brucer reached down and brought himself off, shooting messily all over his own chest. The cabin steward would have his work cut out for him.

After a deep kiss and a long moment, Bruce said, "Cha-cha-cha!" and they both broke down in stoned giggles.

***

It had been, they agreed on their way down to dinner, some of the best sex they'd ever had, with each other or anybody else. They had by now fortunately come down enough to behave themselves at dinner, and the meal was thoroughly splendid. Bruce had read online that the lobster tails could be small and dry, but that certainly wasn't the case that night, and he ate three. Their Romanian waiter brought a sweet little Happy Anniversary cake with a sugar rose on top, and Ira had, as a generous surprise, provided a bottle of good champagne for the table to enjoy.

After everyone had staggered away from the dinner table, Bruce and Brucer headed for the "Grand Atrium" for the champagne waterfall, a Princess Cruises tradition in which a stream of passengers poured bottle after bottle of cheap bubbly over a tall pyramid of stacked-up stemware while cameras clicked away.

And then the ship's band struck up a medley of schmaltzy tunes. Bruce and Brucer were just soused enough to slow dance to the kitsch-laden strains of "The Lady in Red," and if any of the breeders objected to that blatant display of homosexual affection, they kept it tastefully to themselves.

There was one potentially odd moment when Bruce and Brucer found themselves dancing beside the uncut German and his unsuspecting spouse. But nobody said a word or even—thanks to Bruce's superlative self-control—gave a smidgen of attitude. It was, after all, the perfect end to a perfect cruise. The closeted hubby had his own problems to deal with, and he did—in any case—have, as Brucer could attest, a very nice cock.

When the festivities came to a close, Bruce and Brucer made their way to the "Promenade Deck," and walked out into the chilly night, strolling down the teak hand-in-hand. When they were at the stern, they leaned over the railing, arms around each other, and watched the wake sparkle in the moonlight.

"I love you," said Bruce.

"And I you," said Brucer.

And the wake trailed away to the unseen horizon, as endless as love.

A Sea of Lust and Love
John Simpson

It had been almost two years since my last vacation and I decided to make my upcoming trip special. I was leaving on an all-gay cruise aboard the *S.S. Vir Diligo,* leaving out of Venice, Italy. Since I had been single for a year now, I decided to go on the cruise alone so that I was free to be as "adventurous" as I wanted to be.

The descent of the plane into the Venice airport awoke me from what had been a surprisingly sound sleep. As people began to gather themselves together to deplane, one guy in particular caught my eye. He was almost over six feet, and weighed about 190 with a solid body frame. His deep blue eyes were set off by his jet-black hair, and square jaw line. He was wearing tight 501s that were complimented by a brilliant white T-shirt that showed off his impressive biceps. I fell in love immediately while I was saddened, at the same time, knowing I would never see this magnificent man again. Fate could be a cruel mistress.

After clearing the boarding procedures, I was shown to my stateroom by the steward who, I could not help but notice, had a world-class ass. His smile was both seductive and innocent and must have been a practiced art of the Venetians. As the door closed, I smiled to myself in anticipation of what I had hoped would be a relaxing, yet stimulating cruise with over three thousand gay men, for the next ten days.

After the usual abandon ship drill that took place at the beginning of every cruise, I got my first real chance to look around. Men of all sizes, shapes, ages, and degrees of sexual appeal, were to be seen everywhere I looked; it would be a very interesting cruise.

After a short rest back in my stateroom to fully recover from the flight, I dressed and went in search of a bar. As I entered one of the many bars on the ship I felt as if I had just entered a very high-class gay bar in Monte Carlo. There spread out before me was a scene from a James Bond movie, only in this scene, there were at least forty or so James Bonds. One of the most appealing looks for me was a man in a tuxedo, and tuxedos abounded everywhere. As I sat down for a drink, I was able to overhear languages and accents from around the world. One of the most fascinating things about a cruise like this was that it brought together men from all regions of the world making it a truly international experience.

I flirted with several men but was conscious not to get "involved" too soon with anyone in particular. There was no rush, so I was determined to take my time in selecting any potential bedmate, even though my hormones began to tingle at the site of all this man flesh. As usual, I attracted my own share of stares and winks. At twenty-four, I was no slouch either. I stood 5'11, 165, blonde hair, blue eyes, and chiseled abs, with an ass to die for, or so I've been told.

As the crowd began to file out, I noticed that it was almost 6:00 p.m. and time for dinner. On this ship, restaurant seating was assigned so I had to find my particular table to be seated. As I entered the grand staircase of the dining room, a waiter greeted me and asked which table I was seated at.

"Good evening, table 31 please."

"Excellent table, Sir, it's by the rear window of the ship."

As I walked through the dining room, I saw that we were approaching a floor to ceiling window that looked out on the foaming sea that followed the ship as we sliced through the water. It was without a doubt, a million dollar view and I couldn't have been pleased more, or so I thought.

As I took my seat, I introduced myself to four of my tablemates and commented that we were sill missing three people.

As the waiter began to take our orders, the missing three men arrived at the table. As I looked up, I was stunned to find the man from the airplane staring me in the face with a broad smile.

"Hello, I'm Jason. Sorry for being late everyone. These guys are friends of mine, Alex and Ben."

After recovering from my initial shock and excitement, I gathered my wits about me and responded.

"Hi, I'm Jack. I believe I saw you on the plane today, didn't I?"

"Yes, I did notice you. Small world, no?" he replied.

"Indeed, glad to see you're on the cruise," I said barely able to contain my lust for this gorgeous man.

I found it difficult to concentrate on the food during dinner, as I was so captivated by the beautiful man who joined us at our table. I could hardly believe my luck that this man would be dining with me every night of the cruise. By the time dessert came about, Jason began to make eye contact with me more and more. I believe he realized that I was extremely attracted to him. As we got up to leave the table, Jason came over to my seat.

"Jack, would you care to join me at the show tonight? I believe it starts in about ten minutes," he said with a sparkle in his eyes.

"Yes, of course I would, nice of you to ask Jason. Shall we go?"

With that we headed off to the theater, which sat around fifteen hundred people. As we chose seats down front and in the middle, Jason put his hand on my knee and asked,

"Would you like a drink while we watch the show?"

"Yea, that really sounds great. I'll signal for the waiter."

"No, let me take care of everything. You just sit back and relax. What would you like?"

"Thank you, I'll take a Slow Screw," I said blushing.

"I was hoping you would say that," Jason replied with a laugh.

As the drinks arrived, the lights dimmed and the performance began. It was a typical cruise ship show of mixed Broadway songs, only with those songs sung by men being emphasized. Andrew Lloyd Weber led the pack of songs with *Phantom,* sung by a beautiful blonde who performed, "Music of the Night." As the night drew on, Jason placed his arm around my shoulders as we sat in the seats. It was a warm comforting feeling, combined with one of anticipation. My promise to myself not to hook up the first night of the cruise might be broken, but how could I have anticipated that I would run headlong into the Levi's man from the airplane?

Four drinks later, and the house lights came up in the theater to the applause of the crowd. It was an enjoyable experience in that the cast had performed songs that most of the men in the audience knew, and sung along with in many parts.

"Shall we take a walk on deck? It's a beautiful night out there." Jason asked.

"Sure, I would enjoy that."

When we walked through the doors and out onto the main deck of the ship, Jason took hold of my hand as we walked along the railing stopping only to peer into the foaming sea. This was another benefit to being on an all-gay cruise; we could be ourselves and experience life as it was meant to be. A gentle warm breeze blew through our hair as we walked and talked about our lives, speaking as if we were lifelong friends. We nodded to other couples out for a walk as they passed us, before our eyes returned to each other. I was stunned to learn that we lived in towns only one hundred and forty miles apart in Pennsylvania. The world kept getting smaller and smaller.

As we approached the bow of the ship, and began to feel the full force of wind as the ship cut through the starlit night, Jason turned and kissed me. His lips were soft and tender with minimal pressure as he brushed against my lips. It was a tender kiss that was meant to begin what we both hoped secretly would be a night of passion. In response, I kissed him back, but only with an unspoken message that I was fine with his exploration of possibilities with me. I probed his mouth with my tongue searching for his tongue only to feel him push back as he entered my mouth. Jason took control of the situation and communicated with this one action that he was the one in charge of the night's events. He was assuming a more aggressive posture with me, which communicated its own meaning to me.

"Jason, that was nice," I said as I looked up into his eyes.

His hair was blowing around from the wind, which made him even sexier. My mind began to run rampant in the realm of fantasy at what might be.

"Shall we go to your room and relax, Jack?"

"If you wish. I can even offer you a drink as I brought a minibar with me," I said with a laugh.

"Wonderful. Let's catch a movie on the room entertainment channel, or *something*."

I smiled at the praise "or something."

"In fact, I need to stop by my cabin for a moment, what is your stateroom number, and I'll meet you there shortly?"

"Twenty One Forty Seven, I answered. In fact, I will change out of this and into something more comfortable. Please do likewise if you wish," I suggested.

"Nice, I'll see you in a few minutes then," he answered.

My mind raced as I thought of the possibilities for the night's events that lay before me. I quickly changed into shorts and a polo shirt that showed off my chest and made myself a drink. I put on music in my stateroom, instead of the television, as I wanted his attention focused on me and not a television screen.

A knock on my door brought me to my feet and I answered the door to find a vision of handsomeness before me. Jason had changed into the same jeans that he had on when I first noticed him on the plane and a scent of Polo touched my nose.

"Come in, you look stunning as you did earlier today."

"Thank you, Jack. You look nice also."

"Would you like a drink?"

"Sure, I see you have scotch, so I'll take a scotch on the rocks, if you don't mind."

"Please sit down on the sofa while I fix your drink. It might be a little tight there with both of us, but I don't mind if you don't," I said with a smile.

"Actually, tight is good," he replied.

My knees went weak hearing that comment and I quickly fixed the drink and squeezed in next to him on the little sofa next to the bed. The bed commanded the center of attention in most cruise cabins and mine was no exception.

"You know, you really are a good-looking man, but I'm sure you have heard that a thousand times before, Jason."

"Yes, as no doubt you've heard the same thing. May I kiss you again?"

I responded by putting down my drink and putting my arm around his shoulder. He brought his face into mine and began to gently kiss me on the lips as before. Between the aroma of his cologne and the masculine smell of the man, I melted into his arms. I was his, for whatever satisfaction he wanted.

His kissing became more aggressive as we made out on the sofa. He finally broke our kiss, got up, took me by the hand, and brought me over to the bed, which was only two feet away. He once again embraced me and kissed me deeply moving to my neck and throat. I held him tightly as I enjoyed the attention he was paying to my body.

His hands began to travel over my body as we continued to kiss, finally resting on my ass where he squeezed each cheek. Jason began to pull off my shirt as my hands traveled to his ass and felt the rock hard curves that made up his posterior. He then unbuckled my belt as I kicked off my tennis shoes and let my shorts slip to the floor leaving me standing there clad only in my Calvin Klein boxer brief underwear. He stood back for a moment and looked my body over and smiled and simply said, "Delicious."

I climbed onto the bed and lay on my back as he began to undress. His movements were slow and deliberate as he took off his shirt, slid down his jeans and revealed that he was wearing a jockstrap. My attention was riveted on the well-filled pouch of the jock and let out an audible sigh as I found one of my fetishes staring me in my face. I loved men in jocks and here was someone who could have been a magazine model for jocks.

Jason looked down at me and smiled.

"You like what you see?" he asked already knowing the answer.

"Fuck yes, I like what I see. Get your ass onto the bed here and let me give that bulge some attention."

Jason picked up his jeans from the floor, turned around and put them on the sofa. The prime reason for this move was to give me an eyeful of his beautiful ass hanging out from the jock. His ass was nothing short of magnificent. This man knew what he was doing and I couldn't help but think that he was a master of seduction and probably had left a string of broken hearts across the world. But, I didn't really care at the moment, all I knew was I was going to possess this man's sex.

Jason knelt on the bed, and swiftly removed my CKs, leaving me naked on the bed. His eyes wandered over my body once again, resting upon my now erect cock. Just his looking at my dick made me as hard as I could possibly get.

"I think I will enjoy this evening very much," he said.

With that statement he began to lick my pecs and suck on my nipples, which only served to heighten my already high level of sexual energy. I tried to sit up in order to run my hands down towards his ass, but felt myself gently pushed back into the bed. Jason ran his tongue down my chest onto my stomach, and towards my cock. He stopped just short of licking my penis and instead stood up and removed his jock. This caused a rather impressive cock to be set free from the confines of the elastic material and the site of his manhood took my breath away. Jason was endowed beyond that which is normal for the average male and I knew I would have some difficulty accommodating his large phallus. But there was no question in my mind that accommodate it, I would.

Jason knelt down over my chest so that his cock hung right in front of my face, and I opened my mouth and took Jason into my mouth. I found it impossible to swallow Jason's cock as he was just too big, but was able to suck on the head of his dick.

"Just how big are you, Jason?" I asked with curiosity.

Jason smiled as if he was used to answering this question. "I'm just over 10 inches, and 7 around."

No wonder, I couldn't suck his cock into my throat!

"Holy shit, Jason, didn't you have any toys to play with when you were a kid?"

Jason laughed out loud at my statement and simply said, "You got a tongue, use it!"

"Yes, sir."

I pushed Jason onto his back and began to work his entire body with my tongue, ending up on his cock. I licked his entire shaft as well as his balls, paying particular attention to them, as it was one area of his anatomy that I could do justice to. I once again tried to suck his cock, but found I simply could not get past the head of his dick. Jason was used to this problem and had his own remedy in mind.

Jason moved me onto my back and began to suck on my cock. I was of average size and he had no problem taking me all the way down to the curlies. As he went up and down on my shaft, he cupped my balls while gently pulling on them. His other hand roamed between my nipples, tweaking them in response to their rigidness. When my balls began to tighten up, Jason knew that I was building to a climax and so he stopped.

"Not yet, sexy, I got something more in mind before that happens."

Jason rolled me over onto my stomach and I felt his hands part my ass cheeks. A very hot, wet tongue then began to probe my anus, exciting and delighting the nerve endings that were in abundance in that region. I grabbed the pillow and tried not to moan in pleasure, all to no avail. My body withered under the expert tonguing that Jason was giving to my ass, and it went on for what seemed like an hour but in reality was more like ten minutes. As I gasped for air, Jason said he had one question for me.

"Jack, I would love to fuck you. Do you object?"

I had anticipated this question and was ready for it.

"Yes, Jason, I would love that very much, but you have got to use a lot of lube, and take your time. Don't go shoving that telephone pole into me with one stroke," I pleaded.

I heard laughter fill the room, and he got off the bed and removed a small bottle from his jeans.

"Jack, with a dick like I have, the only satisfaction I get when I'm lucky, is to fuck guys. I have made a science out of it."

It was true, after Jason ate my ass out for ten minutes, I felt sexually charged and lose enough to take on just about anything. Jason put on a rubber, lubed up his cock, and then applied a copious amount to my waiting ass.

Jason pulled me up into the doggie-style position, and began his entrance.

"Now, just relax as much as possible, Jack. Believe me, you will enjoy this as much as I will."

I had some doubt as to the veracity of that statement, but was not about to say no to this stud. I felt the initial pressure on my hole and followed all of the procedures I had learned through the few short years of my sexual experience. I had never taken a guy this big, but knew that I probably could.

As the head of his dick passed into my anus, I felt a little panic at the obvious size of the intrusion and began breathing exercises. Jason stopped when he felt his head pass through the initial resistance and he waited.

"Are you okay?"

"Yes, go ahead, slowly."

With that Jason began to push his shaft into where his head had just gone. Jason did indeed know what he was doing, as he stopped every inch or so giving my ass the time to adjust. Finally, all ten inches of Jason's beautiful, but large, cock were firmly planted up my ass. He waited for a moment, and once again asked if I was okay. After hearing my assent, he began to slowly go in and out of my very willing but scared ass. As he picked up speed, I found that I was able to relax more and began to enjoy this beautiful man who was now fucking me better than I had ever been fucked before.

"Jack, your ass was made for me to fuck," Jason said enthusiastically as he thrust in and out.

After about another five minutes of fucking, Jason asked me to lay on my back so that he could continue to fuck me in the missionary position. As I turned over, Jason's cock never left my ass and I simply rotated on it. He began his fucking once again as I lay on my back with a rock hard cock, slowly jacking myself as I was being fucked. It was great to look up at the handsome face and body that was banging the hell out of me. I would be dishonest if the thought of wondering how long it would take him to cum didn't cross my mind. While I was totally into the ass fucking I was getting, I knew that after a while it would become more than just uncomfortable.

Jason leaned down and kissed me deeply as he pumped away on my ass. Apparently this kiss was his usual signal that he was getting ready to cum, because he broke the kiss and sat back up. He then gave me about another dozen hard thrusts and his face contorted into that immutable look of cumming.

"Ahh, fuck, I'm cumming, babe," he said, as he continued his thrusting.

Jason emptied his balls into me for at least ten seconds before collapsing on my chest. It felt wonderful to have this man laying on top of me with his cock still buried up my ass. I could have spent the entire cruise like this and would have been very happy. Finally, he pulled out, took off the rubber and threw it away, and came back to my cock. It didn't take long for me to cum once he started sucking on my dick while fingering my ass. After about a minute or so, I busted a nut and shot all over my chest. Jason looked down at my cum and smiled.

"It looks like we both had a satisfactory conclusion to our gymnastics, and I gotta say, you were fantastic."

"Thanks, Jason, but you did most of the work."

"You have no idea how difficult it is to find a man who can take my cock in his ass and enjoy it like you did. Your ass really was made for me," he said smiling ear to ear.

"Well, who knows who else you will find on this cruise, after all, it's only the first night at sea."

"Who says I'm going to be looking for someone else? Are you?"

I just leaned up and kissed this gorgeous man in answer. I guess it was going to be a rocking week on the ship!

Fate could indeed be a *kind* mistress also!

Romance and Raunch
in the Windward Islands
Jay Starre

Tyler imagined the Caribbean cruise would be romantic. His buddy, Jimmy, snorted at that notion.

"It's gonna be a real sex feast. Over two hundred horny gay men stuck on a boat for two weeks? Fucking and sucking galore!"

The cruise was advertised as "Windward Islands Adventure." From Miami to Puerto Rico, south to the Lesser Antilles and the French West Indies, on to the Windward Islands, and culminating in Trinidad and Tobago off the coast of Venezuela. Exotic islands, sea breezes, and yes, all those gay men. It definitely sounded romantic to Tyler.

Regardless of Jimmy's scorn, Tyler stuck to his preconceptions. It wasn't easy with gay cock and ass available twenty-four hours a day. Especially when the cocks were stiff and the asses willingly spread.

On their first night, it started out as Jimmy predicted. Their porthole opened to the wafting smell of the Caribbean while a gentle sea swell rocked their beds.

Through the thin wall of their cabin, there was no mistaking the nastiness going on next door. Apparently two of ship's passengers weren't wasting any time in the pursuit of raunch.

One of the pair was a real moaner. The guy was not quiet. Jimmy said it best. "The dude's a fuckin' screamer!"

His shouts were graphic. "It's so fucking big! Oh yeah . . . shove it up there! I can take it! Deeper! Cram that big tool up my ass and fuck me with it!"

Their twin beds were barely a foot apart in the cramped compartment. It was easy for Jimmy to jump over to Tyler's. Smirking as he straddled Tyler's lap, Jimmy whipped off his underwear and began fisting his cock.

Jimmy was easily aroused. In his mid-twenties with a dreamy pair of blue eyes and a toned build, he was also easily accommodated. He got plenty of raunchy sex. Tyler and Jimmy weren't exactly fuck buds, but they did fool around now and then.

The squeals and shouts from next door continued. "Take it out and shove it back in! Like that! Yeah! Pound my hot ass!"

Jimmy's eyes shone with mirth as he thrust his free hand into Tyler's shorts and groped his buddy's stiff dick. Tyler couldn't help himself as he co-operated, lifting his ass and peeling down his underwear. Jimmy's smooth butt-cheeks slid across Tyler's thighs. Jimmy's pink cock leaked a stream of pre-cum as he worked it up and down. Tyler's cock, a deeper shade of lust and thicker than Jimmy's lengthy tool, twitched in Jimmy's other hand.

Tyler contented himself with leaning back against the wall, his muscular arms folded behind his thick neck, his cock in Jimmy's pumping hand, and those squeals from next door vibrating through his shoulders.

Jimmy rubbed his naked butt all over Tyler's thighs, winking and grinning as he fisted both their cocks with rapid strokes. "The black dude is really hot, but what do you think the other guy looks like? He's probably got a sweet round ass, and a real hungry hole, obviously. Stuffed with giant cock right now, from the sounds of it!"

Tyler's dick pulsed in Jimmy's hand. He squirmed under the redhead's bouncing naked butt as he imagined what was going on next door. Their neighbor, the one with the big cock, was tall and lean with a short cap of jet-black curls over bright amber eyes. Sculpted features and cocoa skin, he was drop-dead gorgeous. They'd seen him come out of his room and gawked shamelessly at his movie star looks and hot body.

On the other hand, the second dude, the one screaming "Shove it back in! I want it bad," was a mystery. Tyler conjured up an image, but it was mostly of a naked butt spread wide and being gored by a huge black tool, the hole greased and swollen, gaping when cock was withdrawn, imploding when cock shoved back in. The dude's face and body remained a hazy mystery.

It took at least thirty minutes for the hot bottom next door to get off. He never shut up, while Jimmy never stopped smirking as he milked both their cocks in a rhythmic pump that matched the rolling swell of the seas beneath their ship. Several times Jimmy was forced to a temporary halt, or the pair would have blown long before the insatiable bottom on the other side of the wall.

Finally, it came to an end. "I'm so fucked! Oh God! That big black thing is so far up my ass! I'm gonna shoot a load! Oh yeah! I . . . am . . . so . . . fucked!"

Hearing those words, Jimmy took his cue and rapidly fisted Tyler's dick to a nasty explosion. His own pink rod reared and spewed.

Next door, all was quiet murmuring. Jimmy crawled into his own bunk and passed out contentedly. Tyler remained awake for some time in a vain effort to conjure up an image of the screamer from next door. It was strange, because he had told himself he was looking for romance on this cruise, not just hot sex. Regardless, he was fascinated by that disembodied voice, that obviously hungry ass and hole.

It made no sense. It made less sense that Tyler dreamed about the screamer that night as the ocean cradled him in its sensual cocoon.

Jimmy discovered the identity of the mystery screamer first. Their initial port of call was San Juan, Puerto Rico. It was almost evening as they disembarked with the other two hundred gay men. Jimmy insinuated himself beside their handsome cabin neighbor. Tyler watched Jimmy work his magic from behind, unable to hear what was discussed, but sure their laughter had to do with the previous night's raunchy activities.

Old San Juan, a small island connected by walking bridges from the mainland, was their first destination. Crooked streets, sixteenth- and sevententh-century buildings, massive walls, and several forts including the exotic-sounding El Morro, San Cristobal, and La Fortaleza, intrigued Tyler as they strolled through the narrow roads under the garish amber flush of a Caribbean sunset. Jimmy had his mind on other things, checking out the hot gay guys in their group rather than the historic magnificence surrounding them.

"There! That's him. Dan described him perfectly! It's the screamer."

Jimmy's whisper and pointing finger directed Tyler toward a trio of nearby men. The one Jimmy pointed at stood closer to them.

As if he'd heard Jimmy talking about him, he turned and looked right at them. He caught them staring, and offered a small nod and a crooked smile before turning back to his companions.

Tyler's heart beat like a voodoo drummer gone mad. That brief look, the upturned smile and a pair of soft gray eyes, captivated him.

A slim build, deep tan, a quiet poise—he looked like a carefree graduate student with his mop of tousled copper hair. Athletic thighs rose to a taut, round ass beneath clinging green shorts.

An ass that took big cock with ferocious greed!

Tyler's cock stiffened as he gazed longingly at that perfect butt and imagined what had been done to it the previous night.

"I gotta get a piece of that ass," Jimmy whispered in Tyler's ear.

Then, as the redhead noticed the look on Tyler's face, wide-eyed fascination, he realized his buddy had exactly the same thought. "I'm sure I'll get into that ass first, Ty, and it won't be with fucking flowers and poems! His name is Kyle. I'll give you a day or two, but then I'm going for it."

Tyler couldn't help snorting with laughter. Jimmy was probably right. The dude looked so quiet and so . . . innocent, yet he'd been screaming for cock only the night before.

The last of the orange-red sun glinted in the unruly curls of Kyle's hair. His tan glowed across athletic limbs. Tyler sighed, almost certain Jimmy would be proved right in the end.

Together, the friends tried to cruise Kyle, but it wasn't easy. He was always with a group of other men. Kyle caught them staring a number of times and nodded and smiled pleasantly, but that was it.

In the meantime, Tyler enjoyed the sea, the sun, and the ship-load of gay men. The ship was fairly large, with a small pool on the second deck and an equally small stage on the third. Surprisingly good singers and dancers entertained them, while a parade of swimsuit-clad hotties kept their dicks in a near-constant state of erection.

Guadeloupe in the French West Indies loomed on the horizon before either Jimmy or Tyler made any real contact with their elusive prey. Unfortunately, no more nocturnal screaming-fests titillated them from next door.

The town of Basse-Terre was a sleepy village of about 15,000, with mulattoes, blacks, and a small local population of Europeans strolling the streets. It practically reeked of brewing coffee. A hike to a dormant volcano nearby offered a tropical and steamy diversion. It turned out to be a very steamy afternoon for Jimmy.

"There's Kyle. He's alone! You've had enough time to send him love letters, I'm hitting on him now," Jimmy declared and was off.

Tyler watched Jimmy scurry through the fronds toward his prey. Kyle was alone for once, apparently inspecting some kind of gigantic and garish tropical flower on a side trail. Even though envy dominated his emotions, Tyler had to smile. Jimmy was Jimmy, and Kyle, well, who knew what he was really like?

Jimmy met Tyler back at the ship a few hours later. Tyler was lounging by the pool in the late day sun, checking out the available male flesh, while still clinging to his vision of romance, as hopeless as it seemed.

Jimmy tugged Tyler away from the strolling men and to their cabin. "Kyle's fucking hotter than we thought," he reported the moment they closed the door behind them.

Tyler almost refused to listen, but fascination for all-things-Kyle got the best of him. He listened with a stiff cock under his shorts as Jimmy gave a blow-by-blow account of his lusty jungle encounter.

"He sucked me off right there on the path in the fucking jungle! A couple guys drifted our way, but then left us alone when they saw we were occupied," Jimmy said with a smirk.

The redhead was considerate, and nasty enough, to sidle up against Tyler as he spoke and unzip his buddy's fly to fish out his stiffening dick. Jimmy gazed right into Tyler's dark eyes as he offered details of Kyle's hot blow job in the jungle. He jerked Tyler off as he talked.

"The dude didn't waste any time. When I came up to him, he smiled all-innocent like, but then when I introduced myself, his hand snapped out and he fucking groped my dick! I said, 'Why don't you suck it,' and he laughed. Then he got down on his knees and undid my shorts and yanked them down to my ankles! I was bare-butted in a second!"

Jimmy's hand pumped up and down Tyler's cock as the pair breathed in each other's faces in the small cabin. Tyler shook all over, his obsessive fascination uncontrollable. He conjured up an image of Jimmy's pink cock bobbing in Kyle's sweet face.

"Then, the dude just swallowed me fucking whole! To the nuts! Oh man, it was so hot. I've never, ever, had a suck job like that. He deep-throated me while moaning real loud. He went up and down my stiff rod with his lips smacking. He gagged and grunted and slurped like a fucking slut all over my dick!"

Tyler just about shot his load right then, imagining Kyle's pink lips bobbing and smacking. Jimmy stopped pumping and squeezed Tyler's cock, grinning as he allowed his buddy to catch his breath. With a wicked grin, he went on.

"Then, he pulled down his own shorts and underwear and crammed a finger into his own ass-crack! Can you fucking believe it? That ass is too damn hot! All white, with a tan line above and below, the plump cheeks jiggling as he squirmed around on his hands and knees, sucking my cock and fingering his own butt hole!"

"I had to get a feel of that ass myself, so I leaned over and crammed my hand between the creamy cheeks. He sucked me to the root, his face in my belly, while I jammed a finger up his tight slot. We both fingered him while he sucked me. It was fucking amazing. I lasted a lot longer than I thought I could, and he shot his own load first, spraying the jungle path with a huge squirt of goo.

"He kept sucking me and we kept fingering his tight ass until I got off. I shot on his neck and chest with my finger crammed up his butt!"

Tyler shot. Jimmy laughed as the spurt of cum splattered his pumping hand. "We hiked up the trail together after that and he's pretty cool. I think you'd like him. He asked about you."

Tyler, in the aftermath of the intense orgasm, barely caught the last words. "He asked about me?"

"Oh yeah," Jimmy smirked. "What's your buddy's name? He sure is muscular, but he looks kind of shy," Jimmy mimicked as he winked at a gasping Tyler.

Tyler was more confused than ever. The next day Kyle only appeared once, strolling the upper deck with a trio of laughing companions. Tyler couldn't help wondering if Kyle was sucking all their cocks, or taking their cocks up his hot ass, or engaging in other raunchy activities that involved naked bodies and hot holes.

Regardless of those lurid visions, Tyler's romantic notions rose up fresh as they approached the next group of exotic isles. Merely their name, the Windward Islands, sent a shiver of expectation up and down his spine.

On the east coast of Saint Lucia, they put into Port Castries. With a population of 60,000 the town was much larger than their last port of call. Castries bustled with a mostly black population. English was the official language, but a pleasant French patois was spoken by most of the inhabitants. Bananas, coconuts, and mangoes overflowed the market stalls, and Jimmy and Tyler gorged themselves on the fruits.

Twice, they spotted Kyle among his friends. He waved to Jimmy and grinned, then nodded to Tyler and looked directly into his eyes from across a crowded street. Tyler's cock responded by stirring under his shorts, hopelessly it seemed to him.

Back on the ship that night, Tyler scanned the passengers for some sign of the slim, auburn-haired Kyle, but it was a fruitless search. Tyler figured he was probably getting his ass fucked good and hard in someone's cabin. He had to laugh at himself, realizing that just about all the other passengers aboard had probably done something similar by this time.

A little sunburned, and tired from a vigorous exploration of the tropical island, Tyler decided to crawl into his bunk early for a good night's sleep. Hours later, Jimmy barged in to wake him from his deep slumber with two guys in tow.

"Join us? Or are you still waiting for Mr. Right?" Jimmy asked with a nasty wink.

Of all the guys on the boat to choose from, Jimmy had brought back their next-door neighbor, the handsome, black dude Dan, along with a sultry young blond who was already stripping and flaunting his boner.

A moment later, Tyler found himself facing Dan's big, black cock, the foreskin peeled back to reveal a throbbing crown and piss slit, the same black cock Kyle had screamed out his greed to have shoved up his asshole, again and again.

Tyler got up, dressed and walked out. Jimmy called for him to come back and have some fun, but Tyler ignored him. He wasn't mad at his buddy. He was certain Jimmy had brought back the pair fully intending to share them with Tyler. The redhead was not selfish.

The moon hovered low on the horizon, setting over a dead calm sea. It was amazing how large it looked when so close to the curve of the Earth. Tyler leaned over the railing and breathed in the tropical scent of the island behind him and the tangy smell of the sea in front.

It was very late, past three in the morning, and the ship was quiet as the last of the late night revellers retreated to their cabins, like Jimmy, with their conquests. Tyler's mind wandered.

Kyle. He couldn't help himself from dwelling on the guy, and on how he felt about him. Tyler told himself he didn't exactly want a virgin, and would be a fool to expect that in a gay man. But did he want a slut? His aching cock told him "Hell yeah!" but his romantic notions told him the guy for him would want him over another, including Jimmy or the black dude from the cabin next door.

"Couldn't sleep either?"

Tyler heard the soft voice from behind, and even though he'd never heard Kyle speak, he knew it was him. His heart pounded in his chest as he turned around to face the object of his obsession.

That crooked smile. Wide eyes, muted to a soft sheen in the moonlight. The tanned arms and legs in shorts and tank top. A hint of shampoo and cologne, and salt from the sea air clinging to warm skin.

Tyler's cock rose up to throb against his fly. He had trouble framing words. "I was thinking about you," he blurted out, immediately flushing pink.

Kyle chuckled, and then took on a serious look. "I thought you didn't like me. Jimmy was more direct."

It happened then, an irresistible force drawing Tyler against the warm body next to him.

Pushing Kyle against the railing, Tyler enveloped him in muscular arms. Kyle slipped his leaner arms around Tyler's waist and smiled, just before he planted his plump lips over Tyler's, then pried them apart with a darting, wet tongue. In front of them, the moon sank beneath the horizon in a pool of calm, as if it was drowning, just like Tyler as he sank into the hottest kiss of his life.

Kyle didn't hold back. His lips opened wide. His tongue stabbed and swabbed. He sucked Tyler's tongue into his own mouth, hot, wet, and slurping. As their mouths yawned against each other, their tongues twirling and lunging, their warm bodies pressed together. Kyle ground his slender hips against Tyler's broader bulk. Beneath their shorts, stiff cocks throbbed.

Kyle's hands moved purposely down between their mashing hips. Buttons came undone, zippers came down, underwear was pushed south, and hot, pipe-stiff dicks came out. With both arms between them, hands down in their crotches, Kyle pumped their cocks while tongue-washing Tyler's tonsils.

That kiss went on and on. Wet, smacking, stabbing, sucking. They snorted for air through flared nostrils and drool coated their cheeks and chins. Tyler's cock was a piston of heat in Kyle's slender hand, rubbing against Kyle's own swollen dick and flailing fingers.

Kyle was entrapped within Tyler's big arms, squirming against him as he jerked them both off and thrust his tongue deep into Tyler's sultry mouth. Loud moans and gurgles rose above the slap of gentle waves against the ship's prow below them.

Tyler's constant questioning had crashed to a halt. He thought of nothing but the hot body in his arms and the lust burning through his body. He surrendered to the steamy kiss and the hand that jerked him off. He vaguely realized his hands around Kyle's waist had slipped down of their own accord.

He was cupping that amazing ass.

It was a simple matter to push down the shorts that were already unbuttoned and unzipped. Down they went, along with Kyle's underwear. Suddenly, Tyler had that warm butt in his hands!

He gurgled around Kyle's tongue as he explored the smooth mounds, surprisingly full for such a slim guy. He dared to delve between the satin cheeks. The deep crack was slippery with a sheen of humid sweat. Eager fingers discovered the puckered hole and stroked it.

Once Tyler's fingers began their dance across Kyle's sweaty asshole, the slender stud squirmed wildly before he finally broke their incredible kiss.

"I want you to fuck me. Fuck me good," he said in a breathless rush.

Tyler hesitated. "Can we go to your cabin?"

"No. My roommates have company," Kyle said with a smirk.

"Mine too. Jimmy's organized an orgy."

"Right here, then?" Kyle suggested with that crooked grin. He still fisted their cocks, while Tyler's hand was still buried between Kyle's round butt-cheeks and his fingertips stroked the twitching hole.

Again Tyler hesitated. "Uh, you . . . make a lot of noise," he blurted out.

Kyle chuckled in Tyler's face. "I suppose I do. How do you know that? Jimmy?"

"Uh, no, that first night out of Miami—you were getting pumped full of big black cock next door to us. We heard you through the wall."

Kyle laughed out loud, seemingly unembarrassed. "It wasn't black cock I was getting pumped full of. It was a huge, and I mean huge, black dildo. You would have screamed too if that colossal thing was up your ass!"

Tyler's mouth dropped open. He conjured up a nasty image of a massive, greasy, black dildo, plunging in and out of Kyle's puckered asshole.

Kyle didn't waste any more time, coming up with a solution to Tyler's reservations.

He pulled out of Tyler's arms, shoved down his shorts and underwear and stepped out of them. With that crooked grin and a wink, he stuffed his own underwear in his mouth.

He was gagged with his own skivvies!

Immediately, Kyle leaned against the railing and bent over, presenting his milky-white ass.

Tyler realized then what it was that attracted him to this slender young dude. Kyle was totally into whatever he did. The opposite of the reserved Tyler who thought everything through endlessly.

Tyler kicked off his own shorts and underwear and knelt on the deck behind Kyle. Using both hands, he spread those delectable butt-cheeks and dove in for a tasty bout of hole-munching. Kyle squirmed around the lips and tongue swabbing his crack and hole, his groans and moans muffled by his own underwear.

Tongue opened up hole, gaping ass-lips telling Tyler that Kyle was ready for more—for cock. He rose from the slippery feast on shaking thighs and stepped in close. With his hands on Kyle's slender waist, he thrust his thick rod into the wet crack. Kyle heaved his bubble butt up and against the bulbed crown. In one wriggling lunge, the copper-haired stud swallowed Tyler's rod balls-deep.

Tyler thrust against the palpitating heat that encased his shank. The hole was alive with pulsing, clamping heat. He took his cue from the uninhibited Kyle and immediately began to fuck: in and out, pounding his hips and muscular thighs against Kyle's plush butt and slender legs. To the balls, then pulling all the way out with a juicy plop, then ramming home again to Kyle's muffled grunts.

Kyle took it all, responding by slamming his own hips backwards, swallowing the ramming fuck-pipe with gulping anal muscles, and grunting through his underwear with pig-like constancy. Tyler pulled those slender hips back against his thrusting cock, feeding hot meat to the hot hole without a moment's respite. Sweat flew from his brow and dribbled down his torso. Kyle's hips and ass were also drenched in sweat, their colliding bodies making loud slaps.

It was the wildest fuck of Tyler's life. Orgasm hit Kyle first, his bobbing cock erupting between his spread thighs to spray out through the railings and rain down on the waves below. He hadn't even touched his own dick!

Tyler felt the orgasm rock Kyle's body. The slender muscles quivered. The hole he pounded clamped. Tyler yanked his cock out of that steamy slot and sprayed. His purple rod ejected a geyser of semen, spewing all over Kyle's creamy ass.

No one had caught them and, laughing breathlessly, they slid together in a sweaty, cum-drenched embrace. The underwear gag came out and they kissed again, this time more tenderly.

For the rest of the cruise, they were inseparable. Jimmy switched cabins with Kyle, which put the redhead in the middle of a hot four-way with Kyle's former cabinmates, much to his liking.

Tyler, in the end, got the best of both worlds—Kyle's crooked smile offering an exciting dose of romance, and Kyle's sweet ass satisfying Tyler's raunchiest needs.

As the Caribbean breeze blew past, laden with the exotic scents of the tropics, he tried not to ask for more.

Trans-Atlantic, 1955

Curtis C. Comer

Mike Taylor darted from the shelter of the apartment building's fan-like glass awning, waving his hands like a madman at the approaching black taxi, preferring Paris's dreary April drizzle over another moment in Luc's presence. Although Luc, an acquaintance of Mike's friend, Danielle, had offered to drive him to the nearby Gare Saint-Lazare train station in his shiny new Citroen, Mike had politely declined the offer, insisting first that Luc shouldn't be out in the rain. When that failed, Mike had then tactfully suggested that perhaps Luc's time would be better used working on his book. That tact appeared to have worked, for after helping Mike down the stairs with his steamer trunk and portable typewriter, he barely even bothered kissing Mike's cheeks before disappearing back into the apartment building.

The taxi driver, a corpulent man sporting a dirty shirt and a day's growth on his face, grudgingly emerged from his car and into the early morning drizzle to help Mike load the trunk onto the luggage rack on the back of the taxi. An acrid smelling cigarette, Gitanes, Mike guessed by the smell, burned between his lips the whole time. As the neon lights of Pigalle and the Ninth Arrondissement faded into the distance behind him, Mike felt in his pocket for the fifth time that morning, searching for the brightly colored brochure and boarding pass that assured him a first-class cabin aboard the *S.S. Ile de France,* the floating art deco palace. Relieved that he hadn't left the boarding pass behind, Mike settled back into his seat as the taxi sped through the rainy streets faster than he cared for, and he promised himself that he wouldn't be angry with Danielle once he returned to New York. No, he thought, he wouldn't blame her for having tried to set him up with Luc. After all, he reminded himself, Luc hadn't been all bad and had graciously introduced Mike to his friends, all theater and literary types. He had even managed two last-minute tickets for them to see the incomparable Edith Piaf at the Paris Olympia, probably the highlight of Mike's visit. The real reason that they hadn't worked out, Mike supposed, was a simple matter of incompatibility; while Mike had his insignificant job as a bit writer for the *New Yorker* and had had to hoard money like a miser to save money for his Paris trip, Luc, the only child of a wealthy Parisian family, spent his days lounging in Paris cafes and talking endlessly about the great novel he was writing but that everyone knew he would never finish. And, while classically beautiful in the French sense with light olive skin and full, thick lips, Luc had been an absolute bore at love-making, a side-effect of years of Roman Catholic indoctrination, which had apparently stunted his sexual prowess, thoroughly dashing Mike's fantasy of a sensual French lover. Unfortunately, having given up his room at the Pension Henri two nights into his stay to move in with Luc, he could do little else but stick it out even though it became clearer with each day of his visit that Mike was only using Luc as little more than a guide, settling, instead, for sex in back-rooms and dark alleys. Luc, in turn, seemed content showing off his attractive American writer as if Mike were some kind of trophy, and probably knew that Mike was getting frequent blow jobs elsewhere. Oddly, the final insult for Mike came the day that Luc showed up in his shiny new, red Citroen, a gift from his doting parents. For a young man who schlepped his poetry on foot, from editor to editor back in New York, the new car was more than a symbol of their incompatibility; it was, to Mike, downright vulgar.

As the taxi approached the massive Gare Saint-Lazare, its façade illuminated by floodlights, an image of Maurice Chevalier smiled down at Mike from a faded poster, pasted to the side of a round kiosk. Pulled to a stop in front of the station the driver, apparently still angry for having been forced to get out in the rain, allowed Mike to extract the trunk on his own while he sat behind the wheel smoking another cigarette.

Choosing to ignore the driver's impudence, Mike sat his luggage on the sidewalk and passed the fare to the driver through an open window. As the taxi sped away, a one-armed porter approached, and after a quick appraisal of Mike's ticket, expertly loaded the trunk onto a wooden cart, which Mike followed through the cavernous Gare, already bustling with early morning travelers. The sun, though still obscured by heavy clouds, was beginning to rise casting a grayish glow over everything it touched. Although it was nearly a month after the fact, most of the newspapers for sale still spoke of Churchill's resignation, posing the question "What does it mean for Europe a mere ten years after the war?" The porter, a handsome man not much older than Mike's twenty-one years, jerked his head in the direction of the newspaper stands.

"First De Gaulle and now Churchill," he said, his face grave. "It is a bad sign."

Mike nodded, though he really didn't care to get into another conversation about the threat of communism taking over the world, a conversation he had had one too many times in various salons around Paris. Back in the United States the so-called Red Scare was all the papers were talking about and it was enough to make Mike want to remain in Europe. The porter seemed to sense Mike's discomfort and the two continued along the platform, dodging other travelers in silence. When they reached the train, a shiny black locomotive with the destination "Le Havre" chalked on its side, Mike tipped the porter and took his claim ticket before boarding a coach, where he found an empty seat, stowing his typewriter in the mesh overhead bin. As he settled into his seat, Mike suddenly remembered that the trip from Paris to Le Havre was two hours long and he cursed himself for not having brought along a book or, at the very least, having bought a newspaper for the journey. As more people began to board the car, Mike noticed a tall, well-dressed man, probably in his fifties, staring at him from a few aisles away. In no mood for a seatmate and even less of a mood for conversation, Mike rested his head against the cold glass of the window and fell quickly into a fitful sleep, only to be awakened a half an hour later by the conductor, who was demanding to see his ticket. Mike looked around blinking, and realized that the train had already nearly reached the city's outskirts. He passed his ticket to the humorless conductor, a man with a white, walrus-like mustache. The conductor examined the ticket before punching it, and passed it back to Mike with a nod before continuing down the aisle. Mike rubbed his tired eyes and looked out the window at the passing scenery, the blossoming trees and the splashes of purple and yellow visible through garden fences. Relieved that nobody had taken the seat next to him, Mike pulled the brochure for the *Ile de France* from the inner pocket of his sport coat and flipped it open, silently regarding the interior photos of the old ship. Built in the 1920s, the ship's design had always been considered innovative, and Mike looked forward to the solitude of six days at sea, a gift from the ever generous Danielle who insisted that, after Paris, sailing home on a mere freighter would be anticlimactic. Mike refolded the colorful brochure and replaced it in his pocket. As the train continued north-west, the car slowly rocking as it crossed the French countryside, Mike again fell asleep with his head against the window. When he woke again the train sat motionless, and a young brunette in a red and white dress was smiling down at him.

"We have reached Le Havre, monsieur," she said, her voice heavy with a French accent.

Thanking her profusely, Mike arose from his seat, nearly forgetting to retrieve his typewriter before bolting from the then empty coach. Reunited with his steamer trunk on the pier, Mike noticed that several buildings along the waterfront were still gutted, either destroyed by the retreating Germans or by allied warplanes. Seagulls screamed overhead, held aloft by the breeze off of the water. As he neared the ship among the throng of train passengers, Mike noticed that the ship was badly rusted under the davits that held the lifeboats in place, a condition he supposed was caused by the sea air. Despite that initial observance, Mike was truly impressed by the size of the massive red, white, and black liner. Two red and black smoke stacks topped the *Ile de France,* and her bow rose gracefully up toward the sky, a glamorous backdrop for the stylish women waiting to board her, and sporting the most current styles out of Paris and Milan. The stewards, too, many of whom appeared to be mere boys, sported smart, navy blue uniforms, which were decorated with gold embellishments, braids, and buttons. At a row of tables set up on the dock and manned by four men in uniform, clipboards and lists in front of them, Mike presented his boarding pass and passport to a dashing young officer.

"I hope that you have enjoyed France, monsieur Taylor," he said, flashing a winning smile.

Mike assured the young officer that he had, indeed, enjoyed France and he was answered with a knowing wink.

"The French women, they are beautiful, *non?*"

Mike blushed and agreed that, yes, French women were beautiful, although the officer took Mike's blushing to be a sign of collusion, a realization that embarrassed Mike even more. Even in the chilly morning air, Mike could feel himself beginning to perspire under his tweed jacket. The officer, done with his innocent ribbing, checked Mike's name off the passenger list and passed his passport back to him, directing him to the gangway leading to the waiting liner. A steward took charge of Mike's trunk, passing Mike a numbered ticket in exchange, and Mike headed up the gangway, typewriter in hand. Once aboard the ship, Mike was directed by yet another steward to his cabin, where he was surprised to find a real bed, as opposed to a bunk, as well as a luxurious private bathroom. Mike carefully placed his typewriter on a small writing desk just inside the door and, ignoring a sudden urge to shower, decided to explore the ship, picking up from the desk an amazingly detailed legend of the ship to use as his guide. Despite the ship's age, Mike discovered her to be in extremely excellent condition, no minor feat considering that she had been drafted for the use of troop transport during the war. The ship, which boasted accommodations for over 1,700, included a chapel, a shooting gallery, and even a gymnasium. It was the first-class dining room that really impressed Mike, however, with its high ceilings and art deco motifs surrounding the massive room. He made his way back onto deck just in time for the ship to set sail, her horns blowing a massive *bon voyage* that echoed deafeningly through the air while people waved from the pier below. As seagulls screamed their replies, and the ship began to slowly inch away from land, Mike said his own goodbye, not to France, but to Luc, wishing that things could have been different. Tug boats pushed the massive liner toward the mouth of the harbor like hornets harassing a lumbering beast. As the French coastline began to recede slowly from sight, Mike turned and made his way across the deck, its bright red deck chairs already filling up with fellow passengers settling in for the six-day voyage. Still in no mood to socialize, partially because of his hangover from his last night in Paris, Mike went back to his cabin and found that a young steward, no older than nineteen, was just arriving with his steamer trunk. The steward, struggling with the heavy trunk, hadn't yet noticed Mike and Mike stood there, silently admiring the blush on the steward's handsome face and the subtle wave nearly masked by too much pomade in his close-cropped hair. Suddenly, realizing that he was no longer alone, the steward smiled sheepishly and, with one last tug, positioned the trunk at the foot of the bed.

"Take your time," said Mike, removing his sport coat and tossing it onto the bed.

"Would *monsieur* like for me to run him a bath?" asked the steward, sweating from his battle with the trunk.

The thought of being naked in front of the beautiful young steward aroused Mike, and he hoped that the boy didn't notice the growing bulge in his khaki trousers.

"Maybe later," stammered Mike, instantly regretting his choice of words.

The steward smiled, revealing very white teeth, and Mike wondered if he had smiled out of politeness or if he had misunderstood the suggestion. Fearful at what other stupid thing he might say, Mike handed the steward a franc and thanked him for his trouble.

"My name is Didier," said the steward, before pulling the door closed. "Please call me if you require anything."

Assuring Didier that he would, Mike locked the door of his cabin and unbuttoned his shirt, hanging it on the back of the chair sitting in front of the desk. He sat down on the edge of the bed and removed his shoes and socks, carefully balling up each sock and placing them in his shoes, and then stood back up, removing his travel-worn trousers and laying them across the armchair by the bed. His erection, which still hadn't subsided, was poking through the fly of his white boxer shorts and, instead of trying to ignore it, Mike removed the shorts and fell back onto the bed, jerking off and fantasizing that he was fucking Didier up the ass. He came quickly, a hot stream of semen shooting all over his hairy tummy, and he realized, grimly, that fantasy sex with Didier had been better than real sex had been with Luc. Miffed at this realization, Mike walked into the tiled bathroom and wiped the semen from his stomach using a white towel emblazoned with the ship's logo. When he was finished, he tossed it onto the floor and walked back into the bedroom, stopping to retrieve his cigarettes from his jacket. He lit one, and sat down at the chair in front of the writing desk, its seat cold on his naked ass. He removed the lid to his typewriter, pulling a sheet of clean, white paper from a compartment inside of it, and fed it into the typewriter.

Though he wasn't sure what his subject would be, writing after sex was as important for Mike as the cigarette that smoldered between his lips. As was usual for him during these postcoital writing exercises, words came easily, and Mike wrote candidly about his recent observances among Paris's cultural elite, hoping that his editor might like the piece enough to publish it once he returned to New York. After two hours of writing, his eyes tired and his stash of cigarettes depleted, Mike climbed onto the bed and fell into a deep slumber, spent physically and mentally. When he finally reawakened, Mike noticed that the light in his cabin had changed, and he reached to turn on the lamp that stood on the nightstand in order to see his watch, which announced that the time was 5:15 in the evening. Feeling slightly disoriented and amazed that he had managed to sleep almost seven hours, Mike stumbled to the bathroom where he shaved and ran a comb through his light brown hair. He opened his trunk and chose a white shirt and a pair of dark brown gabardine slacks. Having been forewarned about the rules regarding the first-class dining room, he donned a burgundy necktie and finished off the ensemble with the sport coat he had worn on the train. Placing his room key in his pocket after locking his door, Mike walked down the thickly carpeted hallway in search of food. At the dining room, however, he was informed by the polite, yet obviously harried maitre d', that it was not yet time to begin seating, and that perhaps the monsieur would care to have a drink in the lounge. Not having eaten anything since the previous night, Mike strode angrily to the lounge, a room as big as a football field containing countless tables scattered throughout, comfortable chairs grouped around each. A pianist played a grand piano situated beneath a huge tapestry, but he could barely be heard over the animated conversations arising from the crowded tables. Mike made his way to the massive bar and ordered a martini and a pack of cigarettes from the bartender, a redheaded man with a bulbous, red nose. Mike thanked the bartender and was startled by a voice behind him, turning to see the man he had seen staring at him on the train that morning.

"I'm sorry?" asked Mike.

"I said," drawled the man in a heavily affected New England accent, "that it's dreadfully crowded in here."

Mike nodded and took a sip of his martini and taking the empty barstool next to the man.

"I've heard," continued the man, his voice low, "that Montgomery Clift is on board, but the crew," he said, casting a disapproving eye on the bartender, "is being very tight-lipped."

The bartender, smiling amiably, shrugged his shoulders *a la mode Parisienne.*

"I'm sorry," said Mike, amused, "I'm Mike Taylor, I think I saw you on the train from Paris."

The older shook Mike's hand loosely, his own hand incredibly soft with immaculately manicured nails and a diamond pinky ring, introducing himself as Alfred J. Wallace III, and searching Mike's face for some hint of recognition. When none was detected, however, Alfred was all too happy to elaborate.

"You've no doubt heard of me," he said, offhandedly, taking a sip of his own martini.

"Your name does sound familiar," replied Mike, kindly.

"All because I attended a couple of Red meetings in the forties," he said, his voice barely audible, "I mean, really!"

Mike looked at the bartender to see if he was listening, but he was busy serving other passengers down the bar.

"Personally," continued Alfred, "I think this whole thing is just an excuse to go after our kind."

As he finished the sentence, Alfred placed a hand on Mike's sleeve, and Mike visibly blanched at the words.

"I'm not a communist," he managed.

"I don't mean communist," sniffed Alfred, pulling his hand away.

Mike could feel his face flush, and he took another sip of his martini.

"So," said Alfred, his voice cheery again, "what brought you to Paris?"

"Just a little vacation," replied Mike, still stinging from Alfred's astute observation.

"April in Paris," said Alfred. "How very Doris Day and Ray Bolger!"

Embarrassed, Mike laughed at the obvious reference to the movie.

"So," he said, relaxing a bit, "is Monty really on board?"

Mike, like most gay men, had been a big fan of the actor since *A Place in the Sun* and *From Here to Eternity* a year later. Since Clift had not appeared in any new films since *Eternity,* Mike wondered if the actor might not be abroad, thus lending credence to the rumor of his being aboard the *Ile de France.*

"Anything's possible, darling," replied Alfred, rolling his eyes animatedly.

Once dinner was announced, Mike was relieved to learn that he and Alfred were not assigned to the same table, though he was careful to feign remorse as they parted and spent most of the meal making small talk with his tablemates about French fashion and how air travel would soon doom the cruise ship. Fortunately, the subject of communism was left alone.

Full from dinner, and wide awake from his marathon nap, Mike walked out onto the moonlit deck to smoke a cigarette, careful to avoid Alfred as he left the dining room. Passengers strolled hand-in-hand in the cool air, happily sated from drink and dinner and the sounds of laughter and music drifted in the air. Mike decided to go back to his cabin to write and tossed his finished cigarette over the railing before heading back inside. As he walked down the hallway, shoes stood like silent sentinels outside cabin doors, waiting to be polished. At his cabin, Mike followed suit, placing his scuffed wing tips by his door before locking up. He had just undressed down to his boxer shorts and was about to sit in front of his typewriter when there was a short rap on his door. Curious, he opened the door and discovered the young steward, Didier, his cheeks flushed.

"My watch is over," he said, smiling. "But I wondered if there was anything you required."

His heart pounding, Mike pulled Didier into his cabin and kissed him forcefully on the mouth. Didier responded, sticking his hand down Mike's boxers and grabbing his erect penis. Mike began removing Didier's white uniform with a hurried sense of urgency, pushing the boy onto the bed, kissing his neck, his chest, his cock, and his balls. Didier exhaled loudly as Mike licked his asshole, sticking his tongue in and out, then moving back to his uncut cock, which Mike sucked ferociously, his own cock painfully erect and already oozing pre-come. Not to be outdone, Didier pushed Mike over and climbed on top of him, guiding Mike's cock into his tight ass. Mike groaned at the warm sensation of being inside of Didier, and the boy rocked rhythmically up and down on the stiff shaft. Unable to control himself any longer, and sweating from the exertion of the fuck, Mike came, shooting his load in Didier's ass; Didier, in turn, let loose his own creamy geyser, hitting Mike in the face and neck. He fell onto the bed next to Mike and was silent for a moment. Suddenly, he kissed Mike on the mouth and jumped from the bed and began to put his clothes back on.

"This is extremely forbidden," he said, smiling as he pulled on his pants.

"Tomorrow night?" asked Mike from the bed, propped up on one elbow.

Didier nodded and winked, then disappeared, closing the door behind him.

Mike got up and cleaned the come from his face and neck using the same towel he had used earlier and then, still naked, sat down to begin writing, a cigarette in his mouth.

As usual, the words flowed easily.

Rock the Boat
Shannon L. Yarbrough

Never offer to take someone on a cruise for his birthday and try to keep the destination a surprise. He will waste time buying the wrong clothes every single time. Trust me. I know. Three days before flying out to the coast, when I assumed we'd be flying down south, I was hitting the malls and sporting good shops for cute swimming trunks, tight tank tops, sandals, and tan lotion.

As I spent over four hundred dollars in scanty attire, I was lost in daydreams of poolside cocktails and ocean sunsets, all-night dancing and luxury dinners, and orgies of smooth, tanned skin bathing in the endless rows of deck chairs. Seven days at sea with all those hot gorgeous men headed to the Caribbean, here I come!

"Alaska."

"What?"

"We're cruising Alaska," my best friend, Ross, decided to tell me. He had bought the cruise for us as a surprise for my thirtieth birthday, but had just now revealed the destination to me. Our plane was leaving in three days.

"I just spent over one hundred dollars on swimming trunks alone!" I screamed into the phone.

"I know."

"I bought two pair for every day."

"I know."

"I bought an extra suitcase just for them."

"I know."

"I bought every freaking color of the gay pride rainbow. Swimming trunks! I wasn't even going to pack socks or underwear!"

"I know. That's why I'm telling you we are going to Alaska."

"What should I do?"

"Did you keep the receipt?"

"Of course."

"Exchange them for socks and underwear."

The flight out to Washington state was smooth for me, but it put Ross on edge. It was the farthest he'd ever flown anywhere. We took a cab to the dock where stewards, dressed all in white and holding clipboards, were lined up to check passengers in.

"Am I supposed to tip you?" Ross asked, blatantly flirting as the steward handed us our boarding passes, which were also the keys to our rooms.

"Well, I am the last person you will see with your luggage," the steward said in a monotone voice.

"Tip the man," I said to Ross with a tap on the shoulder.

"Did you think that steward is gay?" Ross asked as we boarded the ship.

"Everyone on the ship is probably gay. Blowing the Captain is probably a staff requirement on this cruise."

"God I hope so. I've been holding out for a month just for this trip. I haven't even been jacking off. I can't wait to get laid."

"Somehow I don't think that will be a problem here," I said.

The rooms were bigger than I imagined. I don't know why I expected us to be cramped into small quarters and sleeping on bunks like deck hands in some sea movie. The rooms were comparable to hotel suites with nice comfy bathrooms, all in white with a window looking out over the water. Ross was easily amused by the hand towels folded and shaped to look like a monkey sitting on the bed.

"Let's go look around," I said after we'd checked out our room.

I made him promise not to blow his load at least until we were at sea. He made me promise not to fall in love.

"What's that supposed to mean?"

"This is a vacation. Have some fun. There will be hundreds of horny guys out there. Don't spend more than one day with just one of them."

"It's a deal."

Most of the guys who were already on ship were up on deck checking out the guys who were still boarding. If this were Mardi Gras, they'd be tossing beads. The temperature outside was in the mid-eighties, and I was a bit disappointed to find everyone with their shirt on. Ross and I both were wearing tank tops, showing off our huge arms that all those nights at the gym had rewarded us with. But I knew that as we headed north toward Alaska, the temperature would drop and any sightseeing on board would be over as all the guys would slip into jackets and parkas.

"Let's get a drink," Ross said.

Most of the minibars on deck were not yet opened. We ventured inside to check out the ballroom. The party inside had definitely already started. The ballroom reminded me of some big New York City nightclub with all the smoke, blinking strobe lights, and ten mirror balls hanging from the ceiling. The dance floor was packed and there were even more guys lining the long bars that framed each side.

"Damn! Let's go cruise the cruise," Ross said. I had a feeling I'd be hearing that quite a bit on this trip.

We squeezed our way through the gyrating crowd to get to the bar. Ross insisted on crossing the busy dance floor to the bar on the other side, instead of just going to the bar that was closer. He wanted as many eyes as possible on him.

"Nice tattoo," someone said in my ear at the bar.

I turned to see a hot Latino-looking guy stroking my arm. He was about a foot shorter than me but just as ripped, if not bigger. He was wearing a silky white shirt, unbuttoned down the front, showing off his gorgeous pecs and a set of perfect abs right from the pages of a muscle magazine. He had short, black, buzzcut hair, and brown eyes that were just as creamy as the color of his skin. However, I found it hard to make eye contact with him because I couldn't stop admiring his body.

"I'm Claude," he said.

"Preston. Nice to meet you." We shook hands.

"Is that your boyfriend?" Claude asked nodding to Ross who had already been pulled back onto the dance floor by a group of guys.

"No. Just a good friend."

"I was hoping you'd say that. Are you looking for a boyfriend?"

"Not on this trip," I said with a grin as I took a sip of my drink, thinking of the promise I'd made to Ross.

"I was hoping you'd say that too. So, your tattoo is a cross. Are you a Christian?"

"Why, Claude, I do believe that's a nice way of asking me if I'm cut or uncut."

He laughed. I couldn't help but laugh too, but it was a question I'd been asked many times before in the bars so I knew what came next.

"You got me," he said with a blush.

"No big deal."

"So . . ."

"What?"

"You gonna tell me?"

"Maybe you can find out for yourself later."

"I'd like that. I'm in 20B, two doors down from the steam rooms. You should stop by after we leave the dock."

The music dimmed and there was an announcement that we'd be setting off to sea in exactly one hour. Most of the crowd dispersed to the main deck for a "Bon Voyage" party. I looked around for Ross and found him tucked between two guys on the floor. He was kissing one of them heavily, and the other was kissing his neck and massaging his shoulders. I just laughed to myself, knowing he probably wouldn't keep his promise.

On the deck, Claude and I waved good-bye to land as the crowd cheered and toasted champagne. The sinking sun and endless blue water played a magnificent backdrop to all the men kissing each other with their arms wrapped around one another.

"Wanna check out the rest of the ship?" Claude asked me.

"I've got six days to do that. I think I'd rather check out that steam room."

"I like your idea better."

Claude took me by the hand and pulled me through the crowd. He had a cabin to himself. We undressed in front of each other next to his bed with our eyes glued to each other's bodies. Both of our cocks popped up like springs once we pulled down our briefs.

"Nice," Claude said, admiring what he saw.

I expected to find a thick bush of silky black pubic hair framing a sleeve of foreskin between his legs. To my surprise, Claude was cut as well and his pubes matched his buzz-cut stubble. His beautiful cock was extremely thick at the base with a nice little mushroom head glistening with pre-cum. It stuck straight out at least eight inches, a perfect ninety-degree angle with his body, with a low hanging ball sac that I couldn't wait to throttle with my tongue.

Claude tucked his tool under a crisp, white towel and then handed a towel to me. We slipped complimentary flip-flops onto our feet, and then Claude took me by the hand again and led me down the hall to the steam room door. Gay men certainly don't waste time when it comes to getting laid, not even on a cruise ship. Upon entering the steam room, we were greeted by the hot cloudy air and the smacking sound of someone taking it up the ass. Moans and grunts of ecstasy called out from men hidden along the walls beneath the steam. As the thick air parted and we walked forward blindly, I could just glimpse a thigh or a head between someone's legs.

Thinking of all these men, hidden and having sex all around us, excited me. I felt my own cock rising to attention beneath my towel. Claude and I managed to find an empty spot on a bench along the back wall and sat down next to each other. We immediately opened our towels. He reached over and began stroking my rock-hard cock, his other hand fingering his own. I didn't want to take the chance of someone approaching us to join in just yet. I got up and dropped to my knees between his legs, wrapping both hands around the base of his cock and guiding it down my throat. With both of his hands on the back of my head, Claude slowly fucked my face almost in rhythm with the slow moving ship. I tugged at his balls and fondled them with my hand.

Claude pulled himself forward to the edge of the bench, exposing his ass to my fingers. The glistening sweat from all the steam made it easy to slip a finger into his crack. I stroked his tight, little pucker with the tip of a finger before coaxing it up inside him. Claude flexed his hip muscles as if he were riding my finger. I continued to tease his meat with my mouth.

Suddenly, I felt the heat of someone stepping over me. I looked side to side and saw another set of legs straddling my body. Looking up, I could just make out someone offering Claude their cock right over the top of me. The stranger was lost in the steam from the pecs up so I couldn't see what he looked like, but he was gorgeous from the waist down and had a massive cock that put both Claude and I to shame.

Claude graciously accepted the offer, taking the rod between his lips and engulfing as much as he could. Looking up and seeing him suck cock turned me on even more as I continued to service him. I eventually freed myself out from under the man bridge and sat next to Claude on the bench again. He pulled my face close to his, forcing the stranger's cock into my mouth while he sucked and tongued the sides of it. I ran a hand up the ripples of the man's abs until I had found a tit to pinch. The man pulled my hand to his face and gently began to suckle my fingers with his warm wet mouth. I could feel the tickle of his goatee whiskers against my palm.

I felt someone sit down on my left and rub their hand up my back. I glimpsed over out of the corner of my eyes and saw a young Asian man smiling at me. He pulled my leg toward him and nodded toward my cock. With a move of my eyes, I gave him the go ahead. He leaned over into my lap and took all of my cock deep into his mouth. In the meantime, Claude had started stroking a huge black cock with his right hand, while still helping me to service the tall stranger. I had never taken part in such a diverse cultural orgy before, but if the rest of the cruise was going to be this exciting I was definitely ready for it.

The next day my dreaded jacket finally had to be put to use as we reached the icy waters of Alaska. Despite being on a cruise ship full of horny men, I took time to admire the Alaskan wildlife and terrain from the deck. It was amazing to watch the mini avalanches of ice fall into the water like someone chipping away at ice to fill a bucket for a party.

"It's all the steam from the hot men on this ship. That's what is melting the glaciers today," Ross said. As predicted, he had not kept his promise. He had not even made it to the deck to say good-bye to land yesterday. I was pretty sure this was the first time he'd been outside since we'd been on board. I rolled my eyes at his cheesy comment.

"Catch ya later stud," he said as he walked back inside to search for his next lay. He was singing that old "Rock the Boat" song from the Hues Corporation as he walked away. "Rock the boat, don't rock the boat baby . . ."

I stayed at the railing to admire the chunks of white snow and ice floating in the water, attempting to have at least one single serene moment to myself to take away from the trip. The monotony of cocks would supply me with many stories to brag about back home in the bar with friends; I wanted something else to take home for myself. The raw beauty of Alaska and the tranquil feeling that came over me was it.

"Hey, Preston," a voice called out from behind me.

I turned to find Claude standing there. I blushed a little, but he probably couldn't tell because I'm sure my whole face was already red from the chill in the air.

"How's it going, Claude?"

"Better now that I found you."

"Oh?"

"I was hoping we could finish where we left off yesterday. Just you and me this time."

"Are you always this forward?"

"Hey, I can't help it. I like what I see, and I definitely liked yesterday in the steam room. Too much of a good thing?"

"Not at all! Let's go to your room," I said.

If everything had not been bolted down, lamps and furniture would have been tossed about. Once we reached his room, Claude pounced on me like a tiger just as I was taking off my jacket. With his arms wrapped around me and his lips firmly planted on mine, he wrestled me to his bed. I managed to pull myself away long enough to catch a breath. Claude ripped my shirt open to expose my chest. He then moved down to work on my jeans, which were already growing in the crotch.

I helped him push my jeans down and free my cock. It didn't stay that way long as he immediately swallowed it up in his warm wet mouth. His suction was so hard it raised my heartbeat and almost made me come. I could feel the blood coursing through my veins. I buckled beneath him to get him to release my cock from the confines of his tight lips.

Without missing a beat, Claude flipped me over and cupped my buttocks with his hands. He spread them apart to expose my hole to his face. I tightened my sphincter muscles to tease him. He buried his tongue into my backside and shook his face to force me to loosen it. The pleasure of that sensation made me give up. Claude lathered my pucker with his saliva and was soon gliding a finger deep inside. I contracted my muscles, fucking his hand and eagerly inviting him to slide in a second finger. His fingers and tongue traded places back and forth several times until I couldn't stand it any longer.

"Fuck me, Claude. C'mon. Fuck my ass," I yelled out.

Claude put his huge tool between my ass cheeks and rubbed it back and forth, teasing me even more. I felt him spit onto it a few times and then he gently slid his pulsing rod inside me. I was quiet and relaxed as my muscles parted and let him in. When the thicker base of his meat pushed me to my limits I cried out almost in tears of joy. Claude fell onto my back and shushed me quietly in my ear. He massaged my shoulders and kissed my neck, allowing me to adjust to the size of his cock.

When I started moving my waist to push his cock in and out of me, Claude gladly took that as a sign that I was ready. And I was. With his hands still on my shoulders, Claude rose up and pushed his cock deep within me with one long stroke. His momentum was instant as he pulled his cock almost completely out of me and pushed it deep inside again with one swift movement. A grunt escaped me as the head of his cock tapped my prostate again and again. He continued with these long slow strokes and quick pushes again and again, slowly picking up speed. Each time he forced his whole cock deep inside me, I moaned even louder.

Claude managed to pull me closer to the edge of the bed so that he could stand up. My own feet were halfway hanging off the bed to support me as I was bent over. My shoulders and face were planted on the mattress and my ass was high in the air. Not once did Claude ever pull his cock completely out of me, giving me even a mere second to rest. He continued to pump me, driving his cock even deeper inside until he too began to moan, on the verge of a climax.

Practically in sync with the cruise ship horn we could hear going off outside the window, Claude pulled out and shot a huge load down my back. He was still coming when he flipped me over on my back and began jacking me off. Using his come for lube, he rubbed our cocks together until I was ready to blow. The force of my own climax shot up my chest and across my face. Claude collapsed on top of me in exhaustion, smearing our sticky come between us.

I took a shower with Claude and then returned to my room to rest and change clothes for a "White Party" that night in the ballroom. Upon opening the door to our cabin, I almost walked in on Ross standing on top of his bed completely nude and spilling his load all over some guy lying between his legs. I laughed into my hand at seeing Ross having trouble keeping his balance over the guy. He steadied himself with one hand on the ceiling but was still swaying back and forth.

I quietly closed the door and just sat down in the hallway, leaning against the door and still laughing to myself. For some reason I started singing. "I'd like to know where you got the notion . . . to rock the boat . . . don't rock the boat baby . . ."

Something for St. Jude
Ryan Field

Jude Franklin went to church services on Sunday mornings and played the violin in a small chamber group every Thursday evening. His dark pine bed was the very same twin sleeper he'd slept in since his tenth birthday. Every now and then he'd replace a sticky copy of *Playgirl* magazine with the newest release that he kept hidden between old comic books in the hope chest that rested at the foot of the small bed (no hidden dildo: he preferred his own thick fingers). When it was church picnic time in late April, Jude made his famous sour egg potato salad and everyone begged for the recipe; he laughed and told them he mixed it with his hands. In May he always escorted his next-door neighbor, high-school principal Sally Mae Carter (the town's last old maid), to the prom in a rented tuxedo. And in the second week of August, when he would have preferred to be sailing on a cruise ship to some exotic destination, he'd pack his frail mother into the Dodge and head to Ocean City for a week to stay in the same rental they'd reserved since 1975.

If you didn't know Jude was manager of the only small bank in Martha Falls, Maryland, you'd have thought he was the town librarian. His shirts were white button downs and his bow ties were dark solids. His slacks were either brown, gray, or navy, usually a heavy wool or tweedy material, and always pressed and creased to perfection with a sharp line down the front and back of his legs. He wore either black or brown oxfords with round toes and chunky heels; at the end of his small nose fell black eyeglass frames that were thick and archaic. But more than all this, he was a soaring, handsome man, with a lean swimmer's body and a heaving head of golden hair, and even though his slacks were as dreary as pond waters, his firm, round buttocks turned more than a few heads when he walked down the street.

He had the kind of perfectly round ass that made even straight men pucker their lips when no one was looking.

Though all this attention usually passed him by, the paradoxical concept of a really hot guy dressed in old man clothes caused one young, gay bank teller at work named Ricky to come unhinged whenever Jude was nearby. If Jude stood next to him to explain a bank procedure poor Ricky would break a sweat and clench his fists so his hands wouldn't shake. He imagined reaching over, unzipping Jude's pants and slowly pulling out his dick. More than once, he'd imagined running his large hands across Jude's naked ass while preparing for the mount. Even the way Jude would lower his eyes when he sipped a cup of coffee made Ricky's dick grow hard and thick. His boss was every sexual fantasy he'd ever had, and he was determined to get into Jude's pants if it killed him. Of course, Jude was oblivious to all of this.

He was more concerned about the laugh lines around his lips and the crevices that were beginning to show on his forehead, which caused him to question his entire life and to wonder about all the things he'd been missing. This all happened in the spring, on the way home from a gay cruise spot about forty miles away from Martha Falls. About a week earlier Jude had celebrated his thirty-seventh birthday with his mother and her ancient sister, Aunt Patty. They had dry, homemade marble cake, fruit punch, and weak coffee in cups and saucers that didn't match; his mother gave him a new vinyl wallet from Swank and Aunt Patty gave him a ten dollar gift certificate to the Martha Falls Video and Live Bait and Tackle Store folded neatly into a faded recycled birthday card that read, "Happy Sixtieth" on the front cover. At nine o'clock he thanked them both, went to his bedroom like he usually did, and jerked off to the *Playgirl* magazine with his legs spread wide and two fingers up his ass.

A week later, as a birthday gift to himself, he went to a familiar cruise spot for a little safe action. He did this about three or four times a year; usually when he couldn't control the urge to be touched by another man any longer.

The cruise spot was a rest area off the interstate, and Jude's habits there were as typical as his work schedule; he knew what he liked and almost always got what he wanted. Jude would pull into a dimly lit parking spot next to another car with a guy who was fairly attractive, he'd remove all his clothes except for a white dress shirt and then he'd boldly step out of the car with a paper towel in his hand and start to clean his windshield. While he wiped the windshield, the white shirt would ride up to his waist and expose his smooth, firm ass to the guy in the other car; he'd always spread his legs wide, stand on tip-toes, and arch his back. Of course, the horny guy in the other car would lick his lips and jump out of the car immediately (oh, it never failed). Sometimes the guy would just stand next to him; most times he couldn't help from grabbing a handful of Jude's ass. "What are you into?" the guy would ask. And Jude would reply, slowly removing his white shirt so he'd be stark naked in the shady night, "Quick finger fuck, Buddy, so I can get off." No sucking or exchange of body fluids; just a couple of solid fingers prying his ass while he jerked off, was all.

On that particular night the guy at the cruise spot was an unwashed landscaper in dark, short pants, heavy work shoes, and a soiled white t-shirt. By the time he'd jumped out of his truck to approach Jude he'd already pulled down his zipper and an eight-inch cock with a huge dripping head was standing straight. He told Jude, "Bend over, baby, and I'll fuck you with something bigger and better than my finger. I got eight inches of dirty dick here that will make you beg for more."

Jude lifted one leg onto the hood of the car and smiled; he liked the guys who weren't afraid to talk dirty. "Just your finger is fine." Though he was tempted to suck the whole eight inches up his hole, he'd managed to live without fear of getting AIDS or STDs his entire adult life, and he wasn't going to start worrying at this point. "But after I come I'll get down on my knees and suck your big sweaty balls while you get off." The guy smiled and wet his middle finger with spit; Jude spread his legs as wide as they would go and leaned forward.

On the way home, though he'd enjoyed the dirty talk and being finger-fucked by a rough young guy, it occurred to him he needed to make a change in his life. Not something too drastic; just an alteration that would take him away from his existence for a while. He'd always been such a decent guy, always doing the right thing and pleasing everyone. Now he wanted to do something for himself. So the next morning, after considerable thought, he went on the Internet and booked a two-week cruise for one of those all-gay cruise ships that advertised "The Best Gay Cruise Experience On Earth," with photos of hot young muscle guys frolicking in Speedos beneath blue skies on gleaming white ship decks. The destinations that attracted him the most were the cruises to Greece, Turkey, and Venice; at least, if he didn't meet any men, the trip would be educational and he'd enjoy the scenery.

The bank only gave him two weeks' vacation time each summer. Jude suspected breaking the news to his mother that they would not be spending their time in Ocean City would be difficult, but all she said was, "That's fine with me, dear. Your Aunt Patty can come stay here with me. You know, I've never been all that fond of uprooting myself for two weeks each year to stay in a beach rental that has lumpy beds, a bad air conditioner, and no cable television. I only did it for you. It'll be good for you to get away on your own for a while."

Jude cocked his head to the side and rubbed his chin. "All these years we've been going to the beach every summer and you didn't like it."

"Yeah, well," she said, "Sometimes you do what you have to do to please loved ones."

He smiled. "Yes, mother, we all do that at times."

***

The flight to Europe was trouble-free, but the first two days on the cruise ship were awkward. The hefty ship confused him: There were so many "decks" and everything was either pure white or sailor blue; he kept getting lost and couldn't seem to figure out the floor plan. It reminded him of the time his father had been admitted to a large hospital in Washington, DC; he'd spent hours trying to figure out how to get back to his car every night. Where were all the sizzling young guys running around half naked? Where was all the implied sex happening? All Jude saw were older gay couples in pastel polo shirts and baggy short pants; the single guys were limp-wristed and wore those flowing, blousy polyester shirts you buy from cheap catalogues. But more than that, everyone seemed to form into small clusters as though they'd known each other for years and years. There were some good-looking guys, but they were either lovers or workers on the ship.

He walked the decks in the early morning wearing a plain white shirt and faded jeans, but stared at the floor and kept his hands in his pockets passing strange people who seemed to be laughing and joking about everything. While he dressed for dinner in his black suit, there was a lump in his throat at the prospect of listening to brassy blond queens rave about the elaborate buffet tables as though food were the only thing left in life to look forward to. Oh, by the third morning, after trying to make conversation at breakfast with a tacky queen who waved fake gold rings and tended to embellish (Jude caught him in a lie more than once), poor Jude was ready to swim back to shore.

After breakfast he shoved his hands back into his pockets, adjusted his dick, and started walking face down to his room. As he left the dining room, just turning the corner, someone bumped into his shoulder. "I'm sorry. I wasn't paying attention," said a good-looking young guy with a thick New York accent and a deep voice.

Jude looked up and smiled. "No problem." But when he realized he knew this guy his head jerked and he stepped back to adjust his eyeglasses.

"Mr. Franklin, I had no idea you were going to be here," said young Ricky from the bank. There was a forged lilt in his voice; he spread his arms too wide, and his smile was so animated you could actually see his upper gums. Ricky knew almost everything Jude did by then; the accidental meeting had been well planned.

"Ah well, there you are," said Jude. He could barely speak; of all things! To run into someone from *his* bank in Martha Falls . . . a junior teller no less. What a fine state of affairs he'd gotten himself into now. Not only had he been exposed, but in the most out-of-your-depth way, too. Ricky, who had always been so conservative at work, was now standing there before him wearing nothing but a white tank top and a skimpy bikini bathing suit and there was nowhere to run. Jude's left eye began to twitch and he shoved his hands to the bottom of his pockets to the point where his shoulders shrugged. And as the knot in his stomach grew tighter, he took a deep breath and said, "Ah, well, isn't this some coincidence, Mr. Johnson."

"You sure can say that," said Ricky. His New York accent was brave and obnoxious. "I was just about to jump ship and swim back to shore. I've been so bored. I mean, this is not what I expected. I can't tell you how glad I am to see someone I actually know."

Jude tilted his head and closed his eyes for a moment; it occurred to him that he was vaguely relieved to have run into a familiar face, too. But it was hard not to stare at all the other things he was seeing: The mammoth bulge of meat packed into Ricky's tight bikini (reminded him of kielbasa packed in cheesecloth); the way his white t-shirt scooped down and uncovered the large round muscles of his bronze chest. "I guess this cruise isn't exactly what they advertised it to be."

"Don't get me wrong," said Ricky. "The ship itself is really cool, the weather is perfect, and the skies are bluer than any skies I've ever seen. This place is a paradise, but I'd rather be sharing it with someone I care about? And I haven't seen many hot guys."

"Well, there you are; at least I can say I haven't been sea-sick," said Jude. Oh dear, he certainly wasn't going to start dis-cussing "hot guys" with a subordinate. That just wouldn't have been right . . . best to change the subject quickly.

Ricky smiled. "What are your plans for today? Would you like to meet for lunch?" At the office Ricky was the perfect em-ployee, taking orders, always doing his job as told to do it. But now it seemed as though his true personality was beginning to plane. He wanted to see more of Jude and wasn't going to squander any time.

"Well . . ."

"I'll meet you back here at the entrance to this dining room at one this afternoon," Ricky said. "Right now I'm going to grab a quick orange juice and a banana, go for a workout, and then a long swim." He may have been bored, but he wasn't go-ing to miss out on all the amenities the ship had to offer.

"I guess that would be . . ." Jude began to say.

"See you then," said Ricky. Then he pressed his palm to Jude's chest and slipped into the dining room.

That morning, as Jude walked back to his small cabin in the economy section on one of the lower decks, his arms were swinging and his head was straight and solid. He even smiled and said good morning to a few of the other passengers he passed along the way. For the first time he noticed how blue the ocean was and how lucid the skies above beamed. Everything seemed to sparkle and shine in a way he'd never experienced back in Martha Falls. When the warm breeze hit his face he could actually smell salt from the sea. And for the first time since he'd arrived onboard the cruise ship, he was actually be-ginning to feel like the trip had been a superior decision.

At one o'clock sharp he met Ricky in front of the dining room entrance. He was wearing a pair of brand new black jeans and a white polo shirt. Ricky wore a hot pink polo shirt with the collar turned up, and a pair of those low-rise, hip hugger jeans all the young guys wore on television. Jude had considered buying a pair for himself while he'd shopped for the cruise, but then decided a man his age might look a bit silly wearing something so young.

"Mr. Johnson, you seem to be right on time," Jude said. His hands were in his pockets again and he wasn't sure where to set his eyes. If he'd been wearing dark sunglasses he would have been glancing at the huge bulge in Ricky's jeans.

"Please call me 'Ricky,'" the young man said.

Jude took a deep breath and sighed. "And you can call me, ah, 'Jude.'"

"C'mon Jude," Ricky said, "Let's eat; I'm starved."

Though at first Jude was a bit taken aback at becoming so familiar with one of his tellers, it didn't bother Ricky to open up to the boss. He took full control by placing his large hand gently on the small of Ricky's back and guiding him toward a table in the middle of the dining room. Normally Jude would have opted for a table in the back, in a more private corner, but Ricky hadn't left him much of a choice. The young man couldn't help himself from taking over, and Jude (though his palms were sweaty and his eye was twitching again) submitted completely.

At the buffet table, Ricky crammed his plate with rich seafood smothered in serious cream sauces, gobs of mashed potatoes, and two huge sesame seed rolls basking in melted butter. When he glanced at Jude's plate, sparsely dotted with a few peaches and a scoop of low-fat cottage cheese, he shook his head. "That's all you're eating, Jude?"

"I prefer to eat lightly in the afternoon," was all Jude said. After all, he wasn't planning to go on about his daily eating habits with a junior teller. How and what he ate was no one's business but his own. And that's how it was going to remain.

But Ricky reached across the buffet table, picked up a solid filet steak drowning in a creamy pepper sauce, and placed it on

Jude's empty plate. "Well, you have to at least try this; I had it last night and I've never had a better piece of meat."

Jude's eyes bulged. "Well, I guess I could try it."

While they ate Jude sipped a small glass of prune juice and Ricky knocked down three apple martinis. Jude sat perfectly straight in his chair, sliced his meat slowly and neatly, and then chewed each bite thirty-two times. Ricky's huge arms went everywhere while he ate; he leaned over his plate and filled his fork with so much food it seemed as though he were inhaling his lunch. If Jude managed to finish three sentences it would have been a miracle because Ricky took full control of the conversation, too. He told Jude about his upbringing in New York's Greenwich Village; how he'd received scholarships to American University in Washington, DC; and how he'd worked his way through it all. He had an incorrigible dog, a mix of German shepherd and lab, which ruined at least one pillow a week. But he loved the animal like a child. Jude was surprised to learn that Ricky had taken the job as junior teller in Martha Falls because he was helping his sister and brother-in-law out. She'd been diagnosed with breast cancer six months earlier and he was there to offer support and help with her two young children while she underwent intense chemotherapy.

After lunch Ricky sat back in his chair, spread his legs wide, and said, "How about an afternoon swim?"

"Ah, well," Jude said. "I'd planned reading a bit, and then taking long nap before dinner." He noticed that Ricky had a huge bulge between his legs; the kind of meat mound that made him long to go down on his knees and start licking.

Ricky smiled and clapped his large hands together. "Well today it might be a nice change to go up to the very top deck of the ship and take a swim."

"Oh well . . ." Jude said. He'd heard about the top deck of that particular cruise ship. That was where the men swam clothing optional. He'd been secretly dying to get up there to see what it was like.

"C'mon, let's go," said Ricky, "I'll race you."

Jude stood slowly, and before he had a chance to protest Ricky reached out for his hand and pulled him from the table. They crossed the dining room with Ricky's hand on Jude's lower back again. When they passed two older men, Jude overheard one say, "What a good-looking couple." But Jude wasn't so sure he agreed. He was worried that people would be thinking, "Look at that silly middle-aged guy being lead around by that young twink." Ricky surely couldn't have been older than twenty-five.

When they reached the top of the ship Jude gasped and pressed his hand to his stomach. In the midst of blue-and-white-striped chairs and umbrellas that surrounded a large round swimming pool, men of all sizes, shapes, and ages were lounging in the nude. An emaciated young man with a large nose, a sunken chest, and a dick so large it swung when he walked drove in with a loud splash; two portly, bald, elderly men with large stomachs and boney legs were kissing on the other side of the pool. Both had dicks so small they looked like acorns attached to two small sacks of potatoes. A group of effeminate men were discussing Martha Stewart's sexuality; their eyebrows were plucked and they all wore too many silver rings.

"Oh, I don't know about this at all," Jude said. His hands were trembling and he couldn't seem to keep his feet still.

Ricky frowned. "I guess it's not what I thought it would be either. Kind of a freak show if you ask me. But at least if we get naked and go swimming we'll be the best looking guys up here."

"Ah, well . . ."

"C'mon, Jude," Ricky said. He'd already claimed two empty blue and white chairs and had begun to remove his heavy white sneakers. Even in his state of panic, Jude couldn't help notice that when Ricky undressed he reminded him of a jock in a locker room. His movements were rough and awkward; big feet pounding and stomping . . . the kind of guy who always tasted better before a shower.

Jude placed his hands on his hips and opened his mouth. But just as he was about to protest Ricky reached around and grabbed him by the waist so that he could whisper into his ear. "I know you're not comfortable with this, but I promise I will take good care of you and make sure you're fine. Nothing can happen to you when I'm around; I promise."

Jude looked into the young man's brown eyes. His hands were shaking and his knees were about to fold. "If you agree to leave now, I promise I'll come back after dinner tonight when it's darker."

Ricky lowered his head and smiled. "Okay, but no backing out. You've made a promise and you have to keep it."

That afternoon they walked the ship, took breaks to sit in the sun, and talked the entire time. Jude, as usual, didn't have much to say, but Ricky was an endless chatter machine. His hands flew in all directions when he spoke; there were times his chest heaved and pulsed so hard Jude was afraid he'd hyperventilate. At four o'clock, when they'd reached Jude's cabin so Jude could take a nap and get ready for dinner, Ricky couldn't help saying, "I have to be honest. I knew you were going on this cruise and I booked myself on this ship just so I could run into you."

Jude's eyes bugged. "That's either very creepy or a nice compliment; I'm just not sure which yet."

"I hope you take it as a compliment," Ricky said. His head went down; for the first time that day he couldn't look Jude in the eye.

"But why?" Jude asked. "I don't understand."

Ricky smiled and looked him in the eye again. "Because I have wanted to get into your pants since the first day you interviewed me for the teller job."

Jude coughed and jerked his head to the side. *Did Ricky really just say such a thing?* "Ah well, I'm not sure I know . . ."

"There's no need to say anything right now," Ricky said, "I just wanted to be honest with you right from the start." Then he pulled a piece of paper from his back pocket. "I don't normally carry this around, but I thought I'd take it along today just to show you that I'm healthy."

Jude reached for the paper, opened it up and began to read. It was a recently printed report from a blood lab that said Ricky had been tested for HIV/AIDS and that he was negative. "Well, I must admit, this is a very decent gesture on your part," Jude said. "Actually, I don't carry anything around with me, but I can assure you that I'm negative, too. I haven't been what you'd call sexually promiscuous or active at all. I know I may have missed out on a lot, but I never wanted to take chances like that with my life and my health."

"I like that. I like your name, too. St. Jude is my patron saint," Ricky said. Then he gave Jude a light punch in the chest and headed back to his own cabin.

***

At dinner Ricky shoved passionate forkfuls into his mouth again, barely taking time to breathe. Jude picked and poked around with a salad. "Is that all you're going to eat for dinner . . . with all this fantastic food?" Ricky asked. His mouth was filled with stuffed eggplant; red sauce dripped from the right corner of his lip and down his strong chin.

Jude nodded. "If we're going to do this swimming in the nude thing later tonight, I don't want to do it on a full stomach."

"No problem," Ricky said, shoving a huge piece of roast beef into his mouth, "But don't mind me . . . I like to get naked, rub my belly, and spread out after a full meal."

After dinner, Jude tried to back out of going to the upper deck for a swim. His hands felt shaky; there was a knot in his stomach; and all this with Ricky seemed to be happening so fast. "Maybe we should just stop into the nightclub for a drink, or maybe see one of the shows," he suggested.

Ricky frowned. "You promised. Let's go." Then he placed his palm on the small of Jude's back and shoved him out the door.

At the top of the ship all was calm. The evening was temperate and the stars dotted the dark sky like Christmas tree lights. There were a couple of attractive young guys (not quite as gorgeous as the guys in the advertisement, but certainly better looking than anything either Ricky or Jude had seen so far) swimming in the deep end. They wore loose fit bathing trunks and acted more like best friends than lovers. None of the naked old men or Nelly queens were anywhere in sight. Jude assumed they were all down below watching drag shows or stuffing themselves at the buffet table.

"No one up here is naked," Jude said, "Maybe it's not allowed after dark."

"Up here it's always clothing optional; at all hours," Ricky whispered, "These guys are probably waiting for someone else to have the brass balls to strip down first."

"Maybe we could just . . ."

But Ricky had already begun to unbutton his black shirt. So Jude leaned over and started to untie the chunky black oxfords. Ricky ripped off his clothes, thumped and banged against the blue and white lounge chairs, and tossed everything into a rumpled heap while Jude slowly stepped out of his white shirt and tan slacks and folded them neatly across the back of the chair. All this seemed so perfectly ordinary to Ricky: a couple of guys getting naked in public. Jude couldn't help noticing how Ricky's thick brown cock bounced against his wide, solid thighs when he pulled his white briefs off. He had the urge to reach over, take the big soft thing in his palm and squeeze it gently. Through all this, though he kept his head low, Jude knew the other young guys were watching the strip show.

When they were both undressed Jude couldn't resist. He went down on his knees without warning, pressed his face to Ricky's neatly trimmed groin, and sucked the semi-erect cock to the back of his throat. The cock of his dreams: thick and fleshy and tasting like salt and vinegar. For a long moment, breathing only through his nose, he simply kept his head still and felt the big dick grow inside his mouth. His lips puckered and his cheekbones indented; when he began to suck his soft tongue ran from the bottom of the shaft to the mushroom-shaped cock head that was starting to drip. Ricky placed his palm on Jude's head and spread his legs wider as though he were about to take a piss. He moaned and sighed; his eyes were closed and his head went back. The two guys on the other side of the pool leaned forward and began to rub their balls.

Jude sucked him off for a good ten minutes, and Ricky almost reached orgasm right there, but he knew it was too soon so he pulled out his cock and helped Jude to his feet. Then he placed his hand on Jude's round ass and said, "You don't have much body hair." Then he pressed firmly and led Jude toward the pool.

The two young guys were watching Ricky rub and squeeze Jude's ass. "Ah, no," Jude said, "I'm pretty smooth all over." He had a full erection and his lips were swollen; the taste of Ricky's sweet pre-cum was still on his tongue.

When they reached the edge of the pool, Jude took the stairs and slowly stepped into the shallow end, but Ricky jumped right into the warm chemical water with a loud splash. By the time he came up for air Jude was already leaning against the side of the pool in the five-foot section. The blue tiles felt smooth and easy against his back; his cock was still rock hard from the cocksucking session. Ricky swam toward him, splashing like a donkey, and stood directly in front of him. They were both about the same height, and when Ricky felt Jude's hard cock press against his crotch he smiled and said, "Feels like you're more relaxed now."

"I don't know what's gotten into me," Jude teased. "I'll never be able to get out of the water." It occurred to him there was a naughty thrill to all this; not unlike his excursions to the cruise stops on the interstate.

Jude sighed and took a glance toward the end of the pool. The young guys were now sitting quietly on the pool's edge with their feet dangling in the water and their eyes firmly fixed on Jude and Ricky. They weren't pretending not to be interested anymore; it was obvious they were waiting to see if Jude and Ricky would put on a full show. "Relax," Ricky said, "These guys only want to watch. If it makes you uncomfortable, I'll get rid of them."

Jude pretended to frown. "Well, I wouldn't want to be rude or anything. After all, what harm can they do?"

Ricky smiled. "Well, if they do bother you just tell me and I'll make them go away."

Jude didn't have a chance to respond. Ricky placed both strong hands on Jude's waist and pressed his lips to Jude's mouth. When he stuck his thick tongue inside, Jude wrapped his arms around Ricky's broad shoulders and his legs around Ricky's waist. Ricky lowered his right hand and squeezed Jude's ass hard, and the harder he squeezed the deeper Jude shoved his tongue into Ricky's hot mouth. "Damn," Ricky whispered into his ear, "I had a feeling there was a wild man locked up inside that conservative shell. And so cuddly and soft, too."

Jude smiled and then squeezed Ricky's waist with his legs. "I want you to fuck me right here in the pool." His ass was burning for that giant young dick.

Ricky looked up with a guilty expression to see what was going on around the pool. The two young guys had stripped naked and were holding their erections. "Those two guys are still watching us," Ricky said, "You don't mind? They are playing with their dicks."

He stuck his tongue all the way out and licked the side of Ricky's face. "I just want you inside me right now; as fast as you can."

Jude lowered his legs and rested his back against the fresh blue pool tiles. While Ricky reached down to spread Jude's legs so that he could hoist him up higher by the backs of his knees, Jude leaned his elbows on the pool coping to help Ricky find the perfect fuck position. In no time Jude's legs were spread wide and hanging over both of Ricky's strapping, beefy arms for support. The two young guys were now at the edge of the pool alongside Ricky and Jude so they could watch the fuck session up close; to Jude's right a thin young guy with black hair got down on his haunches and began to tug on a wide, seven-inch dick; on his left a young guy with blond hair kneeled down to play with his own rock hard, curved cock. And while the two guys continued to get off, Ricky pressed the head of his dick up against Jude's tight hole and began to work it in slowly.

"Is that okay?" Ricky asked. His pupils were dilated and he bit his bottom lip.

"Oh, yeah," Jude replied. His mouth was open wide and his eyes were squinting. "All the way; go as deeply as you can." Though it was the first time he'd actually ever had dick, all those years of finger fucking had certainly taught him how to take it.

Ricky quickly inserted the cock head and wasted no time shoving his entire pipe all the way up Jude's stretched hole; the pink hole felt so soft he closed his eyes and pursed his lips as though he were about to whistle. At first Jude winced because they didn't have lube, but once it was all the way up, his ass muscles relaxed and the lips of his hole began to grip the immense dick. He smiled and threw his head back. The two young guys jerking off were gradually inching closer; their naked legs were now touching Jude's shoulders; so close he could smell their musty dicks and hear their hairy balls slapping against their thighs. Ricky began to fuck harder; Jude's legs splashed in the water and his toes curled with each rough knock. Ricky's cock was thick and long and filled him to the point where every inch of his hole felt an orgasmic sensation.

Jude's eyes began to roll around; his mouth fell open. The dark-haired young guy looked down at his cock and then nodded at Ricky, to see if it was okay for him to shove his dick into Jude's mouth (you always ask the top guy for permission). Ricky looked up toward the sky for a moment, and then looked back at the young guy and nodded with his approval. Though Jude hadn't been paying attention to any of this, when the young guy rose to his knees and placed the head of his big dick to Jude's lips, Jude raised his arms and shook his head no. "You guys can watch and do whatever you want, but I'm only interested in the man who is inside me right now." Of course, secretly he was thinking about sucking both guys off. He could have sucked them dry and then lapped up every last ounce of creamy seed. But he liked Ricky and was also secretly hoping for more than just a quick fuck on a cruise ship.

Ricky smiled so wide you could see all his teeth and his upper gums again. It would have been okay with him if Jude had wanted to suck off the other guys, but when Jude refused the two beautiful studs his ego soared. He continued to fuck hard and fast; Jude had turned into a lump of jelly by then. "I'm getting really close," Ricky shouted, now fucking even harder. "I'm gonna blow a load soon, baby."

Jude's eyes met Ricky's and he nodded that it was okay. So Ricky grabbed Jude's dick with his right hand and began to jerk it off. His fucking became quick, with rhythmic bangs that went deep into Jude's body; he jerked Jude's cock with the same strides and in a matter of moments Jude's toes were curling and his eyes were rolling back. Jude had to grab the edge of the pool with his left hand, and then reached out with his right hand so he could hold on to the dark young guy's hairy thigh for support.

"Oh, fuck, baby," Ricky shouted. By then he was pounding so hard and fast there was pool water everywhere.

Jude's breathing became heavier; he opened his mouth and leaned his head forward while Ricky shouted, "AH, YES."

They all came together; Ricky felt Jude's cock swell and release beneath the water. Jude actually felt Ricky's seed shoot up his ass and through his body. Ricky kept going deeper and backing Jude into the tiles, trying to deposit every last drop. The two beautiful young guys blew their loads all over Jude's bare shoulders; a couple of drops from the dark-haired guy hit Jude's chin. When Ricky wasn't looking he stuck his tongue out and licked his chin dry. The two strangers shook their cocks a couple of times to make sure they were empty and quickly stood. They walked away as though nothing had ever happened. But Ricky plunged even deeper into Jude's hole and leaned forward. He grabbed Jude hard and pulled him close so that he could suck his face. Not just a simple kiss; he shoved his tongue all the way down Jude's throat and rolled it around as though he were trying to locate something he'd lost.

"Are you okay, Buddy?" Ricky asked in a stage whisper, placing his hands on the bottom of Jude's ass. "That was some workout."

Jude took a deep breath and spread his legs wider so Ricky's cock could remain inside as long as possible. "Maybe we could do this again later tonight?"

Ricky sighed. "Oh, I think we're going to do it many times aboard this ship. Many times."

Jude arched his back and wrapped his arms around Ricky's shoulders. For the first time in his life he felt as though he'd finally found something that felt right. Something easy and normal and meant-to-be.

Lifeline
Erastes

Ships that pass in the night, and speak each other in passing,
Only a signal shown and a distant voice in the darkness.
—Longfellow

"When will we be in New York, darling?"

"You'll see the harbor lights on Tuesday night without fail."

"That seems incredible!"

"She's the fastest there is. She'll revolutionize sea travel, you'll see."

The couple sauntered past me in the gathering dusk as I watched, sprawled lazily against the railings of the huge boat deck. I gazed after them, admiring their casual intimacy, the way his arm was wound around her waist proprietarily, the loving, trusting way her head was resting against his shoulder.

I loved these tiny snapshots into people's lives. They had sounded so young, so wrapped up in the words of each other and I regretted I had not seen their faces. It would have added a dimension to the memory, something clean to remember.

The dolphins at the prow veered off as the sky darkened and the ship plowed on into the cool evening, and for all the passengers promenading, for all the excitement of the past few days it was surprisingly quiet. Truly a wine-dark sea. A portentous sea, soon to be full of the tales of men and their heroism. But that was to come, and by then my life would be on a new route.

I must have mistimed it, for I am sure he was late, even though I knew that I could not be wrong. He stood next to me on the railing, staring out at the water with a look of pain on his handsome face. I lit a cigarette and offered him one in companionable silence. As he took it I let my fingers brush his knuckles and I know that we both felt the spark between us.

His cheekbones, high and impossibly beautiful, shimmered in the silver evening, and his hair which was dazzling gold on the pier in Queenstown, had turned to liquid moonlight.

"Problems?" I said, leaning back on the rail, letting my obvious arousal show through my tight, high-waisted trousers. He looked up at me, those beautiful eyes filled with an English mistrust of strange men who spoke without introduction.

"I'm sorry . . ." he started, but I cut across him.

"I only meant that I saw you, in Queenstown, in the telegraph office, and you looked worried then. You look worried now." I touched his arm in a conciliatory way and I frowned that it was cloth I touched and not his skin. "I think I know what it is you are worried about. I can help." I was pleased to see he didn't pull away for all of his stiff-upper-lip demeanor. His gaze moved downwards, an involuntary movement, and the musk rose from him in waves as he struggled with his indecision. I closed the gap and claimed him with an arm, pulling him against me. He struggled—oh, a little, just enough to make me want him more—but my mouth was on his ear, reassuring him in the darkness.

"I know what it is you fear," I murmured. My hand slipped between us, over his groin and he whimpered childishly like the man-yet-unknown-to-men I believed him to be. He shuddered, but not from the cold. "I know what it is that you have been hiding." My hand slid between his legs, and I felt the steel beneath the serge and I stepped back, into the shadow of the lifeboat, pulling him with me, thrilling to the sudden acquiescence of him, swaying and pliant in my arms, as if hypnotized by my unprovoked attack on his person and senses. "I know what it is that you *need*." I wrapped one arm around his waist, under his jacket and bent him at the waist, pulling him tight against me. All pretense and coyness was gone. I pushed one leg between his, and ground my hardness against his, now fully erect and as hot as a furnace.

He braced his hand against my chest, but I could see the conflict in his face.

"I . . ." he managed. "I don't . . ."

My mouth plundered his, claiming him as my own and he submitted to me utterly, like I knew he would. His mouth was sweet with brandy and sour with tobacco. His teeth were perfect and his tongue was languid, as if waiting for a call to arms. My own coiled around it, woke it from its dormancy and I burned as he gave a soft wordless groan. He had a sweet, simple naivete, hesitant but then gaining in confidence. His hands joined in the fun, fumbling at my jacket buttons, and wrenching them from their holes. He pulled my shirt free from my trousers with an impatience, which proved that he'd been holding his repression for far too long.

"That's right," I sighed in his ear. "Let it flow from you, be what you want to be." I cast a look up the deck; the young couple was making their way back toward us, together with some late night prowlers. There was only one place to hide and we stumbled toward the lifeboats, our hats flying off and skidding across the deck; both of the same mind, shirts untucked and mouths melded. My fingers popped open the buttons of his fly, certain of the prize within. We scrambled, undignified, up into the boat and I slit the canvas. We slid into the dark, giggling like schoolboys. He hit the damp planks first and his restraint, in the seclusion of the musty sea-scented cave, vanished like morning mist. The moonlight poured, bright as day, through the rip in the canvas and eagerly I finished my work, unclipping his braces, pulling his trousers and underthings down past his hips, and pulling him down with me as I dropped to my knees and took him into my mouth. His fingers tightened—too hard—in my hair and I knew he was on the brink. Another suck, a butterfly touch on the inside of his thigh and he arched, pushing his cock hard into my mouth, which I took, eagerly, greedily. With a hiss of joy and disappointment, he came, and I savored him, swallowing all he had to give then slid up, pulling his arm away from his eyes. I wondered at his eagerness and yet reveled in his shame. I stroked his golden hair with gentle fingers and kissed his eyelids, his soft cheeks, his bruised and pouting lips.

"I'm so sorry," he said, almost to himself. I made reassuring shushing noises, like I would to a child, and began to deliberately and carefully to divest him of every stitch of clothing, not satisfied until he was pale and trembling in the chilly April night. I tore my own clothes from me and then *finally* we were flesh to flesh. Every instinct I had screamed at me to turn him over and plunge deep into his body, but I contented myself with running my hands over his broad chest and kissing him deeper and deeper feeling myself falling hopelessly under his spell like I knew I would.

Hesitantly, like a child unsure if such treasure can really be for him, his hands began to explore my body and I whispered words of encouragement, gratified beyond reason that he was so eager, so soon. I laid flat beside him and allowed him to take a little control; he raised himself on his elbow and ran his hands down my chest. My nipples were hard points and I groaned as he bent to let his tongue taste the flesh of a man for the first time.

He looked at me, amazed. "You like that?"

"God, yes. Kiss me, kiss me anywhere, everywhere." I writhed, possibly more than I would do normally, to show how much I appreciated his attentions, to encourage him to experiment, He obliged me. I felt his lips on my rib cage, my hip bones, my thighs, and it was all I could do not to tangle my fingers into his hair and force his head over the head of weeping cock. He was still nervous; I could tell by his hesitation. He needed one more push to take such a big step, no matter how much he wanted it.

"Please . . ." I whimpered. "Please . . ." It was part artifice, part truth, but it was all he needed. For many, giving pleasure is a twin of receiving it, and I'd known he would be this way. He took my cock in his soft, cool, beautiful hands and kissed the tip, his eyes flickered to my face as if attempting to gauge my every reaction. His tongue flickered and flicked and dragged across the head, and soon all pretense of begging dropped away from me. I begged in earnest; pushing my hips forward—longing to slide my length in and out of that delicate mouth.

"What do you want me to do?" he said, and my control snapped. The sweet compliance was more than a man could take.

I growled at him. "Suck me, or fuck me, whatever you damn well please, but do it now."

"I . . . I want to fuck you," he said. He was so matter of fact about it, I could have laughed, but it wasn't the time. "May I?"

I realized that this option would be easier to manage than for me to breach a virgin in the confined space we had, I kissed him, showing him with my lips and tongue and fingers how much his suggestion pleased me. I brought him back to hardness, rewarding every whimper, every moan with new sensations he'd never had before.

"Like this," I said, shifting to all fours. I found myself absurdly excited at this unexpected turn of events; I had thought that he would be submissive, eager to be had instead of wantonly randy and he delighted me. I love to be taken, especially by a virgin. His hands and lips brushed over every inch of my shoulders and back as I positioned myself for him. I spread my legs, turned my face for his kisses, and let him work it out for himself. He was clumsy as first, pushed in just the wrong place and I muffled a cry, took a deep breath and shifted slightly so his next shot went true. He pushed into my welcoming ass so hard sparks flashed in front of my eyes.

"Oh Jesus." His voice broke like he was crying. "Jesus, I never dreamed . . ." He clutched me as if for balance, his cock twitching deep within me; I could feel his bush scratchy and delicious on my ass, and I wriggled backwards, clenched my ass muscles for him, giving him a taste of the delights to come. He sobbed softly again and began a steady rhythm. His cock plugged me hard with his lust and need. As I relaxed into his happy fuck, he fell forward, still snapping his hips against me. He kissed every part he could reach while he pounded me and soon we were groaning together, neither of us caring who might hear us.

"Do you want me to touch you?" he groaned against my ear, and I shook my head, delighted that even now, he can think of my pleasure; he shows much promise for the life we will have together if he was this thoughtful on his first time. I wanted to wait; I wanted to fuck him so badly I could feel his ass around my cock, could see him in my mind's eye, ravaged and gleaming with sweat as I pound him into my bed. I want to watch him when he comes, watch that perfect face twist as I give him what he wants. But I can wait. This was all for him.

He straightened and grabbed my hips, pulled my ass closer to him, so that he pleasured himself in my tightness. He learned fast. I tightened round him again, and I stayed clenched for his enjoyment and mine and then, then he cried out.

"Fuck! Oh yes . . ." The last words were nothing more than a hiss as his heat exploded into my innards and he fell onto my back for support, his cock slipping from me.

I slid around and held him as he recovered. He was slippery with sweat; damp and panting. I kissed the perspiration from his forehead, and then asked him the question that will affect both of our lives.

"What if I told you that I know the future, and could change yours right now? Could take you off the ship this minute and you'd never have to go back."

He lay motionless beneath me and I kissed his sweat-damp-ened brow again, dipping my tongue into that pretty mouth, tasting the meld of us, smoky and iridescent.

His voice was husky and guarded. "It's bad enough we did what we did, and now I find out you are off your trolley too." He made as to move away but I held him close to me and he didn't struggle—not really—but groaned softly.

"But what if I were to prove it?" I said. "What if I were to tell you that there was going to be a terrible accident and most of the men on board would be killed? Would you come with me then? What are your choices? The new world isn't so new. All that waits you there is a wife who will never understand, a society that will ostracize you. Your choice is that—or taking a risk, and a life of pleasure—with me."

"You *are* mad."

"I said I could prove it," I said. "And I will. Just wait."

"How long for?" He looked a little scared and I wonder which truth scared him.

"Oh," I glanced at my watch. "Any . . . moment . . . now."

I leant down and kissed him again, felt him relax as if accepting I was eccentric. With one eye on the watch I waited for the terrible screaming sound of ice on metal . . .

***

The woman sobbing at the desk was in danger of collapse; the officer was sympathetic but he had seen so much grief over the past few days this seemed light by comparison.

"But he telegraphed me!" she wept. "From Queenstown Pier! He said he had something important to tell me!"

"I can only repeat what I have said ma'am, that your husband was not on board before or after Ireland. He did not even embark at Southampton. He is not on the passenger list. Perhaps," his voice dropped to a low murmur, not wishing the whole hall to hear, "He has left you, ma'am."

Cold Night Visitor Hot
Keith Williams

Skin! What a relief. After days of corduroy pants, plaid shirts, blue jeans, sweaters, scarves, and gloves, it was satisfying to get to see some skin. It was four days into my Alaskan cruise and this was the first time I had visited the ship's indoor pool. It wasn't by chance I finally made it to the pool that day—I went looking for a particular young man I'd named "the colt." When the colt was within sight I couldn't see anyone else . . .

***

To begin near the beginning: I had booked this cruise to Alaska with the understanding that it was a gay cruise—just a *generic* gay cruise, if you could call it that. Not a "gay family cruise," not a "gay senior's cruise," not a "gay couple's cruise," not a "gay men's cruise," not a "gay single's cruise," but just a gay cruise. And that's how it was advertised. But somehow it turned out to be a what you could have called a "several-hundred-gay-male-couples-in-their-early-twenties, plus four elderly gay men, plus a group of about eighteen fifty-something lesbians, plus one forty-six year-old single, gay male (namely me) cruise." Well, by the time I made this observation about the mix of seagoing vacationers, we were already at sea. Though I felt a bit like the odd-man-out, I decided to make the best of it. I had this far-out fantasy that I would be thought of as the "fox in the henhouse," so to speak, among some of the younger men, but it was not to be. There seemed to be an unspoken rule that they were not going to mingle with the middle-aged, the elderly, or any females. I didn't take it personally. Frankly, the women were very friendly, as were the older couples, and so I got to meet and spend time with some very nice people. It didn't look like I was going to get laid, but I always hold out hope.

It was on the first day, just as we boarded, that I spotted my young colt. With his big old hands, feet, nose, and ears he hadn't yet grown into, he struck me at first as an extra-large puppy. If he wasn't a virgin he should have been with his soft full head of brownish-black hair, and matching five-o'clock shadow, a full lower-lip and big blue saucer eyes that added to that puppy feeling. But he was no puppy. He was a colt. He had a firm jaw, a muscular face, and a lean, strong, sometimes skittish quality to his way of moving that definitely made him a colt. *My* colt? Well, in my imagination he was my tall, young colt, but he appeared to be either the friend or the actual boyfriend of a much shorter stocky red-haired guy who was apparently able to read my mind, or more likely he could just read my face, because it seemed that every time I would come close enough to my colt to say "hello," Red, as I thought of his friend, would keeping them moving along.

In spite of Red's quickness, I had plenty of chances to observe the colt and begin to memorize some of his beautiful details. However, it was on that fourth day when things started to turn in my favor. The first surprise was finding out that the colt and Red were in a cabin on the same level as mine, and only about five doors down the same narrow corridor. As I was leaving my cabin that day I saw they had just left theirs and were headed my way. I said 'hello' and they both said 'hello' back but didn't seem to be slowing down, so I thrust out my hand to Red and introduced myself. He stopped and responded politely— his real name turned out to be Chip—and I turned to my young colt, who shook my hand, and in a friendly way said, "My name is Benjamin, pleased to meet you." Well, I was pleased to meet him and told him so. Turns out they were from Chicago—I'm from Milwaukee so we're practically neighbors—and they were on their way to the ship's indoor pool. I told them I hadn't been to the pool yet but that it was as good a time as any to check it out, and that I might see them there. Might! I changed into a bathing suit, threw on a T-shirt, put back on my jeans and shoes, grabbed a towel, and headed off to the pool.

It wasn't too crowded. I took off everything but the swim suit and left it all in a pile in the corner. Red was swimming laps and Benjamin, who had already been in the water, was standing by the pool in a Speedo that was a little loose on him. Heavenly. He saw me and waved. His slender body was even more lithe and solid than I had imagined. Young Benjamin had clearly never seen the inside of a gym and probably didn't play sports, but he was graced with naturally long muscles that would just keep growing as he grew. By now I guessed him to be about twenty-three-years-old, and he continued to impress me with his particular kind of modesty, combined with a distinctly adult male sensuality. His skin was pale from head to toe and he had bristly-looking black hair sprouting from his arms and legs, but nowhere was it growing very thickly. The hair on his chest was a furry diamond with a tail that lead down into his bathing suit. Oh, that suit. I couldn't exactly make out his cock and balls, but they were filling out the suit with a nice lump. Later when I got a rear view of Benjamin, I found that his ass was full and high for such a slim man and, as the loose Speedo showed, as evenly hairy as the rest of him.

Instead of getting into the pool, I walked around to the other side to visit with Benjamin—fortunately my trunks were baggy enough to somewhat hide my growing hard-on. Benjamin smiled and we talked about the cruise and the sights we'd seen thus far. He told me he was a graduate student majoring in history and that he loved teaching. I enjoyed observing how he found ways to check me out—he was clearly interested in my legs and feet, which are all large and stocky, and he also took a quick few glances at my belly, my nipples, and my hands. But mostly, sweet Benjamin the colt seemed to enjoy looking at my face as much as I enjoyed looking at his. The energy between us was a good voltage.

Red was saying 'hi' to me again as he climbed out of the pool and suggested that he and Benjamin were late to meet some friends. Benjamin gave him a kind of neutral look and said, "You go ahead and change, I'll be right behind you." Red went for his towel and began drying off. Benjamin turned back to me and it was when he shook my hand that I noticed his cock under the front of his suit—on the right side it was, but not quite poking out the top. Well, so was mine. Benjamin didn't seem uncomfortable about it in the least, he just said it was great that we got to meet and that he looked forward to seeing me later. Then he went to join Red. For the first time he didn't seem quite so shy, and also for first time I thought perhaps Red and Benjamin were not a couple, or that if they were, perhaps Benjamin had a bit of independence. I jumped in the pool.

That night there was a dance after dinner in the main dining room. It was a casual but pleasant affair and I was happy to see some of the youngsters open up with the lesbians and the older men. Between one senior and a swarthy twenty-something was a bit of romance growing—at least it seemed that way judging from their closeness during a slow dance. My boys, Red and Benjamin, were there and though I didn't get to sit with them, I stopped by their table to chat with Benjamin. We continued to be as fascinated with one another as we were that afternoon. But their table was kind of rowdy so I asked Benjamin if he wanted to dance. I was surprised when he said, "No thanks," and that he didn't dance. He blushed red so I decided not to push it, hoping we'd find another time to talk with more privacy. At about eleven o'clock I wanted to hit the hay—I loved getting up early and seeing the morning come up on the ocean. Just as I got to my cabin I was surprised to see that Red and Benjamin had reached their cabin at the same time, but from a different direction. We exchanged a few words and then

I invited them over for drink. They glanced at each other, then Red declined politely saying they'd take a rain check. I told them, "For you two, my door is always open. Don't forget, always open." Then Benjamin, who never seemed to say too much, piped up and said, "I'll be sure to remember that." Then he smiled and looked back at me as they entered their room and closed the door.

After I got undressed and brushed my teeth, I still had a hard-on from seeing Benjamin the colt again. Thinking about his blushing face, I walked over and unlocked my door. The chances of anyone, including the colt, coming into my room in the middle of the night were slim, so I wasn't worried about a hostile intruder. But I wanted to make sure it was open for Benjamin just in case, just in case . . .

One thing that appealed to me about this cruise in the first place was the cool weather. Especially in early autumn, nights in the waters around Alaska are icy cool. My cabin was well heated, but not over heated, and yet I couldn't help but leave my window open a crack. For me, it is a sensuous pleasure to be lying naked in a warm room with a cool breeze raising my skin. Between that chilly air, the warm room, and the soft cotton sheets I was out like a light.

The digital clock read 1:15 a.m. when I heard the door open. Though I heard it quite distinctly and awoke immediately, I fortunately had the presence of mind to neither jump up nor speak. I peeked quietly through one eye to see who it was, and as the door opened more the silhouette of Benjamin, my sneaky colt, was unmistakable. He was being so careful once he got inside it took him almost five minutes to slowly close the door, come toward the bed, and take off his boxers. I thought of speaking but I didn't want to scare him. I was so intrigued wondering what he might try to do, and how he might try to do it, I tried to just relax and wait.

I was lying on my back with the sheet covering me from the waist down—my left leg and part of my hard-on were outside the sheet. My right arm on the outside edge of the bed was above my head and my left hand was on my stomach. My eyes were closed. I wondered what I would feel. I waited. Then, ever so gradually, I felt the sheet being pulled away toward the foot of the bed. I didn't want to give myself away or chase Benjamin away, so I tried to keep my breathing deep and even, which wasn't easy. After what seemed like ten minutes, but probably wasn't, the sheet was finally off. The next thing I felt was a slight breeze on my legs. It wasn't coming from the window though, so I peeked again. Benjamin—I could just make out his cock sticking up in the dark room—was ever so gently running his hands up and down my legs, just barely touching the hairs. It was a wonderful feeling and once I knew what he was doing my dick bobbed the way a hard-on will when it gets harder. Benjamin proceeded, over the next fifteen minutes to do this all over my body: legs, feet, balls, cock, belly, chest, arms, hands, neck, ears— even my pits and my beard. I'm not an especially hairy man, but Benjamin's ministrations reminded me that we have hair all over our bodies, sometimes very tiny hairs, even where we don't. In other circumstances it might have put me right back to sleep, but I was now very awake and the connection between us was charged. Finally, Benjamin quietly rubbed his hands together to warm them, and then began to touch my skin, carefully, again starting with my legs. I allowed myself the luxury of exhaling heavily and moving my right arm down to my side. Did he really believe I was asleep? Did it matter? I decided I would prefer to continue to "be asleep" for Benjamin and just let him do what he wanted to do for a while. What he wanted to do, and did, was massage my legs and my feet, every inch of them, to lift and caress my balls, to lightly touch my entire penis in a way that would have woken me up had I truly been asleep. He even took the head of my cock in his mouth and soothingly licked away the pre-cum that had been dripping out of it. He tenderly massaged my chest and the temples on my forehead. Then my colt went back down to my crotch and slowly his hot breath warmed my cock. Eventually he had his mouth around the head, not touching it, just letting the warm breath circulate around it. Amazing. When did he think of that?

After a while he backed off for a moment, got his saliva flowing again, and then went down on me—gently of course, but with a force of steady suction that could have had me blowing my load after a while. But instead, Benjamin reached to the ground where he had dropped his boxers. I heard the crinkling of plastic. This bright colt was going to put a condom on me. Fantastic. He rolled it on little by little. Then he proceeded to do some even bolder things, things that made me think perhaps he knew I was a willing participant, but still maybe not. He picked each of my arms up and laid them lightly across my chest, but I wasn't sure why until I felt his weight on the bed. Benjamin placed one knee on the right side of my belly then swung his other leg over to the left side. His bobbing cock once or twice touched the backs of my hands. When he reached back to aim my cock toward his sphincter, I thought he was really risking "waking me up" and I was also really proud of him and turned on by his nerve. Even as the head of my cock was just beginning to push inside his ass, it was going so smoothly that I could feel he had already lubed up. He had come to my room with his ass full of lube. What a boy scout! It must have taken about three minutes, but finally he was sitting all the way back on my cock. His ass was full and he just rested there, without putting his full weight on me. He was breathing heavily and I was dying to touch him or to fuck him, but I didn't. I waited. Occasionally my cock bucked a little inside him. He began to easily rise, but not too far, and then move back down. He repeated this until it had become a rocking motion. He was fucking himself with my cock. I was a live prop in his discreet scenario of a sort of slow-motion rape. It was wonderful. As he continued to rock back and forth, his lips finally came close enough to mine that couldn't hold back anymore and I reached up and kissed him on the mouth. Benjamin jumped and would have jumped right off my cock and off the bed if I hadn't grabbed him by the waist and held him tightly. He was breathing hard and almost gasping. I started to reassure him but he reached out quickly and put a finger to my lips. Surprised, but still totally turned on, I complied with this non-verbal request to keep our activities non-verbal. He rode me for another ten minutes while we made out and pinched each other's nipples and stroked each other's hair. Eventually I just had to ease him off and flip him over onto his back. I lifted his legs over my shoulders and entered him with some force. Benjamin moaned a long and satisfied moan that turned me on so that I started to fuck him vigorously. I continued to fuck him and he continued to moan. I grabbed his lovely cock and began to jerk it up and down as I continued to fuck him. When he shot his load it landed on his chin and around his neck. I knew I shouldn't, but I licked up every bit of it I could find. Then I stuck my tongue in his mouth so his cum would mingle in our mouths as I fucked him harder and harder and shot my load into the condom, my fuck stick pulsing in his ass for another few minutes. I fell to my side, my cock still inside him and we continued kissing for a good while.

Once I had eased out of him and removed the condom, I looked at the clock. It read 3:45 a.m. I was stunned to find that it had been two and half hours since my handsome sex burglar had entered my cabin. We continued to pet, stroke, and kiss each other until we were almost asleep, and then Benjamin got up and quietly left the room.

***

The next day, I got to see Benjamin again, at breakfast in fact, and he was not with Red. Strangely, we made no mention of his night visit to my cabin. We talked about our families and our work. Over the next week and a half I enjoyed the social company of both Benjamin and Red during waking hours. And, for the following nine days, Benjamin and I didn't discuss or reminisce or comment on any of our nocturnal intimacies, even though they went on every night for the rest of the cruise. All but one night that is, when I opened my eyes to find what I was soon to discover was Red's chubby cock hovering around my mouth. Young Red had his charms, I do admit. But I was so happy when my young colt, handsome Benjamin, returned the next night like a cool breeze to warm my whole body and soul.

Two If By Sea
Jeff Funk

"My ultimate fantasy? I'd like to get fucked and sucked at the same time," I said to William, a fellow traveler whose looks were dark and exotic. I could feel his handsome partner's attention shift to my torso and beyond, appraising my body while I answered. This inspired me to straighten my posture and flex my muscles for effect. We were seated in a cozy nook of the "Navigator's Lounge," enjoying cocktails. Dance music from the upper promenade deck was carried by the sea breeze as the cruise ship moved by night to the next port. "My heels in the air," I continued, "taking every inch a hung stud could give me while his buddy goes to town, chowing on my pole. Hopefully, with his ass planted in my face so I could tongue his pucker. Yeah, that'd do it for me." The couple exchanged a look, their eyes sparkling in the candlelight. I got up and said I had to find a bathroom. I figured, best to give them time to conspire and discuss ground rules.

When I first boarded the ship, I wasn't certain I would enjoy myself. This trip was supposed to be a surprise anniversary gift to my boyfriend, celebrating our three years together. As luck would have it, we broke up a month ago. Amicably, I might add. However, I can't help but wonder whether he would have stayed longer had he known about the Caribbean vacation. After discussing it with my brother and his wife, I decided to keep the reservation. Traveling always seems to put my life in perspective and it would be good to get away from the house and the memories. Now that I'm here, on what is basically the Gay Love Boat, I am delighted with the fact that I have a double occupancy room to myself. While I know that a stranger's arms offer hollow comfort, nothing distracts me from a broken heart better than recreational sex, and it has been years since

I've been with anyone other than David. That is, if you don't count what happened yesterday onshore.

**

The day began with me deciding to go to the sports deck for a vigorous workout because I needed to burn off what I had consumed the night before at the midnight chocolate bar. I made a pig of myself, using sweets to take the edge off of my loneliness. Indeed, it would be at least a month until I'd crave anything chocolate. You gotta watch the desserts on these cruise ships. Baked Alaska. Cherries Jubilee. It's a good thing I don't eat like this everyday or I'd be in trouble.

The fitness center was surprisingly empty. All these gym queens on board and no one's working out? They must have been up late. There are two dance clubs on the ship that are a lot like circuit parties, with dancing till dawn. I had my pick of treadmills and took one in the middle of the room, which had a magnificent view looking out onto the ocean. I selected the disco play list on my iPod and gradually increased the track speed until I was at a sprint. At the five-minute mark, sweat began to stream down my face. The room was cooler than I prefer, but I wasn't going to complain. I wanted to savor every detail so I could call upon this memory during future workouts when my mind grew bored. Remember this: running with the waves, out on the open sea.

In the reflection of the window, I saw a beautiful stranger enter the room. Dark hair, goatee. Strong arms. Pecs covered in fur, peeking provocatively from his white tank top. I took in a sharp breath, because at first glance he looked exactly like David. I briefly wondered, *What's he doing on the ship? Did he find out about the vacation from my brother, or more likely my sister-in-law?* As the man moved closer, the mirage lifted like sea mist. I saw that he was taller than my lover and a smidge more handsome. But the resemblance was uncanny. An instant heaviness in my throat threatened to pull down my spirits.

He climbed onto a treadmill beside me. "Good mornin'."

"Hey," I said, reaching to turn off my music. I slowed the machine so I could talk comfortably. "I wondered when I'd have some company. My name's Jesse."

"I'm Brandon," he said with a nod. People who look alike sound alike. He had David's timbre, but with a southern accent. "So are you here with someone?"

"No. You?"

"I came with friends, but I'm single."

Our eyes connected until, suddenly shy, I blinked and looked away.

Just then, the voice of the director gave the morning announcements, letting us know that the ship had pulled into harbor at Blue Moon Cay, the private island owned by the cruise line. On Blue Moon, travelers would have no worries of getting bashed for openly expressing affection, unlike Jamaica. Shit, have you heard about the antigay violence there? It seems that hardly a month goes by without an attack while a mob cheers on or participates. Some modern reggae music advocates the killing of gay men. I find it obscene to pair that message with lilting rhythms, as if murder and hatred go hand in hand with a "good time" vibe.

Brandon asked if I was going to the picnic on the island. I told him I was. "Great," he said. "Maybe you could hang out with me and my friends."

"I'd like that."

We continued working out together for the next hour. I admit, I sneaked glances of his masculine beauty while he was on the bench press. His scent wafted to me and I inhaled deeply, which caused my mind to wander—*would you taste like David? Make love like him? Or would you be better?*—until it was my turn for a set. He was aware of my attention. Several times he suppressed a smile, satisfied with himself for inciting my lust. I was confident the feeling was mutual. We made small chit-chat, exchanging stories about our lives. He encouraged me to go with him and his friends tomorrow on a shore excursion in Belize. I had planned to stay aboard and have that be my spa day, but I promised to stop by the purser's office to make arrangements to join them.

Back in my ocean-view stateroom, I made quick work of showering and changing my clothes. I left quite a mess in my wake since I didn't want to be late meeting Brandon. I would have to remember to tip the cabin boy a bit extra for today's trouble.

On the main deck, I spotted Brandon and his group. I made my way over to them.

Brandon lit up when he saw me. "Jesse, come meet my friends." He introduced me to Doug and Matt. Each nodded. His friend Nathan tipped his hat and said, "Ahoy!" The camaraderie felt good. For a while, I had been a man without a clique.

We boarded the tender that would take us to shore. When it pulled away, I turned and looked at the ship, admiring the rainbow flags flying triumphantly. The sky was a brilliant shade of blue. A smattering of seagulls coasted low to the water along the breeze. Nathan was the talkative one. I listened to his travel stories as we bounced along the waves. I must say, my biggest guilty pleasure of the trip was the simple joy of people watching. There was lots of eye candy. I put on my shades; not to shield my eyes from the sun, rather to hide them. I was too polite to blatantly ogle men. I figured it was best to be sneaky about it.

On the island, the arrangement of food was gorgeous. Fresh fruit, pulled pork, tropical drinks. It was an open air hut with small birds flying about. We each grabbed plates and found a spot in the shade. When most of us were seated, a show began. Comedians, musicians, drag queens. Midway into the concert,

Brandon leaned into me. "Let's go exploring." His soft lips brushed against my ear causing me to tremble.

We held hands as we walked along the beach. "There," he said, pointing. "Nathan's been on this island before. He said we might like this spot." A small wooden sign marked the location: HIDDEN BEACH. We climbed the sand dune and went over to an area of trees and vegetation, a natural covering. A few yards deeper into the grove gave us total privacy.

"Come here," Brandon's southern whisper called to me. His hot mouth covered mine. I chewed lightly on his sensuous, pouty lips before finding his tongue again. As we kissed, my feet kicked blindly at the coconuts on the ground. We needed room. The rim of his white baseball cap kept knocking into my forehead, so he turned it around, which made him look boyish and cute. He held my face with both of his strong hands as though worried I would flee from him. *No chance there, you hot fucker.* A warm breeze found its way inside his shirt, causing it to billow like a sail. I unbuttoned it, letting the shirttails fly free. I savored the sight of his sculpted torso, bronzed from the sun and covered with dark, lush fur. I loved the fact that he didn't shave his chest. It made him more beastlike. Give me a natural, hairy man, I always say.

He pulled my t-shirt over my head and tossed it to the sand. We embraced skin to skin. There's nothing more pleasing to the touch than flesh stretched tightly over muscle; with chest hair, feather-soft; sweat, slippery and primal; warmth, our bodies sticking together; salt, to tempt the tongue; and musk, the sweet smell of masculine sex that makes me swoon. His thick lashes fluttered open. He arranged both of our shirts on the ground.

"Lie down."

I did as I was told. He kicked off his sandals and shucked his shorts. His dick was darker than the rest of his body. It had a hell of a curve to it and pointed skyward. Sun broke through a patch of palm trees and shone upon his hairy leg. He placed a bare foot on my manhood and pressed gently, moving it around inside my shorts. I let out a quiet gasp. Then he knelt in the sand, straddling my chest. I was pinned down. He grabbed the base of his shaft with his thumb and index finger and slowly offered his erection to my lips. I sucked the head and lapped at the piss hole. I lifted my head, eager to take it all. He grabbed a fistful of my hair, keeping me from the inches I craved. I lavished attention on what I was given, watching his eyes, which were closed as if concentrating on the subtle nuances of pleasure. When he wanted more, he pressed further into my mouth. I surrendered to the whims of his domination.

He changed position, letting his fashionably shaved balls fall into my face. I tongued them a while then pulled an orb at a time into my mouth, sucking each gingerly. My saliva gave them a unique aroma, one of my favorite scents. He jacked himself. When his scrotum tightened, I knew he was close. He let out a grunt as his come flew past my head with drops landing in the sand.

His breathing was ragged. "Let me take care of you."

He squatted and took off my flip-flops, caressing each foot. What would it be like to get a foot rub from these strong hands on a regular basis? Some lucky man would know. He pulled off my shorts and put his head between my legs. I felt a slight flicker just below my nut sac. Soon the motion of his tongue grew more insistent. He turned his head to the side and lay on the ground as if he intended to stay in that position awhile. His ministrations were fixed on my nuts. No one had ever licked them so much or for so long. My hard-on throbbed with anticipation. When at last Brandon stroked my sex with the tip of his finger, I popped my load into the air. I don't know how far I shot, but it was an eruption. A drop had landed in the dark whiskers of his jaw line.

"Man, you came so much," he said, flashing a beautiful smile. "Buckets." We kissed. Then I slurped my jism from his face.

Leisurely, we made our way back to the group, walking in the ocean while carrying our shoes. My knees were still weak from our afternoon of desire.

Later that night, there was a party on the island. A blazing bonfire illuminated the beach with an amber glow. Fire dancers, beefy men with strongly built bodies, performed their dangerous ballet for our enjoyment. Torches were at the perimeters of the gathering. It felt like a pagan ritual, celebrating nature, physical beauty and the tribe of men who love men. When a disco beat began pumping from the loudspeakers, a roar erupted from the crowd. Our group danced together. Lost in the music, I closed my eyes and basked in the feeling of brotherly bonding that washed over me. Having grown up in a small, backward town in Indiana and feeling the weight of loneliness for far too much of my life, it was my heart's wish to hold onto the magic of this night for as long as I could.

At one point, Brandon disappeared. I searched for him and discovered him kissing someone with the same passion we had shared earlier in the day. He had simply found another man.

Like David.

***

Now, figuring I'd given the couple ample time to plan their next move, I rejoined them at their table. We had met earlier in the day when I was sitting in a deck chair reading a book. I spotted them from the corner of my eye, whispering between themselves. The bold one, William, approached and invited me for drinks.

I quickly forgave Brandon, by the way. Let that be a cosmic lesson to me: men who look like David, behave like David. I never did make it to the purser's office to arrange an excursion to Belize. Instead, I spent the day in the spa being pampered as originally planned. I wasn't going to waste time sulking. Instead, I wanted to spend the rest of the cruise fucking my brains out.

"Would you like another drink?" William asked.

I shrugged. "Yeah, why not? They're delicious whatever they are."

"Oh, I know," Craig said. "I'm sucking 'em down like they're going out of style."

"Speaking of sucking," William said, steering the conversation back to the topic at hand.

Craig turned to me. "Right, we love your fantasy."

"To get fucked and sucked at the same time?" I scratched my chin and looked from one man to the other. They were both stunning. Hell, I wouldn't kick either of them out of bed. Nor would I have to. In the distance, I heard the sound of laughter, which perfectly reflected how I was feeling inside.

"We do have champagne back in the suite," Craig said. "Don't we, love?"

"Yes," William answered.

I nodded. "Maybe we should go to your room."

In general, I limit myself to a man at a time when I'm on land. But perhaps it's not such a bad thing to enjoy two, if by sea.

The Strange Case
of Brody Thomas Boyce
T. Hitman

So there you are. Your naked ass is pressed against the rail of the "Rainbow Deck" (known as "The Excelsior Deck" when the cruise line isn't catering to its gay clientele, desperate for all those queer dollars). You barely feel the heat that the morning sun over Mexico is already baking into the metal, tattooing bars against the skin of your cheeks, because the hot little blond dude's pouty, perfect cocksucker's lips are wrapped around your Johnson. And he delivers a mean blowjob.

You remind yourself, he's had plenty of experience. After all, you think with the appropriate amount of pride, the same tongue licking your sweaty, loose balls has licked Brody Boneman's; that same throat massaging your dick's been stretched out of shape by Brody's monstrous erection. *Repeatedly.* In that moment, you also think . . . you've had Brody, too, if only via Benjamin McCallister, aka Benjy Dover, the blond angel slurping on your hairy root, tugging on your nuts with one hand, stroking up and down your leg with the other, hypnotizing you.

You don't care that other men have gathered to watch. Three men. Fat men. Hairy, pierced men with Nellie voices, but the weight to make them dangerous.

"Well, look what we have here," one of them, a big walrus, coos.

This must be what porn shoots feel like. I'd ask Benjy, but his mouth is stuffed full of me. And I'm thinking about Brody Boneman, thrusting in and out of that wet, loving suck-hole. I'm so close to unloading, knowing the blond kid won't spit it out, won't waste me. His movies with Brody are a clear indication, but then again, he already has a few jillion of my sperm swimming in his belly as proof.

Readying to add more to the swarm, I fail to realize the mitigating factor in the equation: that Benjy *loves* Brody. So do I. Isn't that why we're both here, strangers on a boat, converging together, guided by fate and circumstance?

I remember this vital fact just as the ground gives out beneath my fuckin' flip-flops, and I'm falling, pants around my hairy ankles, spiraling out of control, with my hard dick slapping against my stomach, spitting its hard-won load into the briny air, across the portholes of a half-dozen luxury cabins on the way down. The fuckin' irony! Had I blasted it into Benjy McCallister-Dover's cock-smoocher, it might have been the best nut of my life. And I was close, so fuckin' close . . .

Blow jobs, lately, tend to land me in trouble. And trouble doesn't get much worse than this. One second, you've got the best cocksucker on the whole damn boat practicing on your flute. You're on the "Rainbow Deck," within sight of the artsy-fartsy Mexican resort of Tulum. A bunch of hairy older queens are gawking at you, and you're sort of getting off on having an audience. And you're thinking of Brody. Brody, with those haunting green eyes, that face too beautiful to belong to any mere mortal; like Medusa's, powerful enough to turn men's hearts to stone.

The next, one of those polar bears grunts, "It's him! That fuckin' gay basher, the one on CNN!"

Just like that, they rush you, and because you're too dopey from the kind of oral sex that could only be better with a can of beer in one hand and the remote control in the other (aimed toward a widescreen that's showing a Brody Boneman fuck-flick, of course!), you don't react quickly enough.

They grab your ankles, push you up and over the rail. And you swear the little blond punk who, only seconds before, was making love to your dick, helps them do it.

Gravity handles the rest.

You're falling, spiraling toward the ocean far, far below. Maybe toward your own death. At least, you think, you died having the ultimate nut.

***

It started out being about Brody Thomas Boyce, a charismatic, somewhat shady character better known in certain circles (and circle jerks) as "Brody Boneman." But from the beginning, I should have realized it would end up being all about me. Christopher John Payne. Most people call me C.J. In some circles, like on the Internet, in newspapers, and a couple of national rags, I'm that *"tall, fugly homo-hater . . ."*

The day I met sleazy pornographer David Woods at his palace in the Hollywood Hills came after the worst week of my life, what people and the media had started referring to as "the Anselmo Incident." I didn't know Woods, and I hadn't seen any of his movies, *movies* being a generous term. Brody Boneman had starred in Woods' most successful fuck-flicks. *Star* is not being generous; Boneman, I learned during our first meeting at Woods' compound, had earned the creepy fuck millions. And he'd skipped out with a goodly percentage of those seven figures.

My cell had clogged with a bunch of nasty voicemails from news vultures wanting more dirt on the Anselmo Incident, mostly with vitriol thanks to some equal rights zealot who leaked my number to the message boards. *Note to self, time to change phone number,* I was thinking, when the Woods' Hole Institute appeared on my caller ID.

I thought it was the famous ocean research society in my native Massachusetts calling, until I saw the area code—818. Not sure why I answered later discovering it was the same fine studio that brought you such gems as *A Hole in Juan, Piddler on the Roof, The Fox Twins Do Tahoe,* and a slew of Brody Boneman strokers, like *The Boneman Cometh, Big Bonin' Brody,* and *Welcome to the Boneyard* (a kinky bit of gay sex celluloid filmed in a gothic cemetery, among the crypts).

"Yeah," I grunted.

"Mister Payne?"

"Maybe. Who the fuck is this?"

"David Woods."

"So?"

"I've got an offer for you."

"Let me guess. Meet you at your house. I show up. Ten angry queers jump me and exact revenge on the big, mean gay-basher, right?"

"No. One of my favorite divas is missing. I need you to find him," he said, his voice containing just a *soupçon* of Long Island.

"How did you get my number?"

"The same way everybody else did."

"Oh."

"Interested?"

"Maybe."

I figured a missing person's investigation would take my mind off Kip Anselmo, and the unfortunate choice of words that had led to my face being plastered all over the Web, thanks to the miracle of modern file sharing and cell phones with cameras. A few hours later, I was at the gate and stabbing "shave-and-a-haircut-two-bits" into the intercom with my fuck-finger.

"Yeah, Christ already. Who is it?"

"Brody Boneman."

Silence. Then, the gate buzzed open.

I putted up a circular drive almost as twisty as Lombard Street in San Francisco, site of the infamous Anselmo Incident, and parked my shitty pickup near a pair of luxury wheels, one of which was getting a gentle scrubbing by a young-twenties muscle head dressed in a backwards-turned baseball cap and little else.

I stepped out of the truck and tipped him my chin, that typical, safe gesture between guys. He shot back daggers. My big toes probably had more hair on them than his entire body. That explained his bitterness.

"You, too, huh?"

"You're not going to gay bash me, are you?" he hissed.

"Nope."

"Good, 'cause I'm a black belt, and I'd kick your ass. Snap you in two, you Lurch-looking motherfucker!"

"The only mom I ever fucked was yours," I said, hands on hips, opening my sports jacket to make sure the kung-fu fuck got a clear look at my shoulder holster. "Still, you're welcome to try."

That deflected his daggers.

"I'm here to see David Woods. You must be his valet. Or chauffer, is it?"

"I'm his *assistant.* Go on up and ring the bell," my new admirer snapped.

The structure towering above us consisted of a main house, supported by white columns, with two wings fanning out on either side. There was a fountain, plenty of palm trees and exotic plantings, a big slab of a door with frosted crystal inserts. It all smelled of money.

I tramped up the marble steps and rang.

Ding-dong . . .

A buzz-cut youth, late teens, if I had to guess, answered the door. Like the asshole washing the car, he was naked except for a pair of loose-fit basketball shorts and a tattoo of a dollar sign—green—whose "S" figure-eighted around his right nipple.

"I'm here to see Woods."

The youth's deep blue eyes sized me up before extending a hand, inviting me to enter.

So what's the first thing they drum into you on the way to getting your private investigator's license? Be aware of your surroundings. Mine were so over-the-top in terms of largesse, especially the marble statues of naked men with enormous semi-erect cocks, I forgot to scan for someone hiding behind the door.

"Hands up, asshole," a gruff voice commanded, as hard steel pressed between my shoulder blades. "This ain't my dick sticking in your back!"

"Good. 'Cause if it was that high up, my own fuckin' pants monster would be feeling pretty fuckin' pathetic right now."

"Rickie, get his piece."

The blue-eyed punk unclipped my Glock and backed away with it in hand.

"Now that we've gotten that out of the way, mind if I turn around? Normally, I like to see the face of the guy dry-humping me from behind."

"Yeah, I *do* mind."

And then, the fucker clocked me.

I think the Karate Kid from the driveway got in a lick or two in the scrum, because my stomach hurt worse than the day after the Anselmo Incident, and my balls ached like they'd been yanked out of their sac.

I came to seeing double, sure I had myself a hell of a concussion. Two versions of the Rickie kid were down on their knees, slobbering on my dick. I was naked, except for my socks. My big toe poked through a hole in one of them. How embarrassing. At least I'd worn clean underwear to the party, even if they were sitting in a big white lump with my pants on the concrete floor. The rest of me was handcuffed to a metal chair whose seat felt slick beneath my ass. I only prayed it was sweat, and that the sweat was my own.

One of the Rickie's moved lower and gently sucked my balls. The other continued polishing my cock, which was as hard and wet as I'd ever seen it. Nothing like a good pistol whipping to give a man a hard-on.

"You like the Fox Twins?" said a voice from the ether. Long-Islandish. Woods.

"Fox Twins?" I glanced up. A trio of figures stood beyond my double-vision duo.

"Ronnie, on the left."

The boy sucking my balls waved.

"Rickie, on the right. You've already met."

The punk with the dollar-sign tattoo who'd relieved me of

my piece grunted something unintelligible around my dick head.

I nodded to the Fox Twins, then glanced beyond their bobbing heads at the apparitions standing unfocused, just beyond my view. Faces materialized. I recognized the Karate Kid, an old apple-waisted fuck with an orange tan-in-the-can complexion, and an Adonis, the kind of dude you'd see playing baseball in the major leagues, or fucking two or three chicks at a time in a straight porn flick. A guy you'd have a beer with, play pickup hoops or beach volleyball with. A real Joe Cool.

Joe Cool had my Glock tucked into the waist of his blue jeans. He was barefoot, wearing a white wife-beater, ball cap (bill aimed forward), sunglasses, hanging down the chest of his tank top by one stem. A bad-ass, handsome dude.

"Mister Payne, I presume," the Orange/Apple said with theatrical flourish. A real drama queen, that one, I already could tell.

"What do you think? I assume you've gone through my wallet."

"Of course. A necessary precaution. We had to make sure it was you, considering who you said you were. The name of Brody Boneman is a very tense subject around here these days. You lied to me."

"That makes us even. You said I wouldn't get jumped the moment I showed at your front door."

"Unfortunate, but my boys tend to be overly protective of me."

The Orange rolled his eyes from the Karate Kid to Joe Cool, then smacked his lips. The twins kept right on sucking.

"You're Woods?"

"*David* Woods. Welcome to my home."

Home was a windowless basement room, bare bulbs hanging from chains, a few sawhorses and oil drums painted red scattered about, in corners.

"Don't think much of the place."

"Oh, this? This is merely one room, beneath the West Wing. We call it 'the Dungeon.' It comes in quite handy when we're filming one of our less . . . *vanilla* productions. Have you ever thought about doing porn, Mister Payne?"

"No."

"Because you're handsome enough. And so tall. Tall sells well. And you've got a big enough dick. A bit hairy, but nothing a good waxing wouldn't cure."

"I'll just heap a leaked sex tape onto my list of recent embarrassments."

"This?" Woods snorted, a thoroughly disgusting sound not wholly in his nostrils, but deep and adenoidal in its timbre. "Oh, relax. Do you see any cameras recording this for posterity?"

"And I believe you."

"I admit, it's tempting. Can you imagine the bucks we'd make?" Woods said this to the Karate Kid. "'Fag-hater does gay three-way with a couple of twinks.' And not just any twinks, but the Fox Twins. That would draw pigs from all across the board. The ones who get off on hot twins *and* celebrity train wrecks, a two-fer. It would be just like John Wayne Bobbitt and *Frankenpenis,* all over again. Oh, the money . . .'"

Woods again faced me.

"And I do love my money, Mister Payne. Which is why you're here."

"You mean I'm not here to have a blowjob forced upon me?" I rattled the cuffs holding me to the chair for effect.

"You don't like it?"

Oh, the fucker. See, while we were having our little badinage, his boys the Fox Twins were doing such an expert job, I didn't care that I was getting my knob polished and my sac sucked. I was sweaty and itchy, and enjoying it so much, I would have let anybody work my junk. Well, not Kip Anselmo, that's for sure. Certainly, not the Orange. I half-closed my eyes and thought about that chick with the red hair and funny Dutch name who solves crime scene murders on that show set in Vegas. If I'd kept gawking at the Orange, I'd have gone limp.

"Are you straight, Mister Payne?"

"Ask my ex-wife's bed sheets."

"You speak in riddles."

"I live in riddles. Here's one for you. What goes up, then comes down?"

The Orange, looking genuinely amused in the slit of gray illumination beyond my narrowed gaze, shrugged. Fuck, of all the times to threaten with a hell of a punch line. Grunting, I thrust my hips forward, burying a few inches of cock into one of the Fox Brothers' faces. Didn't know which one. Didn't care.

"*Me,*" I huffed.

A second after that, my balls pulled up taut around my shaft, and my dick erupted. The rush was unexpectedly powerful—the Fox Twin nursing on my Johnson pulled back, tears in his eyes. Yogurt pissed wildly out of my cock, spraying his face, as well as his brother's. The original suckee snorted. Not as gross as the sound Woods made, and strangely exciting in that I noticed bubbles of milk clogging both of his nostrils, as though he's expelled it through his nose the way you sometimes do with a hasty drink of fizzy soda. The sick side of me waited in anticipation to see if the twins would lick my cum off each other's lips, maybe kiss. They didn't.

"Hot damn," Joe Cool chuckled.

Sweat stung my eyes. My balls ached less. My hose was down to puking out dribs and drabs. "It's been a while. That fuckin' Anselmo Incident's been a hell of a mood killer."

"I'll just bet," the Orange tisked. Then he turned to Joe Cool. "Un-cuff him. Get dressed, Mister Payne, and meet me upstairs."

Under the cover of Joe Cool's gun, I was marched up to a vast room, part office, part killer home theater. Awards and certificates covered shelves, along with porn. Lots and lots of porn.

The Orange sat in a large office chair that creaked and shrieked beneath his ass. Joe Cool waved me toward a smaller, less tortured bit of modern furniture on the other side of the desk.

"Can I have a coffee?"

"Anything you want," the Orange said.

"How about my gun?"

"When our business is concluded."

I shrugged, adjusted my balls, which still felt slimy with the Fox Twins' saliva, and eased back.

"So, where did you hide the camera?"

"What camera?"

"Down in your dungeon," I said. "Don't lie to me. I fuckin' hate liars."

"There was no camera."

"My guess is the Karate Kid had it. In his baseball cap?"

"Touché," the Orange snorted. *Ugh,* so repulsive. "But it was Jason, here, who had the cap-camera."

"Jason?" I snorted. "Why do all of you gay porn himbos have names that begin with the letter 'J'? Jason, Josh, Justin, Jeremy . . ."

"I needed insurance, Mister Payne."

"Call Mutual of Omaha. Or that little gecko dude," I fired back. "Jeremy or Jared or Jake. And then you have the 'B' names—Brady, Boone, Baxter, Boyd, *Brody* . . ."

The slippery smile on Woods' orange face sagged into a reptilian scowl.

"Aah, and now, finally, we're done with the dick-suckery and drama. *Brody Boneman . . .*"

The Orange sagged back into his chair, a sallow-colored glacier of ass and pure evil. The chair screamed in agony. Woods stabbed a button on his computer. The home theater's colossal screen lit. Sex sounds far more harmonious and forthright than anything coming from the other side of the desk poured out of the speakers.

"... *such a hot fuckin' cocksucker,*" a man's baritone sang between gasps.

I turned in my chair toward the screen. Joe Cool stepped back, retrained his aim. Fuckin' loose cannon.

On the screen, one young man was deep-throating another. He spit out the cock being sucked long enough to groan, "For you, I am. Ain't never wanted a man so badly, dude. You're the fuckin' hottest . . ."

Shit, I had to agree. Grudgingly, of course. Eyes wide and unblinking, I studied the action. The suckee, I realized, was the Karate Kid himself.

"I assume the chap getting his ding-a-ling devoured is your boy, Brody."

"'Chap . . .' That's so British of you."

I grunted in agreement. Brit-speak had gotten me into a whole shit-avalanche of trouble recently.

Brody . . .

His hair was short and trim, brown. A thin layer of day-old scruff complemented his lucky-draw of first-rate genetics. His eyes were a rich, hypnotic green. Not muddy hazel, but genuine emerald gemstones. I found myself falling into their pull.

"*I'm coming!*" Brody huffed, through clenched, perfect-white teeth.

To my shock, I realized it wouldn't take much for me to claim the same, a repeat performance of what had happened down in the Dungeon. My dick was up and itching for attention. Mercifully, the Orange hit the pause button. The money shot sailing out of Brody's hairless dick froze inches from the Karate Cunt's mug.

"Brody stole something from me, Mister Payne," the Orange said. "And I want it back."

I turned to face him. His reptilian lower lip ticked at the left corner.

"What did he steal? This little bitch's heart?" I waved at the cum-guzzler in the backward ball cap.

"Fuck you!"

"My mistake. You'd have to have one first to steal it."

Joe Cool—*Jason* Cool—loomed closer. Woods' angry voice stopped him.

"Get out, both of you!"

"But—" the Karate Kid protested.

"I don't want people antagonizing Mister Payne, especially when we need his expert services."

They left. I turned away from the screen, thankful my Johnson had retreated, and faced the Orange.

"I don't think I'm your man."

"You're the only man for the job. Brody Boyce wasn't just my most-popular discovery; he was a trusted assistant. He paid me back for making him a star by helping himself to my checkbook and walking out of here with a million dollars of my money."

"How the fuck did he do that?" I asked, smiling widely, intentionally, to add weight to the man's pain.

"Brody's a charmer. The bank teller knew who he was. He was a fan, you could say—meaning, he pumped his prick to Brody's movies. Brody forged my signature—did a great job—and concocted some story that he'd been paid a huge contract to bottom on screen for the first time. The bank teller believed him. A certified macho stud like Brody letting another young bull top him is always an event in gay porn. Oh, how we love to see our paramours wrangled into submission."

"When was this?"

"A week ago."

"Go to the police."

"I can't."

"Why?"

"I prefer to handle company matters within the company."

"I'm not a company man."

"But you're the man I want."

"Why?"

"Brody's a charmer. I believe you'd be immune to those charms, to him, though I must warn you—I've seen even the most hardened of heterosexuals melt in his presence. Even watched him fuck a few. I have it on digital. We were working on *Brody Bones the Bulls* when he pulled his Houdini act."

I choked down a dry swallow, and didn't comment.

"Given what happened between you and Kip Anselmo . . ."

I held up a hand. "Look, before you reference that total mind-fuck of a melee yet again, allow me to add this little yet vital and completely overlooked footnote to the whole disaster. Kip Anselmo is a criminal. I was hired to take on a skip-trace of him. Fucker is wanted back east under his real name, Michael Mitchell, on a number of outstanding warrants— enough of them so that, when this all gets sorted out, he's doing serious time.

"*Kip* has been out here, hanging out in gay bars and speaking with an English accent, pretending to be minor royalty. What he's really been up to is bilking your kind out of their disposable income and evading the law. I tracked him to a shitty piano bar in the Castro, where he was sipping lime-tinis and smoking Turkish cigarettes and picking pockets. And when I suggested he accompany me peacefully to the sheriff's for a little legal mixer, he threatened to come at me with one of those stinky, lit cancer sticks. 'How'd you like me to singe your eyeballs with my little fag, love?'"

I mimed doing my best Anselmo.

"So, as this convicted felon moved to deliver good on his promise, I knocked the Nellie *faux-mosexual* halfway to China. Just happens that every cock-biter in the place had their camera phones out and ready—right in time to see me clock him, and shout, 'Get that fuckin' fag away from me!' And *voila,* my face is all over the Internet and evening news. They say episodes of the old *Star Trek* play continuously somewhere in the world, twenty-four hours a day. I got Captain Kirk beat.

"So let me be frank, Woods. I'm not a homophobe or a gay-basher. Never have been. If it weren't for you homos, there'd be no rock music and no tight-fitting football uniforms come pigskin time. And I do love my football. Hell, you just video-taped me getting my schlong slurped, and did you see me protest all that much? I love you people!"

My voice rose to a shout as I regurgitated everything the media hadn't allowed me to state in my defense since crucifying me in every format conceivable. Fuck, my head hurt. I closed my eyes, found the egg under my short brush-cut that would probably piss me off and into a blind rage once I was behind the wheel of my truck again, and sucked in a deep breath.

"There you have it," I concluded. I opened my eyes on the Orange.

"Brody took a million of my hard-earned dollars. Finders fee of ten percent if you bring both him and it back to me."

"Fifteen."

"Twelve."

"Deal. I get two grand a day, on retainer. First two weeks, up front."

"You'll get five hundred, and I'll front you one week."

"This isn't a negotiation, Woods."

"Everything's a negotiation. Seven-fifty per diem," he hissed. Like the man said, he loved his money.

"A thousand a day," I fired back, flashing a smile. "And I don't come back here after we settle to do to you what I did to Kip Anselmo for that little stunt you pulled in the Dungeon. What I'm going to do to your boy Jason the next time I see him."

The Orange smacked his lips. My insides knotted at the image of his tongue, the knowledge it had probably wiggled up every asshole that had ever walked through the door. Except for mine, thank the universe for small blessings.

"Done."

"I'll need everything you have on Brody Boyce . . . *Boneman*. Whatever he goes by. Where he lives, his friends, family."

The Orange opened a desk drawer. He withdrew a large, stuffed envelope. "It's all there, including some of his DVDs. So you can get a feel for the man you're hunting. He lived here. Best as we knew, we were his only friends and family."

"What about his fucks?"

"Just what's in those movies."

"I'll take that week's retainer up front. In cash."

"You'll take a check."

The Orange opened another draw, took out his checkbook, and wrote one out to me. I tucked the check into the envelope and stood. At the door, I turned back.

"One last thing."

"Yeah, what's that?" the Orange asked.

"What's he got over you? The nugget that's keeping you from going to the cops?"

The Orange's eyes went dead, with what could have been fear, rage, or a mix of both. His lips started ticking again. Whatever it was, it was big, ugly, just like him.

"Nothing, except for a million of my George Washingtons."

"I told you already, Woods, I fuckin' hate liars."

"I hate people who steal from me. Especially, those I've turned into stars. Good day, Mister Payne."

I crossed the main room, with its gallery of Medusa-stiffened corpses and cocks. Jason Cool waited near the door. He offered me my holster and gun. I put them on, then my jacket.

"By the way," I said.

I tossed the envelope up, into the air. Jason Cool's eyes followed it. On the way back down, I tossed a punch into his gut. All the air wheezed out of his lungs as he dropped to his knees, red-faced and limp as a rag doll. I caught the package.

"At least I did it to your face."

I gave the Karate Kid the bird while backing out. Had the

security gate not opened, I probably would have plowed right through it.

Soon after that, it started becoming clear that the case was less about Brody Boyce, and more about C. J. Payne.

***

Two police cruisers were parked in front of the apartment complex.

Ever since some asshole leaked my address and phone number to the boards and blogs following the Anselmo Incident, my neighbors had kept Emergency-911 busy. A bag of burning dog shit had appeared on the doorstep of sixty-nine Lewis Lane, instead of ninety-six, likely delivered by a dyslexic malcontent. Somebody spray-painted "I'm a fag, too" across half a dozen pickup trucks, no doubt hoping one of them was mine (it wasn't). To date, two jizz-filled water balloons have been hurled at the side of my building. They don't call it 'stucco' for nothing. Which leads me to wonder . . . just how many ejaculating dicks does it take to fill a balloon with ball-snot? Was this some kind of national campaign against me, like what happens when a TV show gets cancelled, and all of its rabid fans unite to make life miserable for the offending network execs who swung the ax?

"Gentlemen," I said to the pigs, firing off a salute from the one hand not laden down with gay porn.

One of the officers gave me the finger. I couldn't tell if he was another member of my gay fan club, or simply pissed off because he'd been forced to drink his coffee in my driveway.

I trudged up the stairs, ever mindful while turning corners. One sucker punch a day, thank you very much. My front door was still locked. I opened it, and walked into the familiar sty of pizza boxes, dirty laundry, and case files on top of every flat surface. After spending the afternoon at David Woods' palatial estate in the hills, my own humble dive was looking pretty tired.

"I wish someone would rob me, just so I could buy new stuff," I grumbled aloud.

Perhaps I could without the B&E to aid me, thanks to Brody Thomas Boyce, the Boneman, I foolishly thought. A twelve percent finder's fee on a million bucks, and I could get some naked statues of my own. But that whole line of mental mastication quickly went out the window. My dick was hard again. I had an envelope full of porn DVDs. *Gay* DVDs. Don't think I wasn't aware of the irony. It didn't matter whether the performers were women, men, or Martians—the star of the show, Brody Boneman, was what counted.

I checked the phone. Twenty new messages, before my voicemail clogged up. I hastily scanned through the love notes, erasing them, one by one.

"Hey, fag hater . . ."

Click.

"Yo, Payne. Guess what I'm doing right now? I'm fucking this picture of you from the newspaper, right through your mouth . . ."

Click.

"I'm so hot for you," lisped a girlish voice. "Thinking about your big, gay-hating cock in my mouth, in my tight little shit-pussy. I'm touching myself over you, Master Payne . . ."

"Jesus Christ," I huffed.

There were ten more of these, then—

"Don't take the Brody Boyce case. Consider this your only warning, dude. If you do, you're fuckin' dead."

I hung up the phone, cycled through the caller ID. Thirteen numbers in: *Unknown Caller.*

I dialed into my mailbox again. With the ringer turned off, I hadn't heard the two new calls that had come in during the latest scan through the blatherings of my vocal fan club.

"Suck my dick, Payne!"

The next caller insulted me with epithets concerning dogs,

my mother, and something about wanting to insert a Blue Hub-
bard squash up my ass before I clicked his rant into oblivion.

". . . only warning, dude," that other caller repeated. "If you
do, you're fuckin' dead."

Fuck the squash. Now *this* was food for thought.

***

As porn goes, David Woods was a lousy auteur. The awkward, shaky camera angles were enough to make a person sea-
sick. Half the scenes looked like a cross between *NYPD Blue*
and the canted super villain pads in the cheesy old *Batman* TV
series from the psychedelic 1960s. Slow-mo money shots, repeated from a variety of angles. Shitty disco soundtrack. Way
too much kissing. Men beating their meat over watching two
men fuck don't want romance; they want mouths on dicks, and
tongues up assholes. Even I knew that.

Where Woods excelled was in his mega-star, Brody Boneman.

By the fourth squirt into the nasty tube sock I keep at the
side of the bed, I took serious notice of someone other than
Brody Boneman in Woods' fuck-flicks. Spunky blond kid,
looked younger than a zygote—but of course, he had to be at
least of legal age. A little boy-chick, with *Jimmy Neutron* hair
and a pouty, cocksucker's mouth that found its way around
Brody's donkey dong in half the DVDs Woods gave me.

So here's where it started to get clear to me, and more than
a little weird.

I'm fast forwarding through this one scene in *Boneman Bones
the Brothers*—the fucker's cock puts his horse-dicked African-
American co-stars to shame—feeling sort of inadequate, even
with my own above-average fuck-monster, when the action
slows, shifts. One instant, Brody is balls-deep up some black
dude's shiny pink asshole. He looks up, and in mid-thrust, pulls
out. Another brother arrives to stuff the space. Brody crosses

the room, his dick tick-tocking ahead of him, just like an elephant's trunk.

We, the viewers, see that which has beguiled him: it's the waifish blond, standing at the door. Naked. Erect. Youthful balls hanging like two ripe peaches in a loose, hairless sac. More cocksucking ensues. More rimming. Brody stuffs the blond's pussy full of stallion. And a few thousand more of my potent swimmers throw themselves to their deaths against the crusty, discolored cotton in the toes of my cum-sock . . .

In the power outage that followed, it struck me. The tenderness those two shared was nothing like the rough-fuck interaction Brody forced upon his other co-stars.

Dick hanging out of my shorts, I popped the DVD out of the player and reinserted one I'd already sprayed two loads over. There they were again, Brody and the blond kid, listed in the credits as "Benjy Dover." A tender scene, filmed mostly over Brody's shoulder. Benjy-blond's eyes were cast upward, at Brody's. Contained within them was that look a puppy dog gives its master, the sweet, dopy love seen in the bottled gazes of young lovers.

That was when it struck me; they *were*.

I scrolled through the contact sheet Woods had provided. No Benjamin Dover, aka, blondie.

The movie continued, muted, in front of me. I picked up the phone. Big surprise—there were a dozen new messages waiting for me. I ignored them.

"Hello?"

"Put Woods on the phone."

"*Mister* Woods isn't available."

"He is for me. It's Payne. My rate goes up ten percent for every ten seconds you keep me on hold."

Three seconds later, the Orange slurred, "Payne?"

"Tell me everything you know about this kid in the Boneman vids, goes by the name of Benjy Dover."

Silence.

"Yo, you there?"

"He's nobody," Woods said.

Despite the dick-shriveling power of the Orange's voice, my Johnson was up again. Woods' nobody had Brody's left nut between his lips and was hard-sucking it like a calf to its mamma's teat. Brody silently howled out in response.

"Give."

"Benjamin McCallister. He doesn't work for the company anymore."

"Why not?"

"Creative differences."

"How creative?"

"Let's just say, he wasn't a team player."

"Really? I just watched him get double-penetrated by a pair of mutant pants snakes."

"Well, he *was* a *tag*-team player."

"I think he's the key. Were he and Boneman a couple?"

"You mean, an 'item?'"

"Item, couple, fuck-buddies?"

"I suppose, but nothing beyond your typical porn industry couple. They fucked on film, thought it was something real, dated for a while, and broke up. It happens all the time."

"You say they're not together anymore?"

"They had a falling out. A very ugly public one, on the set of a movie, maybe a month ago. A real hissy fit. I had no choice but to cut Dover loose."

Loose. I snorted into the phone.

"Something funny?"

Brody was again buried balls-deep in the blond's shitter on my jizz-stained TV screen. Talk about loose!

"No, ironic. Give me the details."

"Real name's Benjamin McCallister." Woods then rattled off an address and phone number. I jotted the intel on a notepad, the pen glued to my palm in a glaze of clotting sperm.

"And that's all of it, I swear."

The moment Woods said that last bit, I knew he was lying. There was a lot more to the Benjy Dover angle than he was letting on to. I fuckin' hate liars.

"One more thing."

"Yeah?"

"Who else knows I took this case?"

"Just my trusted staff. The boys you met today. Oh, and by the way, I'm docking you a day's pay for decking Jason. That little assault of yours is going to cost you."

"You just try to collect on it and I'll be assaulting *you*."

A sigh breezed through the line. "I don't take threats lightly."

"Back to the question. Who knows about our arrangement besides Jason Cool and the Karate Kid?"

"Just the twins."

"Nobody else?"

"No, why?"

"Somebody doesn't want me to find Brody Boyce. You think one of the boys in your entourage also had one of those typical porn biz romances with Brody?"

"Why, Mister Payne, we all have."

***

The door to Benjamin McCallister's one-bedroom apartment on North Whitley sat unlocked. Nobody answered the door. I turned the knob. The door opened. Breaking half a dozen serious laws, I strolled in, mindful of corners and closet doors. At least I didn't break another by falling back on my lock-picking tools.

It was your typical Hollywood apartment: not quite a dive, but stale with the odor that comes from temporary living. It was the sort of place wannabe actors and musicians and dreamers inhabit while waiting to be discovered, and where they commit suicide when their big break fails to materialize. It wasn't much of a step up from my shitty place, but I had too many overzealous fuck-wads gunning for my scalp to consider putting a bullet in it myself.

The place was noticeably bare, even for a fly-by-night porn actor. I found one t-shirt and a couple of mismatched socks in the stack of milk crates in the bedroom that no doubt passed for a bureau. A bunch of stroke magazines and copies of *Daily Variety* littered the closet floor. There were some toiletries in the bathroom cabinet, but no toothbrush, toothpaste, or deodorant. The place had been abandoned—and recently, if the expiration date on the carton of milk in the fridge and the latest ish of the industry rag were to be trusted. In his haste to escape, Benjy McCallister hadn't even bothered to lock the front door.

I paced the bedroom. The idea that Brody had fucked the apartment's former occupant in that small, drab bed left my dick—raw from so much recent attention—swollen and itchy. I found a cum stain on the sheets and sniffed it. Brody's? As soon as the question passed through my mind, I was licking at that crusty fossil, too, and milking a few drops of my own DNA onto the bedclothes.

Nutting helped me to think clearly again. I tucked my aching length of dick-tartar into my pants and returned to the living room. The phone. I lifted the receiver. A dial tone rolled out. I hit the caller ID.

Van Landingham Travel. I jotted the phone number down. The electric company. A pizza parlor on Sepulveda I've ordered from. The Wilver Court Hotel.

Next, I hit the redial. There was a delay, and then the phone began to ring with a hollow, distant tone. A shiver teased the short hairs at the nape of my neck. It felt like I was dialing into a cell phone based somewhere at the end of the Earth.

On the fifth ring, "Hey babe, you're still there?"

The voice, deep and masculine, sent a chill tripping fully down my spine. The entire apartment rippled out of focus as it tumbled. I knew that voice. I'd heard it ordering some adoring bottom to, "*Suck my dick!*" or "*Lick the sweat off my cum-tanks, dude!*" It was Brody.

"Hey," I sighed, the lone word carrying up a desiccated throat, across a tongue that had become a strip of rawhide, and through sandpaper lips. "Yeah, still here, babe."

The hesitation from the other end of the line was palpable. "*Rocky Mountain,*" he said, the coldness in his voice filtering through the line, into my blood, making my balls pull up tightly around the base of my achingly hard cock.

"High." The word was out of my mouth before I could stop it, or consider the right response to what was obviously private code, a test.

The line went dead.

Long seconds later, I thumbed the redial.

"Leave a message," a voice grumbled. *Beep.*

I called three more times, but I only got voicemail. Brody, though . . . I'd located Brody. But he was at least a million light-years away.

***

"Yes, Mister Payne?"

I hated the sound of the Orange's voice, especially when he said my name. It was like the slither of a snake; each click of his tongue, castanets, the unholy sound some segmented creature like a scorpion or crab makes as it moves to strike.

"Get ready to open your purse again, Woods."

"Extortion, Mister Payne?" He smacked his lips together and scolded me with a tisk.

"No, you're sending me on a little trip."

"Excuse me?"

"I told you the way to Brody was through your former boy-bitch, Benjy Dover. That catfight on the set was staged. Turns out, Benjy's a better actor than you ever gave him credit for."

I explained what I'd discovered in the kid's apartment, the Hollywood trade dailies, and the info I'd gleaned from the telephone—a call to Van Landingham Travel and a higher-pitched voice had yielded unexpected results.

"I pretended to be McCallister, and the travel agent was pretty helpful. Yes, they confirmed 'my' reservation on Jewel of the Seven Seas Cruise Fleet, the *Queen America.*"

"You think Brody's on that boat?"

"No, but I do think McCallister's on his way to meet Brody. The *Queen* is being rainbowed-out for a special gay cruise, with stops in all the tourist ports in Mexico, including Tulum. Tulum has a big gay community, and it's a celebrity hotspot—they film a bunch of Spanish soap opera tele-novella things there. I'd bet a carload of testicles that your pal Brody's hiding in that port, waiting for his bend-over buddy to show, to start their new life together."

"How romantic," Woods said. There was an edge to his voice that unleashed a foul taste in my mouth.

"I'll need a ticket and some traveling money. That's if you want Brody and your share of the million dollars he stole returned."

"You're sure about this cruise ship?"

I told him I'd gotten as far as a cabin number onboard the *Queen America* before the travel agent started asking questions too detailed for me to answer. I then told him about the Wilver Court. "McCallister had a room there, until this afternoon. The Wilver Court is the hotel of choice for travelers when Jewel ships drop anchor near L.A. He just checked out. I assume he's now onboard the *Queen,* which sets sail for Mexico in ten hours. So if you want Brody, you'd better get me onboard—and fast!"

***

Here's more irony for you: the most-hated man in Queer America, trapped on a cruise ship with over a thousand of would-be assassins, all of them feeling very liberated, bold, and horny, on vacation . . . and more than a few with serious chips on their shoulders.

I shaved my head, sculpted a mustache out of two days worth of scruff, and hoped sunglasses and a baseball cap would do the rest. And they did, at first.

Woods. The cheap orange-faced mother-fucker booked me into the shittiest cabin on the ship. It was an airless, claustrophobic shadow box with a dollhouse-sized bed and a head I could barely stand up straight in; located, I imagined, somewhere between the boilers and the septic tank. The place stunk of industrial cleaner and old ejaculations. Just how many loads had been blasted into the walls of this high-priced prison cell, I dared not imagine. But I was sure that if you shined a black light around the place, like they do on those yellow journalism investigative TV shows, you'd find the place whitewashed and crawling with junk.

I tossed my bags onto the floor, then tossed a pint of my own wiggling spermatozoa onto the fitted bed cover. Jerking off, as always, helped me to think, and settled my nerves.

Somewhere on this ship, Benjy Dover-McCallister was dreaming dreamy dreams of Brody. Fuckin' Brody . . .

I opened my laptop, popped a DVD into the tray, and found my stick hard again at the image of him.

Brody Boneman-Boyce, I admitted, shaking my head, was without question the handsomest face I'd ever laid eyes upon. There was power in those lips, those eyes, voodoo emanating out of that dick. ⌐

My mind wandered, my cock dripped, lubricating the cup of skin between my forefinger and thumb enough to negate the need for spit or help from the microscopic bottle of complimentary hand lotion on the tiny counter near the sink. Suddenly, it was me in the graveyard, sucking on Brody's balls. *Balls, me?* All nuts *stank.* That's why chicks were so reluctant to get up close and personal with them. My own reeked, thanks to the amount of distance my feet had traveled to find this fuckin' cabin—the length of a football field. They were loose, itchy, musty. And here I was, fantasizing about sucking his?

I scratched my balls, raised my fingertips to my nostrils, and imagined the heady odor as belonging to *his* low-hanging twins. Brody, eating my asshole, stabbing his tongue in and out, entering me, unleashing icy-hot chills through my insides, then searing cramps as he pushed the wrong way into a channel that had only been designed by Nature's Architect to function in a single direction. Pulling out. Painting a mustache across my upper lip . . . we would soon be headed South of the Border, so a visit by the legendary Dirty Sanchez seemed appropriate in this masturbational daydream.

And then, right before I nutted so hard, the first stream of batter flew over my shoulder, splashing the wall, I imagined Brody squirting a ribbon of piss across my face, as I'd seen him do to the blond kid during one of their more-telling scenes. *Ownership.*

It pissed me off to think it, but it was true. I wasn't so immune to the stud's wizardry skills. Brody now owned me, too.

***

I hitched up my pants and headed out of my cell for some air and sunshine. The dank corridor opened on a bright day almost too vibrant to face. Salty air, sweetened by a dose of coconut suntan lotion, blew away the stale funk I'd breathed for the past several hours.

If Benjy McCallister was traveling on Brody's dime (and considering how shiny that dime was when Brody stole it), I knew he wouldn't be camped out in steerage with schmucks like me. No, McCallister was cruising in style, up on either the "Victory" or "Rainbow Decks," among the Hollywood and Park Avenue greenbacks crowd.

I strutted along the deck, past the pool and a couple dozen Greek gods frying under thin layers of butter. Everywhere else in America, the dude-thong is an invitation to get a man's hairy ass kicked; here, apparently, that look was all the rage. I was feeling seriously overdressed in my camouflage cut-offs and flip-flops. An army of dicks, leaving little to the imagination, sweated in deck chairs under tiny, revealing triangles of crotch-hugging fabric.

The air was ripe with the promise of sex and cum. Loads of cum, and lots of sex, in every way, shape, and form, from the sweetly vanilla to the kind of kinky that's illegal in most states. Maybe there was something to this whole gay lifestyle worth pursuing, after all.

I figured that crowd-watching among this crowd was a given, so I slowly navigated the deck, lifting my shades on occasion.

"Take a picture, it'll last longer," one bicep-bitch grumbled.

I huffed out a, "Fuck you," and continued on. I could take him, if it came to that. I didn't care. He wasn't Brody Boneman.

The *Queen America* had been decked out in pink triangles and rainbow bunting for the voyage. She cut water, I imagined, like the cruise ship version of some heavily made-up drag queen.

The first day, while hunting for McCallister above deck, I came across a small crowd that had gathered around a pair of god-bods who were offering their stiff pricks to any willing mouth that wanted a taste. I dined in the George Washington Grille. Masturbated over Brody Boneman DVDs . . . fuckin' Brody . . . until my cock was rubbed raw. I slept in that bed, with my feet and half of my legs from the knees down hanging out over the edge. Woke stiff on day two, and not only in the dick department.

I went on my morning prowl, figuring that Benjy Dover was spending the lion's share of the voyage in his suite, ordering room service and keeping a very low profile. The little punk had packed up his life and dreams, hauling them into foreign waters for the man he loved. So why risk that to the multitude of temptations waiting in every corner of the boat?

I encountered a gaggle of transvestites on the "Rainbow Deck," a few of them so hot they could pass for the real deal, some so hideous, I guessed it had to be late October, and enough glistening, naked flesh to fill one of the outer rings of hell. But no Benjy Dover.

After ordering a fruity drink with an umbrella and getting my dick sucked in the men's head by a lovely he-she after said drink cycled through me, I moseyed back to my cabin, feeling drained in more ways than one. Because the cocksucker who'd guzzled me dry had done such a thorough job, what I was seeing didn't dawn on me at first.

I reached the part in the long, dank corridor where somebody had drawn in bold red lipstick: *is aboard*. Perhaps twenty feet from my cabin door, where a group of men had gathered.

Stopping, I turned back. Behind me, in bright red strokes, was: *C. J. Payne, the notorious fag-basher.*

Beyond the part in the text that had originally captured my attention—*this cruise ship!*

Punctuating the caption perfectly, the graffiti artist had drawn a red lipstick bull's-eye onto my cabin door.

I counted six men. One stood in a bitchy pose, hands on hips, mouth pursed in the tight pucker of a very constipated asshole. Two men were banging on the door.

The Constipator's face-rectum unclenched, discharging a litany of verbal diarrhea. "Just let him open that door! I'm going straight for his devil's eyeballs!"

"Honey, that's the only 'straight' you'll ever be!"

"Cut the squawking and keep on knocking!"

I dug in my flip-flops, revolved, and miraculously got out of there before anyone noticed my presence.

***

I reported the incident to the cruise director. He promised they would clean up the graffiti and promptly move me to a different cabin, which they did. But the damage was done. The gossip would spread throughout the boat like wildfire, and in less time than it had taken to sink the *Titanic*. The gays knew I was onboard. Somebody had rolled me over.

I remembered the phone call, and knew the man who'd threatened to kill my ass was also onboard.

Some cabin boy packed up my bags full of gay porn, the dirty underwear I'd left at the side of the bed, and the rest of my things. All were waiting for me, in pretty much the same arrangement, in my new digs, which weren't much better than the previous accommodations. The threat of legal action would keep the crew in line; the problem was that I now had two problems nipping at my ass: finding Brody, and whoever it was that didn't want me to find him.

I spent most of the next day in my cabin pacing, jerking off, waiting for some angry knock to disrupt my pacing and jerking off, and ordering my meals in. In my excitement to see what the he-she had hidden under her micro-mini, I'd removed her man-t-hose, stuffing them into my pocket. They smelled sweetly of the he-she's cologne/perfume, and I masturbated with them clutched in my teeth, thinking of him/her.

A day shy of Tulum, I formulated my plan and called the Orange.

"Mister Payne, any progress?"

"Working on it. Look, there's been a problem with my room."

"What sort of problem?"

"Pipe burst, flooding my crapper. They moved me to a different cabin, up on the "Rainbow Deck." Got a pen?"

I rattled off a fake room number on the "Rainbow Deck," right around the corner from the men's john where I'd released a few jillion of my potent swimmers down the gullet of a tranny who looked like Shakira.

I hung up and exited my cabin. I grabbed a newspaper, paid a middle-aged Mary fifty bucks for his Panama hat, and headed toward the "Rainbow Deck." There, I waited.

But not for long.

Peering under the brim of the hat and over the top of the sports page, I tracked the lone figure's furtive movements toward the dummy cabin. Cold rage sucked on my balls, while magma boiled in my blood. Woods was having me tailed!

Worse, it was Jason Cool who'd been sniffing around my butt-hole.

Though a violent hurricane lashed me on the inside, I was the picture of coolness externally. He wouldn't be armed; I'd left my Glock behind in L.A., so this would be mano–a-mano, appropriate for the cruise. I calmly folded my newspaper, tucked it under an arm, and pursued Jason Cool.

When he reached the men's head, I calmly removed the Panama hat, and, glancing in both directions to ascertain that we were indeed alone, calmly tapped him on the shoulder, then clocked the fucker as hard as I could.

Jason Cool's nose collapsed under my knuckles, like warm fruit compote. He stumbled ass-backwards, howling at the limit of his lungs.

Very little after that was calm.

***

Lightening-quick, I bound his wrists together with Shakira's man-t-hose—waste not, want not—and hauled him into the same toilet stall where I'd sprayed my nuts in his/her mouth a day earlier. There, I forced him to bob for apples. Luckily for him, the stall's previous visitor had flushed.

"*Fuck*," he screamed around a mouthful of toilet water.

"You don't tell me what I want to know and you will be. *Fucked*, that is."

"Go fuck yourself!"

"If I was Brody Boneman, I probably could."

I shoved him down again, held him under the bowl, kneed him in the nuts from behind, and lifted him out of the drink.

"Next time, you'll be face-first in that weak lemonade until you pass out and drown. Now sing!"

"Okay, okay," Jason Cool cried, his voice nasally, clotted. "I'll tell you."

"That's more like it." It was also easier than I'd anticipated. "Why does Woods have you following me? The money?"

"That . . . and something else," Jason Cool said, all cockiness gone from his voice.

"I'm not a psychic, tough guy. Spill the beans or I'm gonna shove you back in that toilet and piss on you myself."

"No, *please*—"

"There's a new one for your vocabulary. So why the shadowing act?"

"He's afraid. Afraid you'll learn the truth."

"About what?"

"Why Brody really bolted."

I drew in a deep breath, held it, waited, and when the information wasn't quickly forthcoming, re-gripped the fucker's collar.

"W-wait! Brody was blackmailing Woods. He didn't steal the money. Woods paid it to him."

"Blackmail? Over what?"

Jason Cool sobbed something unintelligible.

"I'm running low on patience, my friend."

"Brody, he wasn't . . ."

"Brody wasn't what?"

"He wasn't of legal age when Woods used him for his first movie. Woods'll tell you that Brody lied, but the film . . . you know how Woods likes to video everything."

"So I noticed," I huffed.

"I've seen that video, the two of them joking about it. Woods knew, but he went through with it, anyway."

I absorbed this new intel. "So Brody soaks the Orange—"

"Orange?" Jason Cool babbled through a cascade of toilet water and nosebleed.

"*Woods*. Woods wants his money back, hires me to get it. I'm this close to finding your boy Brody, but that still doesn't explain why you're here."

But then it all made terrible sense.

"Woods sent you to clean up his mess, didn't he?"

Jason Cool didn't answer. His silence was proof enough.

A shiver teased the nape of my neck. My hands clenched into fists on the other man's. "Son of a fuckin' bitch . . ."

Before I could stop myself, I shoved his head back down, beneath the water, and held it there for what seemed a very long time. Jason Cool thrashed. His screams echoed with a distant, dreamy underwater quality. To my horror, my cock was as hard as my rage.

I'm not a religious man. Don't believe in the All-powerful or the afterlife. But I am superstitious, enough to know that I could be wrong about it all, and if I do end up burning in the lake of eternal fire, it won't be over Murder One.

I hauled Jason Cool's mug out of the piss-pot. For a very long second or two, he was purple in the face, and not moving. Then he sucked in a desperate breath. His eyes bulged so far out of his skull, I worried they'd start swinging by their optic nerves.

The terror on Jason Cool's face matched the bile-tainted revulsion within me. The silver lining was, I'd struck fear into my adversary's soul. For the next few minutes, I didn't have to ask a question twice.

". . . you were sent to find Brody. Once you reported in, I was to eliminate him, and anybody else who was involved."

"Including me?"

"No. I was to set you up to look like the hand that did the deed," Jason Cool chattered. I shrugged. Fearing another dunk, he offered, "Evidence that you decided to keep Brody's money for yourself. In a fit of anger, you killed him and the other kid.

Woods figured we could play on your bad press, that you really hated gays and snapped when Brody gave you 'tude."

"Convenient," I said. "So tell me, tough guy. You the dude who's been leaving me threatening messages, the one trying to get me strung up by my nuts?"

He nodded. I found myself reaching for his throat, but caught myself.

"A double agent? Why?"

"I ain't no killer, man. And I ain't that loyal to Woods. The man's a monster. But I got a stake in things, you know. Brody, he's such a fuckin' rock star, dude. The kind that comes along once every ten years. Like Zeb Atlas, Lukas Ridgeston, Jeff Stryker, Ryan Idol . . . those stars burn out quickly, go supernova, man, and when they do, it opens the door for other, lesser stars to shine . . ."

He recited this while on the verge of fresh tears, like it was an internal monologue he'd practiced to perfection.

"I wanted Brody to disappear, not die," Jason Cool sobbed. "Just go away, so my star could shine!"

Jason Cool wasn't very cool in the moments that followed. He broke down completely. Tears sprinkled the tinkle-water. Jason Un-Cool's howls echoed off the head's drab, cold walls.

"Listen up," I growled.

He didn't, so I smacked the side of his face before reaching for his neck. Then he did.

"And listen closely, pal. I'm gonna give you something even bigger and better than stardom. I'm gonna give you back your fuckin' life."

Jason Un-Cool mewled in response. His scolded puppy dog eyes locked with mine.

"I ain't gonna off you. I ain't even gonna stuff your own socks in your mouth and invite every stiff dick on this cruise ship to come in here and fuck you in the shitter, tempting as that sounds to me right now. But these little kindnesses don't come free. There's a price. We got an understanding, son?"

Jason Un-Cool nodded, cried.

"That didn't sound real convincing."

"Yes, *Sir*," he emoted, real convincing.

"You're going to head back to L.A., first chance you get to hop this tub. Put it on the Orange's expense account. Next, you're going to drop a dime and report him to the Morality Cops, tell them exactly where Woods keeps that tape. And when that's done, you're going to send out your headshot and dick-pix to some other porn company, one that will utilize your pretty face and tight ass in front of the camera, and leave the be-hind-the-scenes action to the professionals. Is that an Affirm?"

I stood, whipped out my dick, and pissed into the bowl, inches from Jason Un-Cool's mug. I tipped a squirt at him, just to seal the deal.

That was that, and we both knew it. Endgame. Checkmate. I untied the man-t-hose holding him in place as my bitch, then strutted out of the men's head, resigned that things were pretty much over. There wasn't much sense now in pursuing the blond kid, or Brody. The Orange had set me up to take a fall, only he'd be the one rolling down the hill when I got done with him. I'd milk out my fee for the rest of the cruise, get the money wired to me, do my best to keep a low profile, wait for the Anselmo Incident to blow over when a new celebrity shit-storm rele-gated it to yesterday's news, maybe start over some place new. A place like Tulum, perhaps.

Brody. That's what I'd do. I'd lock myself in my cabin for the next week and beat my meat raw to Brody Boneman's stroke flicks. Just the idea made my dick swell. I'd start right now, put the rest behind me, vanish into that magnificent pornographic fantasy world where it was just him and me, his cock, my mouth. Heaven.

If only it had worked out that simply.

I turned the corner, cut through a crowd of well-dressed, cologne-soaked cock-smoochers, and was halfway down the "Rainbow Deck" when I saw him.

Benjy McCallister, the love of Brody's life.

***

It was like a kick to the scrotum; that pain that doesn't hit you all at once, but in staggered doses. Worse than stubbing your big toe.

I did a double-take, then froze. Some disenchanted queen tisked and rounded the wall of my back. My front, turned toward a little deck bar serving colorful concoctions the human digestive tract hadn't been designed to process, transformed into stone. Especially, my cock.

The adorable little fuck sat alone, nursing a cocktail bluer than my balls. Eyes cast toward the sky, a dreamy expression on his face, I could easily guess the nature of his secret euphoria.

"Brody," I whispered.

Saying the magical name unlocked my paralysis. Legs shuffled forward, stone feet became flesh again. Breathless seconds later, I was standing beside his barstool.

"Buy you a drink?" I heard my lips mumble.

Benjy McCallister pulled his gaze down from the Brody-soaked blue sky to me. "No, thanks," he said politely.

"Then how about you buy me one?"

"I don't think so."

Benjy abandoned his drink, got up, and started to walk away. I figured he'd been hit upon *ad nauseum* from the instant he'd set foot on the *Queen America*.

I wasn't just another horny trick, however. I wouldn't take no for an answer.

"It's not like you can't afford it, Benjy."

Now, he was the one who froze in place. My cock twitched at his surrender. Slowly, Benjy-boy revolved to face me, fear replacing his day-dreamy whimsy.

"You know who I am?"

"I know who you're going to see in Tulum."

Benjy gasped. "Who sent you? Woods?"

"The Orange? Hell no, relax. You could say that Brody sent me. Now, how about that drink?"

***

I must have fucked him a dozen times that night, and at both ends. Didn't so much ask him as much as tell the little fuck he was going to put out for me. Benjy was my link to Brody, and if I couldn't have the real deal, I'd at least claim the next best thing.

It went like this:

"The Orange hired me to hunt you dudes down, but he secretly sent one of his cock-ninjas after me, so he could feed Brody a dirt-sandwich. You, too. See, I know all about the blackmail thing, and I don't have a problem with it."

"So, you're here for . . . what? A cut of the quarter-mill?"

I sent my scariest smile across the table. Benjy shrank before my eyes.

"I know it's a cool mill. Don't lie to me, kid. I really fuckin' hate liars. Do it again, and I'll see to it that you never make it off this boat at Tulum."

"Okay," he said, mouth screwed into a quivery scowl.

"Yeah, I want a cut. But not of the money."

"Then what do you want?"

Ten minutes later, we were at the door to Benjy's suite on the "Rainbow Deck." The place was twice as big as my claustrophobic cabin. A dozen blood-red roses draped in satin ribbon sat on the bed stand, along with a card. A pile of baggage and duffels were stacked along one wall.

"What I want," I growled, my mouth suddenly, completely dry, my tongue turned to desert, "is details. Get on your knees, but tell me *everything* . . ."

While jerking on my cock, he spilled the beans.

"His balls have this nutty, funky smell, even after he showers. His asshole tastes . . . *fuck* . . . so fuckin' good. His cum is salty, so delicious. And so's his piss, especially right after he's just busted a load in my mouth . . ."

He extolled the joys of licking the hot, buttery stink from between Brody's toes, his feet sweaty, right out of his sneakers after a jog.

He revealed how Brody's thickness, when shoved up his shitter, often massaged his prostrate enough to make him squirt, without even touching himself.

He talked about their flirtations with kink, leather, public sex. Eyes wide, in a moment of near-religious adoration, he revealed he'd once blown Brody while his big-dicked messiah was seated on the toilet. How Brody would sometimes suck his own cock, how they would lick it together. How Brody loved to chow on his asshole post-fucking, slurping out his own cream pie.

And how Brody always, always said those three little words, always, after climax. Before climax. Just because.

"'I love you,'" Benjy whispered.

I felt my yogurt bubbling up from my balls. The room around me fazed out of cohesion. God, how I envied him Brody's devotion. Resented him. Even hated the lucky fucker.

I tossed Benjy onto the bed and fucked him bareback, without added lubrication beyond the brush of my tongue and the dribble out of my dick.

Brody had fucked that pussy.

I fucked it, aware of this intimate, exciting fact.

***

An hour before sunrise, I dribbled the last of the juice in my nuts down Benjy's throat. Spent, soaked in sweat, I figured I'd sleep for a week following the previous night's fuck-fest. Oh, the irony.

"I need one more bit of info."

"Yeah?"

"Rocky Mountain," I said, my voice trailing to a whisper. "What's the rest of it, the right answer?"

"Retire," Benjy said.

"Huh?"

"That's where we planned to retire, when we were old and gray, after a lifetime of being together."

My stomach knotted. Gore threatened to rise at this revelation.

The boy sat in a naked hunch, not showing his face. I wasn't the only guy besides Brody to throw a load or twelve into his cunt or throat, merely the first to do so away from a porn set.

"You're in love with him, too?" Benjy asked, his voice barely audible.

"No," I lied.

"I thought you said you hated liars," he fired back.

Guilt flooded over me. I did love the phantom of a man I'd never met, but had gotten intimate with on a deep, spiritual level over the past week. And I had busted my load, all over his mate, his relationship, the one he loved and planned to spend a lifetime with, until old and gray in the fuckin' Rocky Mountains, just for the chance to have some physical connection to him.

I staggered into the bathroom and puked.

"You okay?" asked the voice at the door.

"I will be. Give me a moment."

My stomach, empty except for the taste of Benjy's sweet little pucker, cursed me again. I retched.

"I probably just need to eat something, other than you."

"Want to order in?"

I rinsed my mouth. The room stunk of betrayal, desecration, and sweaty balls. "No, I need air."

***

So that's how we wound up on the "Rainbow Deck." The fresh air, the sight of distant Tulum, a line of coral-colored light, just breaking over the horizon to signal sunrise . . . I felt spent, but also strangely alive and hopeful. It was as though I'd puked up all the toxic waste of recent weeks force-pumped into my system. The Anselmo Incident, the Orange, his cronies, the fact that my father never really loved me, and my pet hamster died over Easter vacation one year back in Massachusetts, and the time in fourth grade when I snagged my pecker in a zipper—all of it.

Fucking Brody's boy-bitch at both ends had left me reborn.

"Suck me," I ordered.

"Huh?"

"Right here, in front of the whole world."

"But—"

I strong-armed Benjy onto his knees. Half an hour earlier, I'd sworn I couldn't milk another drop out of my stones. But facing Tulum, my dick was rock-hard, and my balls felt like puddles of warm flesh, sagging down to my ankles.

I wasn't just in love with Brody, I'd become him.

I was Brody.

Benjy lowered to his knees, unzipped my cammies, hauled out my Johnson, and made love to it with his mouth. Cock stiff, balls swinging low and mighty for all to see . . . and a small crowd soon gathered around us on deck to take in this sight . . . I surrendered to the illusion. I was a millionaire. I had my beautiful bottom-babe, for life. I was safe, in Tulum. I was—

"It's really fuckin' him!"

That's right, I thought. It's me, Brody Boneman, Big-Dicked Eighth Wonder of the World. King of Gay Porndom. Emperor of Tulum, and one day of the Rockies, of—

"That evil fucker, C. J. Payne!"

My eyes flew open, and reality quickly sank in, a split-second too late.

By that point, my adoring public had pitched me over the rail, leaving me falling, flailing, spiraling toward oblivion.

***

I don't know how I made it ashore.

I hit the water so hard, it knocked the air out of my lungs, and the shorts off my ankles. Struggling to breathe, my limbs feeling as though they'd been ripped out of their sockets, I scrambled to break the surface. The *Queen America*'s propellers, was all I could think about. So I started paddling, for fear of being drawn under and shredded in the cruise ship's wake.

The next nightmare I called up from my psyche was the school of sharks. Every tickle that brushed my legs or bare ass was a Great White.

I paddled, gasping, panicking, screaming until hoarse.

My bare foot, the flip-flop long gone, kicked against a giant of the deep. I screamed some more. Then the surf tossed me onto the beach, and I realized the monster was really solid ground.

Naked except for my shirt and spitting my guts out, I staggered ashore.

I wasn't sure when it happened. Time had lost all of its meaning by then. The man leaned over me, tapped my shoulder.

"Hey, you," he said. "I hear you've been looking for me."

I rolled over, winced. My butt-cheeks were sunburned to the color of boiled lobster.

Through my pain, I saw him. Brody, the superstar. The stud. Lover and vampire and thief and soul-stealer and fantasy and reality and—

"It's C.J, right?"

I shrugged. I'd shaved my head, lost my shorts, and with them, my wallet and proof of my identity.

"I'm not sure, anymore. For a moment, I thought I was you."

"Naw, there's only one Brody Thomas Boyce, the Boneman, and he's larger than life, a legend."

He leaned down, as if to kiss me, and my cock pulsed, my sunburned ball-sac loosened, my heart galloped.

"*A real fuckin' supernova* . . ."

His kiss never reached me. Mustering the last of my strength, I lifted my hand and shielded my eyes. Through slitted fingers, I saw that he was only an illusion, a fantasy, and that I was alone on a garbage-strewn beach, untold miles from Tulum and the man who'd taken all that I was, body, heart, and soul.

Ocean in His Eyes
Christopher Pierce

I had never been on a cruise before, it was very exciting for me. The huge, majestic ship; the endless ocean; and my fellow passengers—gay men all—it was breathtaking. Although I'd heard that all-gay voyages were fertile cruising grounds, I'd actually come aboard for some relaxation and time to think, not to get laid.

I was shy, in my mid-thirties, with a decent body and a plain face. I hoped to blend in and disappear among the crowd of much-younger, much-flashier guys and just enjoy the sights and consider my options.

But despite my best efforts, I did not go unnoticed.

A few nights into the cruise, I was standing alone on one of the high decks, just looking out at the expanse of dark blue that went on forever. The music from the disco below pounded a steady rhythm into me as I looked. At that exact moment I was wondering if there was enough water in the whole ocean to wash away all the mistakes I'd made, all the problems I'd created for myself.

It was very dark, the moon was behind some clouds. I didn't hear him as he walked up beside me, didn't even notice him until he spoke.

"You're a loner," he said, and I jumped in surprise.

"I didn't mean to startle you."

"It's okay," I said, "I just . . . thought I was alone."

His features were shrouded in darkness, but I could see that his face was handsome, chiseled, and that he was wearing a necklace of some kind. His chest was bare despite the late-night chill, and his legs were nearly hidden behind the sarong that was wrapped around his waist. His feet were bare.

"I like to be alone too," he said, "even when there are others around, it's nice to be by yourself sometimes."

"Yes."

I turned back to look out over the sea.

I felt his eyes on me, but strangely, I didn't mind. His presence was comforting, he could look at me all night.

"Something weighs heavily on your mind," he said.

"You can tell, huh?" I said with a grin. "I've just got a lot to sort out before we get back."

"What troubles you so?" he asked.

"You don't want to hear all my problems," I said, hoping that he did.

"I'll listen if you'll talk," was his response.

I took a deep breath.

"Well, I guess the simplest way to explain it is that I've wasted my life."

He didn't say anything, so I continued.

"Looking back, it seems like I've squandered every opportunity, ignored chances I should've taken, lost or given up everything worth having."

He watched me in the dark. The noise of the disco seemed far away, and as the great ship sailed on it felt like we were the only ones on that ocean, just him and me.

Finally I broke the silence.

"I know what you're going to say," I said. "It's all in the past, right? I should just let it go and go forward from here, forget the past."

"No," he said, "that's not something I'd say at all."

"You wouldn't?" I asked, surprised.

He shook his head.

"I revere the past," he said. "Its lessons are priceless, its experiences invaluable. I'm in a place where I'd rather look backward than forward."

I noticed that even though there was a wind blowing and I could see the fabric of his sarong flapping in it, it made no noise.

At that moment, the moon emerged from behind the clouds and I saw him clearly for the first time. He was beautiful, as I'd guessed, with hypnotic eyes that were the same dark blue as the ocean that surrounded us. From the cord around his neck hung a perfect nautilus seashell, pearly and glowing in the moonlight. His chest and abdomen were tanned dark from the sun, their contours statuesque. The thin material of his sarong barely concealed his cock, which hung long and full between his legs.

"Don't be afraid," he said. I stared at him, his face bright in the moonlight, not believing what I'd just seen.

His mouth hadn't moved when he'd spoken.

That was what had been strange about his face, but I hadn't been sure in the darkness. His mouth had *never* moved the whole time we'd been speaking! I started to say something, but he stepped forward and put his fingers to my lips, silencing me. At his touch warmth flowed through me and blood raced into my cock, hardening it almost painfully fast. Feeling him was like being attached to a live wire. His eyes seemed to glow in the night, stormy oceans within them.

"I need to show you something," his voice in my head said. "Will you take me to your cabin?"

I nodded stupidly—how could I refuse him? He removed his hand from my mouth and I instantly longed for his touch again.

"Take me there now."

I obeyed him, and headed back below decks. Guys that passed us smiled knowingly, thinking that they knew exactly what the stunning stranger and I were on our way to do. Looking back I realize that they had no idea what the night had in store for us.

When we reached my cabin, I unlocked the door and opened it for him. He walked inside and I followed him silently. Even though he wasn't touching me, my dick was hard and I could feel energy crackling between us. When the door was closed and locked again I turned to him. We faced each other, only inches apart in the tiny room.

His sarong fell to the floor and I finally saw his magnificent penis, full and erect and pointing like a divining rod right at me. "Remove your clothes," his voice whispered in my head. I did what he said and my shorts and tank joined his sarong on the floor. My cock jutted out from between my legs, as if wanting or needing to touch the amazing creature that stood in front of me.

"What's happening?" I asked.

"I need to show you something," he repeated. Stepping forward, he was only inches away from me. His body was so beautiful, his face so haunting. And his eyes, they had seen so much, they were full of memory.

So close I could smell him.

My nostrils flared as I breathed in his scent, the scent of the sea—salty and clean and deep. His odor was instantly addictive, it made me want him so badly, even more than before. I stood there in front of him, longing for his touch, desperate with need yet paralyzed.

"Please . . ." I said helplessly.

He kissed me then, pushing his tongue gently into my mouth. The touch of his lips was sublime and our mouths moved together, probing, exploring, caressing. Instantly I raised my hands to his body, feeling every angular plane. His body felt like none I'd ever touched before. There was no trace of softness, no pliable flesh, as if he were all muscle like a sea creature, a dolphin or a shark. Immense power was contained within his body, yet he held it firmly in his control, his body an instrument which would do exactly as he desired.

Then his hands were on me, and my skin tingled and rippled where his fingers touched. His arms wrapped around me, squeezing me tight. Our cocks met and rubbed together, communing and exchanging sensation as if they were alive with their own intelligence, flesh become sentient. Being held by him was like being held by the wind—nature incarnate, capable of supreme gentleness as easily as supreme force.

He moved me to my cabin's tiny bed and I melted down onto it with him on top of me.

Effortlessly he maneuvered himself between my legs, lifting them up onto his shoulders. He turned his head on its graceful neck to the light fixture on the wall and blew as if extinguishing a candle. The light flickered and went out. I would've gasped in surprise if I hadn't had a much better reason to gasp—he was pressing his cock against my asshole.

I started to close my eyes, but his voice in my head stopped me.

"No, look at me. Look into my eyes. It's time to go."

"Where are we going?" I asked breathlessly.

"The past," he said, and as I looked up at his face, he entered me. His powerful dick slid into my ass and pleasure unlike anything I'd ever known flowed through me.

I stared into his eyes and it seemed they were getting bigger, but I realized that it was me who was shrinking, smaller and smaller until I could fall right into his eyes. Their pupils, instead of being black, I saw now were the darkest green, the green of the deepest ocean.

Our bodies fucked, and as they did our hearts and spirits plunged into a world of mystery and excitement and danger.

It was so strange—I could feel him on top of me, his cock thrusting into me, and yet we were also somewhere else, somewhere close by or far away, I had no idea. We were swimming under the waves, we were both naked except for the shell necklace that was always around his neck, his hand holding mine as we went deeper and deeper. I breathed normally, even though we had left the surface and its life-giving air far above. The water was our whole world, a liquid universe I'd never fully understood or appreciated before. The sun's rays penetrated the water, shooting down into the depths. We swam through them and the light made our skin shine and glow. I glanced over at him and he smiled at me, his mouth full and generous, his hair streaming out behind him. I was safe as long as he kept hold of my hand. I trusted him—he'd wanted to bring me here and I knew that he meant me no harm.

We came upon a vast school of fish, and I marveled at their shiny silver bodies that shimmered in the water. They turned and moved together, as if sharing a single mind. My lover pulled me into the school, which briefly broke apart then reformed around us. He moved with the fish, twisting and turning through the water as if he shared their group mind, his hand tight on mine as we swam. We traveled with the school for a while, just loving the feel of their bodies streaking over, under and around our own.

High-pitched squealing noises reached my ears and I was startled, not having heard anything distinct under the water until now. A group of larger shapes was heading for us from below—I wondered if I should be frightened, but when I turned to my lover he was laughing. I laughed myself when he started making the noises himself, and as the creatures swam closer I could see them clearly—dolphins! They surrounded the school of fish and started gobbling them up, swallowing them whole with their elongated mouths. The dolphins nipped and chirped at us, playful as puppies, as they happily snacked on the school. Panicking, the fish tried to escape, but there were too many dolphins. Within minutes the whole school had been devoured.

My lover chattered and squealed with the dolphins, speaking their language as if it were his own. He seemed so at home, like this was where he belonged.

The dolphins swirled around us, rubbing against our bodies with their own.

He guided my hand to one of the dolphins' dorsal fin, and did the same with his own hand on another.

"Hold on!" his voice spoke in my head.

Suddenly, we were streaking upwards as the dolphins powered toward the surface. Faster and faster we swam and the light from above grew brighter and brighter until we broke and soared joyfully into the air. It was like flying for a breathless moment, then we crashed back down into the water. Again we rose, the dolphins taking us with them as they jumped spectacularly into the air. Better than any amusement park attraction, the marine mammals gave us the ride of our lives as they leaped and spun and twirled over the waves.

My lover fucked me, pushing himself in deeper and deeper, our bodies fused in passion as our hearts and spirits flew through the ocean with the dolphins. I became aware of a sound, a thumping that matched the ecstatic beating of my heart. It was the sound of his seashell necklace, bumping against his solid chest as he moved in and out, in and out. But even that sound was drowned out by a new sound, a trumpeting blast as loud as a foghorn.

"Look!" my lover said.

I followed his pointing finger and I saw a huge column of misty water shooting upward from the surface of the ocean. Confused for a second, I suddenly realized what was causing it.

A whale!

"Come on!" his voice said in my head.

We left the dolphins and swam for the whale. I had never been a terribly good swimmer, but with my lover by my side I was able to swim with the best. Which he was. I was awed as we got closer and closer to the whale. It was gigantic, the largest animal I'd ever seen. I guessed it was probably a sperm whale if I remembered my college marine biology class correctly. Its dark blue—almost black—hide was encrusted with patches of barnacles that looked like tiny piles of snow on top of the animal. Swimming over on top of the creature, the two of us grabbed a hold of the some of the barnacles.

After a few more seconds on the surface, the whale dived, taking us along for the ride. It was breathtaking as we soared down into the ocean, the color of the water getting darker and darker as we left the sun and the surface far behind again. As before, I had no trouble breathing. I glanced over at my lover and the excitement and joy on his face was addictive. He was loving every second of this, as was I, and as we went on this journey our bodies continued the frenzied fucking that had started this whole thing off.

We were further down now than we had been before, and it was a little scary to realize how deep we were—I had no idea, but I knew it was probably miles below the surface. The ocean is the last unexplored part of the world, we've only mapped a small portion of it, and we were definitely in an uncharted area.

The whale continued downward, master of its domain, and we held on for dear life as it went deeper and deeper. The pressure of the water, which would have killed me normally, was only a slight discomfort. Now the water was nearly black. I couldn't help being frightened, but my lover's hand found mine and held it tight.

I could hardly see, overwhelmed by how tiny I felt in the enormity of the ocean.

Strange lights appeared in the darkness.

For even this deep, life flourished.

There were creatures all around us, generating their own biochemical light. They were strange and wonderful, some of them recognizable with their fish- and eel-like shapes, others unlike anything I'd ever seen before. Some were small, some as large as us, some almost as big as the whale, but I knew we were in no danger. I stared with wonder at animals any scientist would kill to see—giant squids, fish thought extinct since the age of the dinosaurs, honest-to-god sea serpents that were a hundred feet long . . . it was breathtaking.

"What do you think?" his voice whispered in my head.

"I don't believe it," I thought back at him, knowing he heard me.

"There's more," he said. "Let's go."

Holding my hand firmly, my lover let go of the whale and I did the same. We left the giant mammal and swam through the darkness. Then he was swimming fast, pulling me along with him, streaking through the water faster and faster until we were shooting through the ocean like torpedoes. We started heading upward, and little by little the light of the sun returned.

As the light returned I looked at my lover, and for the first time, really saw him. I was stunned, even though I'd somehow known all along this moment would come. His head, face, and torso were the same, with his long hair and beautiful features and chiseled physique, but below his waist, where his legs should have been, was a muscular fish's tail, at least six feet long, green and shimmering, every scale a sparkling jewel in the water.

He was a merman, I realized. I was being fucked by a merman. I was on this extraordinary vision quest with a creature that was not human, not of the earth at all, but of the sea.

"Where are we going?" I thought to him.

"My home," he answered, and an explosion of color appeared above us.

A coral reef!

The merman led me into the forest of coral—growths that were small, growths that were big, in a rainbow of different colors—it was stunningly beautiful. As we swam through the forest, we passed schools of glittering fish, shy octopi, sea turtles that twisted and turned like playful otters, anemones, strange crustaceans of all shapes and colors, deadly Moray eels that stayed away from us when the merman sent a warning look their way . . . it was a dizzying array of beautiful life, and at the center of it all: my merman. He took me into a cavern hidden amongst the coral, and I knew that it was his home.

It felt like him inside, it was dark but somehow warm and welcoming.

He took me in his arms and kissed me, and back on this ship I could feel his fucking speed up—he was getting close to climax, as was I. It was amazing to be in two places at once, having passionate sex with him in one place, and in the other watching him pull the seashell necklace from his neck and placed it around mine. The shell started glowing and our orgasms broke at the same time. The merman grabbed my cock and pumped it for all it was worth.

We howled in ecstasy and our bodies glowed like the shell necklace as our loads exploded out of us, his into me and mine onto my chest. It was like a huge wave that I rode, pleasure flowing to every part of my body. All my muscles tensed and relaxed as the wave seemed to bear me far away, out of the cave, out of the reef, out of the ocean, all the way back to my bed in the cabin on the cruise ship.

"Sleep now . . ." the merman whispered, and warm darkness enclosed me.

When I woke up the next morning I wondered if it had all been a dream.

But the shell necklace was still around my neck and there were watery footprints on the floor. Curious, I held the shell to my ear, and heard the merman's voice whispering to me.

"My love. Thank you for accompanying me last night. It is a custom among my people when one of us is near death to share our favorite memories with someone, so those moments are never lost. We call it the Rite of Showing. I am very old, and will be gone by the time you read this. But the memories I relived with you will burn forever inside you, until such time as you decide to share them with someone else, so in a way I am not really dead. Again, thank you. Good-bye."

I laid back on my bed, filled with love and longing.

Here at last was a chance I had taken, an opportunity I hadn't missed, a gift I could treasure.

I laid back on my bed, and cried.

About the Contributors

A native Californian, **BEARMUFFIN** lives in San Diego with two leather bears in a stimulating ménage à trois. His erotica has appeared in many gay publications. He now writes for *Honcho* and *Torso* magazines. His work is featured in several anthologies from Alyson Books and Cleis Press.

LEW BULL's stories have appeared in such publications as *Ultimate Undies: Stories about Underwear and Lingerie, Secret Slaves: Erotic Stories of Bondage, Tales of Travelrotica for Gay Men, Ultimate Gay Erotica 2007, Treasure Trail, Dorm Porn 2,* and *Fast Balls.* When he is not traveling in search of exotic places, he's living in Johannesburg, South Africa, with his partner of twenty-nine years. He welcomes any comments and can be contacted at lewbull@hotmail.com.

CURTIS C. COMER lives in St. Louis with his partner, Tim, and their cat, Magda, and lovebird, Raoul Gomez. His writing has appeared in numerous anthologies, including *Starf*cker* (2000), *Best Gay Love Stories* (2005, 2006, and 2007), *Ultimate Gay Erotica* (2005, 2006, and 2007), *Dorm Porn 1* and *2, Treasure Trails* (2007), *Fast Balls* (2007), and *My First Time, Vol. 5.*

ERASTES is the director of the Erotic Authors Association and a member of the Historical Novel Society. His work has appeared in many anthologies such as *Ultimate Gay Erotica 2005* and *2007, Treasure Trail,* and *Fastballs.* His first novel, *Standish,* has been an Amazon best seller since its release in 2006 and was nominated for a Lamda Award. His aim in life is to make the gay historical novel as mainstream a genre as the heterosexual kind.

RYAN FIELD is a thirty five-year-old freelance writer who lives and works in both Los Angeles, California, and New

Hope, Pennsylvania. His work has appeared in many short story collections and anthologies, and he is working on a full-length novel. He also interviews bloggers from around the world for www.bestgayblogs.com.

JEFF FUNK has written hundreds of choral works published by Warner Bros. Publications, more than 1.7 million copies in print. His stories appear in *Dorm Porn 2, Tales of Travelrotica for Gay Men, Vol. 2, My First Time, Vol. 5,* and *Ultimate Gay Erotica 2008.* He lives in Auburn, Indiana.

TODD GREGORY is a proud pornographer from the city of sin, New Orleans. He is the editor of the anthologies *Blood Lust* (with M. Christian), *His Underwear,* and *Rough Trade,* and the author of the novel *Every Frat Boy Wants It.* He has published numerous stories in various anthologies, and lives to do research in the French Quarter every weekend.

T. HITMAN is the nom-de-porn for a full-time professional writer who has published numerous short stories and novels. Always writing his first drafts using trusty Sheaffer fountain pens (some of them 24-years-old), he lives with his awesome partner, Bruce, and their two cats in a very small bungalow on a very large plot of land among the pines of New Hampshire.

DAVID HOLLY is the pseudonym for a writer who is nothing like Dave the genial rogue pictured in this story. (Somewhat unlike Dave anyway—the Gay Marco Polo, Bare-Assed Leap-Frog, and Choo-Choo games were drawn from actual experiences, but they happened some time ago and in another county.) David Holly's fiction has appeared in publications such as *Guys, First Hand, Manscape,* and *Traveller's Tales: Hot Shots.* His work has also appeared in *Dorm Porn 2, Tales of Travelrotica for Gay Men, My First Time,* and other anthologies.

JOEL A. NICHOLS lives in Philadelphia. His fiction has appeared in *Velvet Mafia, Distant Horizons 2007,* and in numerous anthologies from Alyson, Cleis, and others. Joel studied German at Wesleyan University, Creative Writing at Temple University, and was a Fulbright fellow in Berlin. He teaches college English.

CHRISTOPHER PIERCE is the author of the novel *Rogue: Slave.* His erotic fiction has been published most recently in the anthologies *Working Stiff, Muscle Worshippers,* and *Ultimate Gay Erotica, 2007.* He co-edited (with Rachel Kramer Bussel) Alyson's *Fetish Chest* trio of anthologies. You can write to Chris at chris@christopherpierceerotica.com and visit his world at www.ChristopherPierceErotica.com.

ROB ROSEN is the author of *Sparkle: The Queerest Book You'll Ever Love,* and the forthcoming Haworth Press novel, *Divas Las Vegas.* His short stories have appeared in such noted anthologies as *Mentsh: On Being Jewish and Queer, I Do/I Don't: Queers on Marriage, Best Gay Love Stories 2006, Truckers, Best Gay Love Stories: New York City, Best Gay Romance, Superqueeroes, My First Time, Vol. 5, Son of PORN!, Best Gay Love Stories: Summer Flings, Ultimate Gay Erotica 2008, Hard Hats,* and *Best Gay Romance 2008.* His erotic fiction can frequently be read in *MEN, Freshmen,* and *[2]* magazines. Please visit him at www.therobrosen.com, or email him at robrosen@therobrosen.com.

SIMON SHEPPARD is the editor of *Homosex: Sixty Years of Gay Erotica,* and the author of *In Deep: Erotic Stories; Kinkorama: Dispatches from the Front Lines of Perversion; Sex Parties 101;* and the award-winning *Hotter Than Hell.* His work also appears in over 250 anthologies, including many editions of *The Best American Erotica* and *Best Gay Erotica.* He writes the syndicated column "Sex Talk" and the online serial "The Dirty Boys Club," is

a member of the Princess Captain's Circle, and hangs out at
www.simonsheppard.com.

JOHN SIMPSON is the author of *Murder Most Gay,* a full-
length e-book. Simpson has also written "The Virgin Marine,"
"The Acropolis of Love," "The Tower," "The Serpent," "Locker
Room Heat," "Campus Steam," "Lust in the Sand," and now "A
Sea of Love and Lust," all short stories, for Alyson Books. Ad-
ditionally, he has written numerous articles for various gay and
straight magazines, and two full-length non-fiction paperback
novels. Simpson will soon be starting a new novel involving a
gay president of the United States.

Living on English Bay in Vancouver, British Columbia, **JAY
STARRE** writes fiction stories for gay men's magazines including *Men* and *Torso.* Jay has also written gay fiction for over
45 anthologies including the *Friction* series for Alyson, *Travelrotica, Ultimate Gay Erotic 2005* and *2006, Bear Lust,* and *Best Gay
Love Stories, New York City.*

KEITH WILLIAMS is a freelance copy-editor, and writer
of non-fiction and erotica. Williams also works as a carpenter
and makes furniture. He lives in Milwaukee with his Airedale
Terrier, Angus. His sex stories have been published in *Travelrotica 2, My First Time, Vol. 4,* and *Cruise Lines* from Alyson
Books, and *Dangerous Liaisons* from Haworth Press.

SHANNON L. YARBROUGH's short stories have been
featured in several recent Alyson publications, including *Best
Gay Love Stories: New York City, Dorm Porn 2,* and *Fastballs.* He is
the author of the book, *The Other Side of What.* He lives with his
partner in St. Louis, Missouri, and is currently at work on another novel.